A Lonely Road

Rachel Fitzjames

ISBN: 978-1-967700-02-8 (Paperback)
ISBN: 978-1-967700-03-5 (Ebook)

Library of Congress Control Number: 2025909938

Book Cover by Maldo Designs

Editing by Melissa Rotert – Wordplay Copy & Line Edits

A note to readers

Each book in the Spruce Hill series features on-page, open-door steamy scenes, along with swearing and some degree of suspense. There may be a limited amount of on-page physical violence as well as the threat of peril facing one or more characters. Specific content in this story that might be of concern to readers includes stalking and vandalism. As a general reassurance, no animals or children are ever harmed in my books.

For more details, please visit my website at https://rachelfitzjames.com/ or use the QR code below.

*To all the prickly black cat types
who some might call
unlikable—don't ever change.*

Contents

Chapter One

NORA

"You can do it, Baby."

My murmured encouragement was compounded by stroking the furry steering wheel cover, like maybe affection alone might keep the car moving.

"We're almost there, just hold on one more minute. You can do it."

Unfortunately, Baby disagreed with that assertion. The car stalled just as we reached the address on my rental agreement. I'd had to get a jump from a family of six in a cargo van at a rest stop in Ohio, determined to avoid calling roadside assistance if I could help it, but I made it to Spruce Hill, New York, without further incident.

Until now.

Ten more feet would've put us at the driveway, but at least I was close enough to the curb to pretend I'd meant to park on the street. I sighed as I stroked the steering wheel again. This car was my one constant, my prized possession—my only real friend.

What a sad commentary on my life.

Shaking off that gloomy reality, I took the key out of the ignition, not that it mattered after Baby had given up the ghost, and looked toward my new home.

The main house was white with red brick accents, green shutters, and careful landscaping, but the garage apartment about fifty feet behind it was my ultimate destination. It would've been nice to park right at the bottom of the stairs leading up to my new home, but there wasn't much to unload from the car.

Only a handful of houses lined the little dead end street. My landlord had left for a six month sabbatical in Florida just that morning, hiding the key for my rental under a potted plant by the door of the apartment. When I mailed back the signed lease from my last place in Columbus, Mr. Jenkins had sworn up and down that Spruce Hill was the perfect place for me to start fresh.

Best of all, it was quiet. Blessedly, wondrously quiet.

It certainly seemed perfect, this small town nestled along the shore of Lake Ontario in the middle of New York State. The views of the lake after I left the highway soothed my travel-weary soul, and the stretch of town I'd driven through to get to the rental was adorable, in a bustling-but-off-the-beaten-path type of way.

Spruce Hill was tucked away from the surrounding cities, bordered by the lake, farmland, and forest, but not so far from civilization that I couldn't grab a pizza or hit up a coffee shop in under ten minutes.

Scanning the mostly deserted street—it was the middle of a weekday, after all—I caught sight of someone in the neighboring driveway, a tall man in faded jeans and a white t-shirt. He was half hidden under the hood of a red, late model pickup truck. It was impossible to guess at his age, though he looked trim and fit in the way of someone used to working with his hands. My father had a similar build, so I knew this neighbor could be anywhere from sixteen to sixty.

Uncertainty warred with logic for a moment before I shook myself out of it. I couldn't sit there at the curb all day long. This town was tiny, and for however long I stayed here, it would be perfectly adequate.

Maybe not *home,* not if my years of searching and failing to find a place like that were any indication, but safe enough for a while so I could put it to the test.

I puffed my cheeks as I stepped out of the car, pulled my suitcase from the back seat, and slung the messenger bag holding my laptop and work notes over one shoulder. By the time I was halfway up the driveway, a rare sort of optimism bubbled inside me. The sun was shining, the birds were singing, and the smell of freshly cut grass hung in the air like the sweetest perfume.

God, I loved summer. I'd spent too much time losing myself in the anonymity of big cities lately and had forgotten all about the beauty of a little suburban town.

Just as I reached the stairs, the man next door straightened and I stumbled to a halt, nearly tripping over my own feet. Definitely *not* my father's age, but a lean, beautiful man in his prime with cropped caramel curls and an easy smile that crept across his face when he spotted me.

Though he studied me with interest, it seemed perfectly benign and neighborly. There was nothing creepy or sinister about him, so why was my heart pounding so hard?

The man wiped his hands on a greasy rag and said, "Howdy, neighbor."

I merely raised a startled brow at the drawled greeting and his smile widened. His voice was smooth and deep, his blue eyes sparkling with good humor. Had my love life really been so pitiful that a smile like that could tempt me so hard? I actually had to stop myself from leaning toward him.

Get a grip, Nora.

"Sorry, my granddad used to greet all our neighbors like that. I figured I'd give it a try." A dimple appeared in his cheek. "After that unenthusiastic reception, I promise I won't do it again."

"I'll hold you to that," I replied, then bit my lip when I realized I was teasing a stranger.

He grinned. "You must be Mr. Jenkins' new tenant. I'm Jake Lincoln. Welcome to Spruce Hill."

Clearing my throat, I said, "Yes. Thanks. I'm Nora Cassidy."

He nodded like I was a perfectly normal new neighbor instead of a bundle of nerves and neuroses. Maybe I could manage small town life, after all. Then Jake held out his hand and, after a brief hesitation, I reached out to shake it.

"Well, Nora Cassidy, it's a pleasure to meet you. Mr. Jenkins asked me to keep an eye out for you, so if you need anything, just give a holler."

With a tight smile, I pulled my hand back. His skin was rough but warm, his grip strong and sure. I reminded myself that part of avoiding undue attention in this town was fitting in, and fitting in meant not making a spectacle of myself over a silly handshake.

Even if my new landlord had implied to this handsome stranger that I was some helpless damsel who needed looking after.

My jaw clenched, and I had to force the muscles to relax.

"I hope you like the apartment," he said, his tone friendly and casual. "Mr. Jenkins had me renovate the place about a year back as a graduation gift for his grandson, but the kid ended up moving out to California with his girlfriend. It's been vacant all along. Seemed like a waste of such a great space, all that light coming in."

"I haven't been inside yet," I replied, shifting the bag on my shoulder as my face heated. *Real smooth, Cassidy.*

"Right, of course." Jake glanced from me to the car. "Do you need help unloading? You can pull into the driveway, Mr. Jenkins won't mind."

"No, no," I protested with a forced smile. "I've got it. There isn't much. Nice meeting you, though."

Before I turned away, I saw his golden brows draw down. Maybe he thought his vow to look out for the little lady next door would be broken if he didn't help me haul my crap inside. He said nothing, however, just moved back a few steps so his feet were on his own driveway by the time I glanced down from the landing.

I nabbed the key from beneath some kind of potted fern—hopefully fake, because I had yet to meet a plant I couldn't kill simply by trying to keep it alive—just outside the door and heaved myself inside. With a loud exhalation, I leaned back against the door and looked at my new home.

The furnished apartment was far more spacious than I'd imagined, airy and well-appointed, with plenty of windows to let in light all through the day. Even though the kitchen was small by most people's standards, it was a definite step up from the places I'd lived in before, with glossy countertops and shiny new appliances. Everything looked fresh and bright, like it had simply been waiting for me all along.

Jake the Neighbor had clearly done an amazing job on renovations.

Cute and capable, I thought as I surveyed my surroundings. The walls were a pale gray, the windows sporting sheer linen curtains that shimmered in the sun. I set my laptop bag on the low coffee table and wheeled my suitcase into the bedroom, which was moderately sized and done up in impersonal but attractive decor all in shades of mint and baby blue. On one wall hung a large, slightly abstract painting of a lighthouse in darker tones of the same colors.

Leaving the suitcase by the closet—which had enough room for ten times more clothing than I possessed—I wandered back through the living room, letting the quiet settle me.

Before leaving to fetch the single cardboard box of foreign language dictionaries and translation guides that I'd left in the trunk, I peeked through the curtains covering the glass portion of the door. Jake was still there, back under the hood of his truck, and I steeled myself with a deep breath before opening the door.

The staircase leading down one side of the garage was sturdy and freshly painted, each solid step beneath my feet providing me with another ounce of confidence.

Jake's curly head lifted as I reached the driveway. "What's the verdict? You like it?"

"It's beautiful," I replied without thinking, then my face heated. "I mean, it's very well done. Much nicer than I imagined. You're right, it does get great light. I wasn't expecting that."

His friendly smile widened at my rambling praise, his eyes glinting with amusement. "Well, I'll take that as a compliment. I'm just glad someone is finally around to appreciate it. My sister is a realtor, so I called her in for most of the decorating. She loves that stuff, wanted to turn it into a private little oasis."

"It's all lovely, thank you. Both of you." I took a single step toward my car and his dimple deepened.

"And you don't have to worry about anyone popping by unexpectedly," he went on, like he hadn't noticed my eagerness to flee even though I was dead sure he had.

"Oh. Okay." *Nora Cassidy, what the hell is wrong with you?*

"We're pretty friendly here in Spruce Hill, but most of the people on this street are young couples and families, not part of the drop-by-with-a-pie-for-the-new-neighbor generation. Mr. Jenkins was the only one who showed up when I moved in a few years ago, armed with cookies from the grocery store."

"Right. That's good to know." Floundering for a way to bring the awkward conversation to a close, I said, "Well, I should go. I need to pick up some groceries, get settled in."

Jake leaned one hip against the front of the truck, crossing his arms over his chest in a way that blatantly flaunted the ridiculously firm muscles under his tee. "How exactly were you planning to get to the grocery store after your car stalled?"

Before I could prevent it, I scowled at him. "Baby just needed a rest. Her battery isn't what it used to be."

"Baby," he repeated, the corners of his lips twitching. "I think *Baby* needs a little more than rest, Nora. I'd be happy to help."

My shoulders straightened as I said, "Thank you, but I'll be fine on my own."

"I have no doubt about that," he replied.

Those pretty blue eyes of his danced with humor in a way that both enchanted and annoyed me. Just when I started to stalk toward my car, however, he dangled a carrot that I couldn't refuse.

"I have a jump starter box you can use. There's an auto supply store around the corner, they'll install a new battery for free if you buy it from them. Though I'm sure Hank won't mind if you want to replace it yourself. There's also a woman-owned garage called Saucy Wrench on the other side of town, if you're more comfortable there."

The garage's name threatened to break through my commitment to giving him my darkest glare, but Jake continued to smile. It took a great deal of effort for me to finally grind out, "Sure, the jump start would be lovely."

With a smirk that clearly stated he wasn't put off in the least by my tone, Jake disappeared into his garage to get the box. I dragged my hands over my face, wishing for a complete do-over to this entire day.

What was wrong with me? It wasn't like I'd never had an attractive neighbor before. Hell, my last apartment building had thrown two beauties my way—Audrey from 6F and Jamal in 4B. Maybe that situation was different, since all three of us were clear about not expecting anything other than a good time, but I'd never felt as nervous or off-balance as I did in meeting Jake Lincoln.

He returned and passed it to me without comment, which I appreciated immensely. At my muttered thanks, his lips tilted upward and that damned dimple peeked out from one cheek, then he gave a quick salute and returned to working on his truck.

I spun on my heel and forced myself to assume a natural gait as I walked toward the car, resisting the urge to hurry away like a scared little mouse.

The jumper box worked perfectly. I considered banging my head against the steering wheel but refrained, just in case Jake was still watching, and made my way to the store he mentioned, conveniently located barely a half mile from the apartment. I'd have to scope out the other place, Saucy Wrench, some other time. Baby probably needed more than just a battery—and sooner, instead of later.

"Another magical first impression made," I muttered aloud, disgusted with myself for getting so flustered in front of Jake.

I'd spent years developing a polite but distinctly unfriendly persona for interacting with strangers. Within minutes, this new neighbor started edging his stupid, handsome face past my defenses. It had to be something about the warmth in his eyes, the easiness of his smile.

It had been a long time since I'd *wanted* to let someone in and now that the thought had taken root, I found the urge intensely irritating.

With a determined scowl, I forced Cute Neighbor from my mind.

Hank, an older man with a thick head of white hair and a bright smile that rivaled even Jake's, sent someone to install my new battery the minute the words were out of my mouth. By the time I'd paid and shoved the receipt into my purse, Baby was ready to roll. I thanked both employees profusely before heading back toward the grocery store down the street.

By that point, I had my game face on. I offered murmured greetings to fellow shoppers, made small talk with the cashier, played the part of the new girl in town like I was a trained actress. It was utterly ridiculous to have to encourage some friendly interactions in order to not draw even more unwanted attention, but blending in was the key.

I would do whatever was necessary to achieve that, Cute Neighbor or no. My quest to find a place to call home was my priority, and this town checked a lot of boxes.

On my way back to the apartment, I took a detour along Main Street to scope out the rest of the area. It was a typical small town, populated by a mixture of family-owned businesses and a few chain stores. In the stretch of a mile or two, I passed three cozy coffee shops, two pizza joints, and a trendy local restaurant-slash-bar that had two golden statues of mermaids on either side of the front door. I snickered at the creatures but made note of the location.

While others flocked to cafes with their laptops in hand, I liked to work in a place where the sounds blurred into white noise and I could lose myself in a crowd, usually some kind of pub or a restaurant with a bar that didn't mind me lingering at a table in the corner. The only other option nearby was a dive bar

I'd passed on the way into town. Its lack of windows and dingy exterior had been an immediate turnoff.

I liked noise, not being surrounded by sketchy potential assailants.

The flutter that rose inside me as I turned onto my new street unsettled me, but Cute Neighbor appeared to have gone inside by the time I pulled into the driveway.

I told myself it was relief I was feeling, and I almost believed it. Hefting all of the grocery bags into my hands, I shouldered the trunk closed and returned to the blissful solitude of my new home.

Chapter Two

NORA

JUST AFTER SEVEN THAT evening, I eyed the sign overhead, my gaze caught on the swirling script that proclaimed this place *The Mermaid Gastropub & Grill*. I reached out to stroke a fingertip along the curved fin of one of the golden statues on my way through the door.

I blinked as my eyes adjusted to the dim lighting, smiled at the young hostess who led me to a small booth along one wall, and took the opportunity to glance around the restaurant's interior.

This was definitely a step up from my usual choice of venue.

There were a dozen or so tables already occupied and another handful of people seated at the gleaming oak bar that stretched across the back of the restaurant. I studied the tasteful decorations and slightly eccentric art adorning the walls. A framed article about announcing plans for a new local art gallery hung on the wall at my side, next to a sea glass mosaic depicting a lighthouse on the lake.

This place was as far from a dive bar as it could get, but bustling enough that it might do quite nicely for my purposes.

My gaze drifted to the bar, which looked like a slab from some ancient tree that had been polished to a warm glow. With a sharp intake of breath, I recognized the man behind it as none other than my new—and terribly attractive—neighbor.

In brazen contrast to his torn jeans and stained t-shirt of earlier that day, Jake was in a crisp white button-down, rolled neatly to his elbows. He was joking with one of the customers seated at the bar, currently unaware of my presence.

That man sure cleans up nice, I thought, then kicked myself for the observation. It didn't matter what he looked like, it was better to avoid him.

After a server with a thin, braided beard and purple hair took my order, I pulled out my notebook, forcing myself not to look back toward the bar. The atmosphere in the restaurant wasn't quite the din I usually sought out, but the low hum of conversation around me would do almost as well. I'd written out several pages of translation notes before the server returned with my meal. Once he left, I scribbled down more thoughts as I ate.

This place was actually perfect. I was already impressed with how much work I was getting done, even with the distraction of Cute Neighbor lurking at the edge of my awareness.

Just as I was finishing my stuffed mushrooms—which were heavenly enough for me to excuse the golden statues out front—the server reappeared with a plate of strawberry shortcake that I definitely hadn't ordered. When I opened my mouth to protest, he shook his head to silence me.

"Compliments of the owner," he said with a sly smirk, glancing toward the bar.

When I followed his gaze, Jake raised a hand in salute, smiling just enough for that dimple to pop.

"Jake Lincoln owns this place?" I asked numbly, tearing my eyes from his stupid, adorable face to blink down at the exquisitely crafted confection laid before me. Glistening berries were piled high atop the crumbly shortcake and crowned with whipped cream that inspired a few too many rapidfire fantasies in my head.

Had I walked under a ladder? Desecrated a field of four-leaf clovers? How else could I explain this sudden run of unfortunate luck?

"Oh, yeah," the server replied, grinning at me before he disappeared.

Reluctantly, I dragged my gaze back to Jake, whose crooked smile suddenly did strange things to my pulse. I raised a hand in thanks, shot him a lightning quick smile, then stared blindly down at my notebook until my heart rate calmed.

It was just dessert, nothing to get worked up over. Damn him, I'd never turned down a free dessert in my life. I wasn't about to start now. Especially when it looked so very delicious.

Of course. Of course Cute Neighbor owns the perfect writing location in this tiny town, for fuck's sake.

Without glancing back in Jake's direction, I tucked the notebook into my bag and picked up my fork. Even if I had wanted to, I knew that leaving without sampling at least a bite of Jake's sweet offering would be unspeakably rude, and hadn't my goal been to avoid drawing attention to myself?

It was just dessert. A nice, neighborly gesture to the new girl in town. Surely that was all he intended it to be.

Oh. My. God.

I closed my eyes as I took a tiny bite. I couldn't even remember the last time I'd tasted something so decadent. At the very least, I was grateful Jake was the owner of the place and not the chef. Being able to actually concoct treats like this might sway me dangerously close to warming up toward him.

Hell, I was already thawing as the delicate shortcake melted on my tongue.

I smiled weakly at the server when he returned with the check, then tucked cash into the vinyl folder and slung my bag over my shoulder. Before I could slip out of the booth, I spotted Jake heading straight toward me. He wore fitted khaki pants and they were just as flattering on his long limbs as the ripped jeans.

A memory of the lean muscles of his arms popped unexpectedly into my head, reminding me of what was now hidden beneath his pristine dress shirt. I swore under my breath and stood quickly, preferring to meet him on closer-to-equal terms.

Considering he was nearly a foot taller than me, it was probably moot, but it made me feel slightly more in control.

"Good evening, Ms. Cassidy," Jake said smoothly. "How was your dinner?" The corners of his eyes, which shone crystal blue in the dim light, crinkled slightly as he smiled.

I lifted my chin, feigning a confidence I didn't feel. "It was excellent, thank you. I had no idea you owned a...gastropub." It came out more like an admonition than a statement of fact.

Jake's grin widened. "Family business. My dad made the mistake of letting my sister choose the name, so she's responsible for the mermaids. She was obsessed with them as a kid. Before my family bought the place, it was called Smugglers Den, in honor of the town's history during Prohibition. Legend has it there was a fair amount of rum-running and smuggling going on in Spruce Hill at the time."

"Oh." I was surprised by how freely he shared information. And by how interested I was in everything he had to say.

That was entirely new for me, and I wasn't quite sure how to feel about it.

"I hope my presence didn't detract from your visit," he said conspiratorially, like he was trying to win me over. "I promise I'm not stalking you. I didn't want to sound pushy by suggesting you come in right after you got here."

With a resigned sigh, I adjusted my bag and allowed myself a tiny smile. "I guess my night was not entirely ruined," I replied. "And the shortcake was delicious."

"Chef Bea is an absolute godsend."

It was difficult to keep my eyes from the unbuttoned collar of his white shirt. He was extremely attractive and I was overcome with the desire to observe him, to study every facet of the man—physical and otherwise.

As a woman in a new town still trying to get the lay of the land, I desperately wanted to avoid the distraction this handsome neighbor posed.

Jake Lincoln owned a restaurant that seemed to be a pillar of the community. He was friendly, helpful, respected by his staff. Involvement with the town's golden boy would plant a spotlight over my head, and that was the last thing I needed while I settled in.

"I'm glad you came by," Jake said, his voice low, soft in a way that threatened to summon goosebumps along my skin.

"I like it here." I didn't mean to blurt the words, but they escaped nonetheless.

His smile bloomed like the sun from behind a cloud, and my regret withered immediately. For a moment, it looked like he was searching for the right thing to say, then he gestured toward the bag where I'd stowed my notebook. "Are you a writer?"

"Sort of. I'm a translator, actually," I replied. Surely work was a safe topic of conversation? "Freelance stuff, for the most part."

I tried hard to keep my expression neutral, but I saw the way Jake studied my face. Work was something I loved, something I found intensely fulfilling. Now, I felt dangerously close to babbling out more than I ever intended to reveal to him.

Jake nodded, a small smile curving his lips "Very cool."

"It's getting late, I should probably head home." Relieved that this interaction went smoother than the last, I took a small step back, then I remembered seeing his truck in the driveway when I left the apartment. "Did you walk here?"

"Yeah, I did. After the rain earlier this week, it turned into a beautiful day. We get such a small window of nice weather, it's hard to resist the chance to enjoy it."

Nodding, I hummed in response. I'd put too many miles on my car in the last few years. If I wanted her to survive, it might be worth cutting the poor girl some slack, new battery or not.

I gave myself a swift mental shake. Was I truly considering coming back? I'd gotten more work done in the past hour than I had in a single day in months, sure, but could I knowingly subject myself to his curious gaze while I worked?

The answer didn't come quickly, so I flashed him another brief smile. "Right. Well, I'll see you around. Thanks again for the dessert."

Jake smiled. "Any time," he replied. "Have a good night, Nora."

The sound of my name on his lips did something strange to my insides. "You too, Jake," I said, forcing myself to use his in return.

I watched as he strode back to the bar and couldn't bring myself to regret the sight of his stellar ass as he walked away. The man definitely cut an impressive figure. It was a moment before

I recovered my senses and left the restaurant, then drove home with the radio off, allowing a pensive silence to surround me.

Starting out in a new place was no easy feat, as I knew only too well, but I really hadn't expected it to be any different this time around. As I turned onto my street, I thought back to the last few places I'd lived—a big city, a tiny rental house in the middle of nowhere, a suburb of endless cookie cutter houses and carefully manicured yards.

In total, I'd made a bare handful of personal connections throughout my adult life, and the most notable were Audrey and Jamal, who'd never really known me as anything but "Nora from 4F." After college, I'd set out to see new places, to figure out where I truly belonged, but the endless quest was growing tiresome.

And it was pretty freaking lonely, if I was willing to admit that to myself.

I parked in the driveway and turned off the ignition, gazing absently at Jake's truck next door. Was I thinking about *dating* him, for heaven's sake? Maybe he wasn't even interested in me—maybe he had a girlfriend. Or a wife! I knew next to nothing about him. So what if he looked at me the way I'd looked at the strawberry shortcake after that first bite? It didn't have to mean anything.

"Girl, you have been alone for too long," I scolded myself. "How can you even think about getting involved with someone right now?"

My hormones must be out of whack, I concluded—biology didn't care about logic. If I'd wanted to get laid, I should have taken it up with Audrey and Jamal back when I could still get lost in the bustling population of a city much larger than Spruce Hill, New York.

I kept that mantra on repeat as I invented excuse after excuse not to return to Jake's restaurant over the next week, but no matter what music I blasted or how many channels I flipped through, the silence of the apartment became overwhelming to the point where I could barely think straight, nevermind get any significant amount of work done.

"Normal people like quiet while they're working," I told my reflection one evening. "Only freaks like to drown out distraction by working in a bar."

Unfortunately, my reflection stared mutely back at me until I sighed and turned away from the mirror with a huff. I tucked my notebook and laptop into a canvas messenger bag, slung it across my chest, swallowed an oath when I couldn't resist checking my hair one last time, and walked out into the warm evening.

It doesn't mean anything.

I repeated those words to myself as I strolled down the street toward The Mermaid. Jake Lincoln was probably not interested in me, anyway. I sure as hell wasn't looking for a relationship—or even a hookup. This was simply because I needed a place to get some work done. That was all there was to it.

Jake was not behind the bar this time. Just for one mad moment, I felt a rush of something that I'd swear was relief but which felt suspiciously like disappointment.

A second later, my quick scan of the restaurant found him seated at a table with a ledger and calculator before him. His gaze had already locked onto me, and the air sizzled around me the moment our eyes met. That slow, crooked smile of his started a low burn deep in my belly.

Hormones or otherwise, I was in deep trouble.

Chapter Three

JAKE

A S NORA FOLLOWED A server to a booth tucked in the back corner of the restaurant, she offered a tiny little wave, which I returned with a friendly smile. Unable to hide my interest, I tapped my pencil on the tabletop and watched while she passed by, trying not to be too blatant in my perusal of her long legs and rounded hips once her back was to me.

This new neighbor of mine was inexplicably intriguing, in a prickly sort of way.

When Mr. Jenkins told me about his plan to rent out the garage apartment to this woman, he was uncharacteristically vague about where she was from or how she'd happened across his tiny little ad in the local paper. The old man had left town that morning with nothing more than a gentle reminder to me about watering his plants and keeping an eye on his new tenant.

Jenkins had lived in Spruce Hill his entire life—he only rarely ventured outside the town limits, at least that was the case until he'd planned this sabbatical. He was the sort to trust everyone to uphold the same small town values he had lived with for eighty-some years.

I'd been raised in a big city and knew better than to take anyone at face value, especially a beautiful woman who could scarcely bring herself to shake my hand.

A ripple of regret worked its way through me. It was impossible to miss her chilly reaction that first day, but I hoped her return to The Mermaid meant she might warm up to the idea of becoming friendly, at least. My own neighbor feeling the need to avoid me ruffled my feathers enough that I decided I'd simply make it impossible for her to hate me.

I wouldn't be pushy or obnoxious about it, just...patient. It had always been my strength.

As I tried not to stare toward her booth, I thought back to our meeting in the driveway. When she first walked up, I'd assumed she was young, maybe mid-twenties, but the way she handled herself changed my mind. By the end of the conversation, I guessed her to be in her early thirties.

With her chestnut hair thrown up in a curly ponytail that day, she'd looked very much the classic girl next door, fresh-faced and pretty, with eyes the color of rich, dark chocolate. She was delightfully curvaceous, which made for a beautiful contradiction—all that glorious softness against the thorny shields she kept in place.

A pretty woman with secrets. Right up my alley, if she weren't so obviously disinterested. That was a crying shame, but I wouldn't pressure her. That flash in her eyes when I mentioned Mr. Jenkins asking me to keep an eye on her was particularly telling.

Nora Cassidy was definitely not a damsel in distress. More like a warrior, maybe.

While she'd seemed terribly shy at first, nervous about even greeting me, it was clear there was fire underneath. That was what drew me like a moth to a flame. Above all else, I wondered what the real Nora was like when that fire erupted and burned away the thorns.

It would be incredible to witness, that much I was sure of.

With a glance to confirm she was still tucked away in the corner booth, I considered a number of possible backgrounds for the woman next door. These ranged from innocuous to fantastical, and I stared sightlessly down at my ledgers as I weighed the options.

Fleeing from a jilted ex-lover? Wanted for a crime? Hiding from the mob? None of it seemed to fit, but was the truth more complicated or simply more mundane?

Even from our brief interaction, I got the distinct sense that she was trying to mask her emotions but hadn't quite perfected the technique, that she wanted to remain aloof but also craved conversation and connection. Her spark of interest in my work on the apartment had been an enticing glimpse behind the veil—the sudden light in her eyes and color in her cheeks, the unguarded praise. The same thing happened when I asked about her job. It gave me hope that I just might be able to learn more about her.

With time, anyway. I wasn't going anywhere.

Once Joanna left Nora's table to take her order to the kitchen, I sauntered over to the booth as casually as possible.

"Hey, neighbor," I said, keeping my tone intentionally light.

This woman still seemed as likely to spook and run away from me as to smile or wave, so I forced myself to play it cool. I could have sworn I saw real pleasure in her dark eyes when she thanked me for my dessert offering the other night, even if the expression was fleeting. To me, that was as good a sign as any that there might be a thaw in the future.

The smile that flitted across her face now was tiny, but it was definitely a degree or two less guarded than last time.

"Hi, Jake," she replied.

I nodded toward her bag. "Did you come in here to work again? Isn't it a bit loud for that?"

"I like the noise, actually. For some reason, it helps me to be more productive than when it's too quiet. It keeps me from overthinking things. Like white noise, I guess." A faint, alluring blush rose in her cheeks, but her dark eyes shot to my face with sudden concern. "Is that okay? I know I'm taking up a table for longer than I would need it just to eat. I'm sure I can find somewhere else in town to work."

I held up my hands in a gesture of peace. Nora's gaze caught on them for an instant, so quickly I almost missed it, then she forced her eyes back to my face as I grinned.

"Easy. Of course you can work in here. If you want to let me know when you're coming in, I can even have the hostess keep this spot free, if you like it. We don't fill up completely too often and this booth is not generally a favorite—too loud, too close to the bar. If that's what you like, though, it works out on both sides. And hell, please don't feel like you have to order anything just to sit here and work. It's the least I can do for a neighbor."

Her expression changed instantaneously as a full, radiant smile lit her features, taking her from pretty to stunning so fast that my heart tripped a little.

"If you're sure," she said, "but please promise you'll just say the word if you need the space. I really don't want to take advantage."

You can take advantage any time.

The thought coursed swiftly through my brain, but I caught myself before voicing the sentiment. Every moment in this bewitching woman's presence was like a test of my wits, a challenge to balance my interest in her with keeping myself from saying anything stupid that might scare her away.

"Deal," I replied instead, offering her my hand to shake on it. I pretended not to see Nora's fingers curl into a fist before she forced them open and shook my hand. She drew hers back quickly, but before she could open her mouth to speak, I took the hint and said, "I'll leave you to your work, then. Let me know if you need anything."

I carried the ledger back to the office behind the bar, since the dinner crowd would be filtering in soon. Once I was seated at my desk, though, I couldn't focus on the numbers in front of me. Instead, I laced my hands behind my head and leaned back in the chair, summoning up a perfect image of the fascinating Nora Cassidy.

She was probably only a few inches past five feet, with luscious curves a man could sink his hands into. Her hair was different today, braided back from her face on one side so the rest fell in rich waves down her back. Even dressed as simply as she was now, in jeans and a cream sweater, she looked divine.

For some odd reason, I liked the idea of her working here, seeking refuge in my restaurant. Even better, I liked the fact that I'd be able to keep an eye on her—though perhaps not in the way Mr. Jenkins had intended. I was determined to learn everything I could about her, everything she'd allow me to learn, and having her close at hand would make it a whole lot easier, given the mile-high walls she had built around herself.

I had a feeling the payoff would be high enough to reward my patience.

Half an hour later, my phone gave several chirps in quick succession. I rolled my eyes when I saw the texts were all from my twin sister, inquiring about the new arrival in town.

If I so much as admitted the woman was attractive, Samantha would never give up pushing, not until she'd slipped a diamond ring in my pocket and arranged a date at the only swanky restaurant in town—or done it herself. Nora was a little too reserved to be Sam's usual type, but stranger things had happened. My sister loved the same way she lived, with wild abandon, while I'd been so caught up in work and home renovations that I hadn't been out on a date in over a year.

I responded with a casual observation about the weather, grinning when she shot back half a dozen colorful expletives. We might have been in our thirties, but needling my twin never got old.

On the other hand, I knew Sam would not let the matter drop without a real answer. She'd be over there ringing poor Nora's doorbell by tonight if I didn't say something to quell her interest, and I'd promised Nora no one was likely to drop by.

She drives a heap of scrap metal. Battery died as soon as she pulled up.

Sam was not amused. *You know that isn't what I meant, you jerk. Details. NOW.*

Cocking my head, I wondered what I could offer to assuage her curiosity. No way was I telling her the woman was sharp, beautiful, standoffish, a bit prickly. I pictured the dark curls and smattering of freckles across her nose, the guarded brown gaze that flared with interest so quickly I'd almost missed it—she was certainly all of those things and more.

My sister didn't need to know that, not yet anyway. Those points were all fodder for matchmaking and I was determined not to pull my interfering sister into the mix. Not until Nora got her footing and felt comfortable enough to tolerate a little friendly conversation.

Of course, I'd probably need all the time I could get just to teach my twin *how* to engage in friendly conversation without bowling Nora over.

She's nice, I replied, adding a smiley face.

My sister would just have to take a chapter from my book and learn how to be patient. I silenced the phone and tossed it down on the desk. Let her stew over it—Spruce Hill was a small town, and she'd surely run into Nora sooner rather than later.

Besides, it was perfectly clear that Nora could handle herself. I just hoped I'd be there to see it when she finally encountered my boisterous twin.

Chapter Four

OVER THE NEXT FEW days, Nora seemed determined to learn the rhythms not only of the town, if my sister's ridiculously well-connected gossip mill was any indication, but also of The Mermaid in particular. She showed up at different times of day, and she never took me up on my offer of a free table—she always ordered something, whether it was a meal, an appetizer, or just dessert.

I made a mental note that the strawberry shortcake was her favorite.

Though our prices were reasonable, I quietly instructed the staff to give her the employee discount. For all I knew, she could be an heiress, but I had no clue how much a translator made for their work. Even if she was independently wealthy, that didn't mean I couldn't be a good neighbor and give her another reason to keep coming back.

One night, when I was tending the bar until closing time, I noticed her narrowing her eyes at the bill. When she glanced up, I gave a benign, friendly smile. If she wasn't willing to ask about it—and I was pretty confident she wouldn't—then I sure as hell wasn't going to bring it up.

Much to my disappointment, Nora didn't show up to the restaurant the following evening or the next. While I consoled myself with the image of her tucked safely in a corner booth, dark hair cascading over her shoulders and veiling her face as she worked, a familiar voice called my name and I shook myself from my daydreaming to greet my best friend.

"Casey, hey. I thought you guys were camping until Wednesday," I replied as she slid onto a stool at the end of the bar.

"Came back early. Tommy and Angelica's baby has an ear infection. The poor kid couldn't stop crying, so we decided to call it quits and head home. Such is life now that we're old enough for shit like marriage and families, huh?"

Casey McDonald was as close to me as my own sister, a near constant in my life since we first moved to Spruce Hill. If Sam was a tornado, Casey was the calm, deep water of Lake Ontario. She'd been in love with Sam for as long as I could remember, but somehow the two of them never quite managed to get past the fear of ruining their friendship in order to take the plunge.

At sixteen, I'd been pretty happy to learn Casey was only interested in women—she was stunning and teenage me might very well have ruined my own friendship with her in the way my sister had managed to avoid for so many years.

Now? I'd give my left arm to lock the two of them in a room together and not let anyone out until they finally confessed their love for one another.

I laughed as I handed Casey a cold beer. "Next thing you know, we'll be sitting in rockers on a porch together, talking about the olden days. I'm sorry I missed camping, though. When's the next trip? Maybe I can manage a few days away to join you."

Casey took a long pull on her beer and raised a brow. Her startling, fire engine red hair was combed back like James Dean and there was a teasing light in her eyes—tiger eyes, Sam always called them, a fierce hazel that missed nothing.

"Sure you won't be too busy with a certain newcomer in town?"

Groaning, I said, "You were out in the boonies and the news still managed to travel that fast?"

"C'mon, man, you've lived in Spruce Hill long enough to know how that stuff gets around. Especially with Sam involved. She's been texting me for days. So, spill. You two hook up yet?"

I shot her a warning glance. "No. She's barely been here a week."

"Sure you're not losing your touch?"

Silently cursing my sister, I served another patron and waited until the older man walked away before saying in a low voice, "I'm not losing anything. Nora is…cautious. Skittish, maybe. A little jumpy. She reminds me a bit of Angelica back in college."

One of our closest friends had been assaulted walking back to the dorms during sophomore year. We'd all closed ranks in the aftermath, committed to keeping every member of our little crew safe.

Casey blew out a breath, her expression growing somber. "You think she's been hurt?"

I thought about it for a long moment, then ran a hand through my hair. "I don't know. Maybe not like that. Could have been a bad relationship, a bad family situation? She doesn't talk about the past much and I don't think she's ready for anyone to pry."

"Duly noted. Well, I look forward to meeting her." When my eyes narrowed slightly, Casey grinned. "Easy, cowboy. I won't encroach on your territory, don't worry."

"She'd probably kick all our asses if she heard herself referred to as 'territory,' so watch your mouth around her," I warned. I glanced toward Nora's usual booth for probably the hundredth time in two days and felt my spirits fall a little at seeing it still empty. "She comes in most evenings to work, but it's been a couple days."

"Let me guess, you're afraid you scared her away," Casey ventured.

Before I could reply, my gaze caught on the figure slipping through the front door and my heart inflated like a balloon. I felt Casey's focus sharpening on my expression—there was no doubt she saw it written on my face, all the signs that my interest in Nora wasn't strictly neighborly.

When I glanced back at Casey, she smirked. "Oh, hell, Lincoln. You're into her."

Casually, she turned to look at the woman who'd just entered the restaurant. At first glance, Nora was certainly pretty, but it wasn't until those deep brown eyes locked on mine and a small smile curved her lips upward that I suspected Casey might understand. That smile, the little hint of mystery, was so startling in its beauty that even Casey did a double take.

"Can you behave like a respectable adult for a minute while I say hello?" I asked, barely looking back toward Casey.

"You know I'd never cockblock a friend," Casey teased under her breath. At that, I shot her a brief glare, but she only grinned in response. "Go on. I do expect an introduction eventually, but heaven forbid I interrupt a reunion of lovers."

I barely heard her as I filled a glass with root beer and brought it over to Nora's table. "Hey, stranger," I said lightly. "I was afraid you'd found someplace else to work."

"No, I've just been…ah, busy." Though she looked calm and composed, a faint blush highlighted her cheekbones. I cocked a brow at the weak excuse and she wrinkled her nose at me without elaborating.

"Right, of course. In any case, I'm glad you're back," I said smoothly. I waited until her eyes lifted to meet mine and then had to fight down the urge to touch her. "There's a bachelor party coming in tonight, just so you know."

She closed her laptop. "I'm sorry, I can go if you need the space."

"No, no, not at all. Stay. Please stay. I just wanted you to be prepared. It'll probably be louder than usual tonight."

I couldn't help myself—I laid my hand over hers on top of the computer. The warmth of her skin seeped through my palm. *Just as soft as she looks,* I thought, and my heart thudded when she didn't pull away from me. Still, I was afraid to test my luck, so I reluctantly drew back my hand and smiled at her.

"Bea's got a new dessert special tonight, you should try it so you can give me an honest review. Let me know when you're ready for a refill."

Nora didn't respond, but I felt her eyes on me as I strode back to the bar, like she was as surprised as I was that the physical contact hadn't caused her to jerk away. It wasn't until I flashed her a warm smile from behind the bar that she opened the laptop again and turned her focus to her work.

At the other end of the bar, Casey raised her brows comically high. "I haven't seen that kind of sexual tension since—well, ever. Shit, man. She might actually be into you, too. I really expected some kind of unrequited love here, based on your puppy dog eyes when I came in."

I gave a short laugh, but my eyes strayed back to Nora every time I had a free second throughout the evening. Something about her presence calmed me, like I could finally relax.

The bachelor party showed up just after the dinner rush ended, a group of six guys from Oakville, the next town over. It became clear pretty quickly that they'd already consumed a fair amount of alcohol, but not so much that anyone needed to be cut off yet. The group would require watching, though. I had no problem kicking out a bunch of rowdy drunks, even if Sam and I had been making an effort to bring in events like this.

When Casey eyed the group and offered to stay to help me keep a handle on things, I was aware enough of my own distraction to gratefully accept. We'd worked as bartenders together at The Mermaid after college, a perfect weekend gig for two recent graduates. My father had been happy to have the help and even happier to keep a close eye on us.

Casey washed up and joined me behind the bar. "Just like old times, huh?"

For the first hour, we were much busier than usual, even with Casey's help. The two of us, with the ease of long practice, moved seamlessly around one another as we mixed drinks, opened beer bottles, and poured wine. In addition to the bachelor party seated at the bar, familiar patrons flowed in and out with a regularity that I usually appreciated.

The rush gradually slowed, leaving only the bachelor party and a few regulars at the bar. I was already extremely grateful for Casey's help, but even more so when I noticed one of the groomsmen eyeing Nora toward the end of the night. The man was seated at the far end of the bar, pretending to pay attention to his raucous friends as his gaze slithered over Nora in a way that made my skin crawl.

"What's up?" Casey asked quietly. She'd known me long enough to detect even the most subtle change of mood, and it must have been clear that I was suddenly on edge.

"I don't like the way he's looking at her," I replied, my voice low.

Casey surveyed the scene and set a hand on my arm. My tension was a palpable thing, my eyes focused on the man watching Nora as I bit back the urge to growl. While I had no right to place any claim on her, I damn well wasn't going to let her be subjected to the kind of leer that had taken up residence on this sleazeball's face.

"Given what I've heard about our new resident, I'm not sure she would appreciate your interference, Lincoln. Stepping in might do more harm than anything, if you want to stay in her good graces. I'd hate to see you throw it all away over some macho misunderstanding."

I gave a reluctant nod before turning to serve a customer who'd squeezed in beside the groom. Casey shifted toward that end of the bar, trying to engage the bachelor party attendees in conversation. I was torn—I didn't want that kind of attention directed at Casey, either, but I knew she was well trained in handling drunks. Hell, we'd trained together in that field. She was more than capable of dealing with them.

When I glanced over again, I caught sight of the man at the end of the bar sliding off his stool and walking unsteadily toward Nora.

"Shit," I muttered, tossing the towel in my hand to Casey.

We'd find out soon enough if my interference would piss Nora off. I couldn't sit back and do nothing.

Chapter Five

Nora

WITH MY HEAD BENT, intent on my computer screen as I debated appropriate idioms, I didn't notice the man coming toward me until he rapped his knuckles on the lacquered table and scared the living hell out of me.

Reflexively, I closed the laptop and slid it into my bag, rising from the booth as though I'd planned to leave at that particular moment anyway. I had enough experience with drunks to know it was better to cut my losses and get the hell out of there.

"Hey, baby," the man slurred.

When I glanced at him, my body jerked in surprise and my heart slammed into my throat. He looked a little too much like a ghost from my past, but the resemblance faded as I took in the details—the hair was a similar light, mousy brown, but his face was too narrow. This guy was thin and wiry, with bloodshot eyes and a look on his face that I knew only too well.

One couldn't make a habit of working in bars without dealing with his type now and again.

"How about a drink, pretty girl?"

My muscles tensed, more at his smarmy tone than the words themselves. *Stay calm, stay calm, stay calm.* "Thanks for the offer, but I was just leaving."

"Aw, come on, just one drink. I'm good company, baby, I promise you that." His gaze traveled over my body in a way that made me feel like I needed a shower. "Oh yeah, we'd be good together. You'll see. I've got all night."

"Thank you," I said woodenly, "but no. Like I said, I was just leaving."

I started to turn away, but the man's hand shot out to grab my wrist faster than I expected, given the way he was weaving on his feet.

The reaction was ingrained; without thinking, I rotated my arm around to break his hold, grabbed the man's wrist in return, spun him around, and twisted it hard behind his back until he dropped to his knees with a sharp, startled cry.

"Shit, okay, I'm sorry!" he shrieked. "Fuck, let go!"

I released him immediately, drawing my hand back to my chest in an attempt to slow my racing heart. The man scrambled to his feet and scurried back to the bar, leaving me staring at Jake, who approached us just as the guy hit the floor. The laughing taunts of the man's friends pounded in my ears, keeping time with the loud thud of my own racing pulse.

"I have to go," I whispered, reaching for my bag.

"Nora, wait. Please wait. Let me walk you home. Christ, are you okay?"

Jake grabbed the bag before I could, slinging it across his chest as he studied me. I wasn't sure what exactly he was seeing, but even after years without a panic attack, I could imagine well enough—white as a ghost, my eyes too wide against my face, breath coming in little gasps that threatened to give way to hyperventilation.

That pathetic image shook me out of my panic, at least a little bit, and irritation rose in its place.

"I don't need you to protect me," I snapped.

"No," Jake agreed easily, "I can see that you don't. But it's dark out, so I'd feel better with you at my side for my own protection. Let's go."

My brain was buzzing so fast, I didn't even flinch when he set his hand on the small of my back and steered me out into the night air. It was easier to breathe out there, but we only made it half a block before a strangled sob tore from my throat.

"I think I'm going to be sick," I gasped.

Jake grabbed my shoulders and gently guided me down until I was seated on the curb. He crouched in front of me, and the familiarity of his face—even with the dimple nowhere in sight—was enough to quell the nausea.

"Breathe for me, Nora, you're okay. You're safe. It's going to be okay."

The shuddering breaths that whistled past my lips were all I could manage, leaving me lightheaded and shaky. Jake shifted to sit on the curb beside me and cupped his hand around the back of my neck, easing my head downward until it rested between my knees. He released my neck to smooth his hand in a wide arc across my back. Beneath his palm, my entire body trembled, but his warmth seeped into my skin, covering me like a blanket.

"Just breathe," he murmured. "There you go. Keep on breathing for me, just like that. You're safe now."

Slowly, the shaking waned and the tightness in my lungs eased. It was only then that embarrassment flooded me, replacing both panic and adrenaline. I knew I should move, scoot away or stand up maybe, but the way he was stroking my back was so soothing, I couldn't bear to make him stop just yet.

"I'm sorry," I whispered, my voice hoarse. "Oh, Christ. I just attacked someone in your restaurant."

Jake's short laugh rumbled deep in his chest. "No. Hell no. Nora, you defended yourself. He put his hands on you first. I saw the way he was looking at you. I'm so sorry, I should have gotten to him before he ever had the chance to touch you. What you did was in self-defense. You were amazing."

As soon as I could draw a decent breath, I sat up slowly and covered my face with my hands. I didn't tell him to stop, so Jake continued that slow sweep of his hand over my back. It felt

good. Right, even, like some internal magnet under my muscles had latched onto one in his palm and refused to let go.

After a long moment, I finally managed to draw a deep
inhalation into my lungs. The breath still trembled through
my frame, but at least I was confident that I was finally getting
enough oxygen.

"I should get home," I said quietly. "You really don't have
to escort me. I'm sorry, Jake."

Part of me wanted to cry, another part wanted the concrete
below to swallow me and my humiliation in one gulp. The
final, tiny part that I fought so hard to resist wanted nothing
more than to lean into Jake's warm, reassuring touch.

As if he'd heard those thoughts, Jake's hand slid up to
the back of my neck so he could tip my face toward him.
He waited until I met his eyes to say, "Stop apologizing. You
were just assaulted in my restaurant, so I'm damn well making
certain you get home okay. Are you sure you're ready to stand
up?"

I nodded and gratefully grasped his other hand when he
held it out to help me to my feet. "Thank you," I whispered.

Mortification trickled painfully through me, weighing
down my limbs as I stood, but it slowly gave way to a numb-
ness that settled in my brain. Still, I didn't pull my hand away
as we continued toward home, clinging to the comfort Jake
seemed so ready to provide.

Low profile: gone.

"You're pretty badass," he murmured.

My laugh was barely more than a rush of breath, but a relieved smile ghosted across his lips at the sound.

"Or pretty neurotic," I replied. "He was probably harmless."

When he didn't respond right away, I glanced up at him and saw his features harden into an expression I'd never seen on his handsome face before. Cute Neighbor had transformed into a knight ready to avenge my honor, and for once, I wasn't insulted by the thought of someone else trying to protect me. Those blue eyes softened when he looked down at me and shook his head.

"You said no. If he was harmless, he would've left it at that and kept his fucking hands off you."

I fell silent, thinking as much about Jake's reaction as about the scene I'd caused. It had been a long time since I'd been comfortable enough to hold hands with someone, but I was afraid if I broke that small connection, lost even that tiny point of contact, I might fall apart again. We walked the rest of the way in silence, until we reached the wooden stairs up to my apartment. I reluctantly dropped his hand and turned to take my bag from him.

Jake handed it over, but he shook his head again when he saw my expression. "If you're planning to apologize again, don't. You did nothing wrong. *Nothing*."

Standing there in the falling darkness, I suddenly felt achingly lonely. Jake hesitated for only a heartbeat, then pursed his lips like he was throwing caution to the wind before he reached out and touched my cheek. It was only the barest brush of his fingertips against my skin, but my eyelids fluttered at the gentle intimacy of it.

That reaction seemed to embolden him, so he cupped my face in his warm palm and waited for me to open my eyes again.

"I'm sorry you were hurt."

The way he said it sounded like he meant something beyond the evening's mishap, like he could see into my past. I lifted my hand to cover his. "I'm okay," I replied, even as I wondered if it was true.

"Nora," he breathed, his thumb stroking my cheek. He closed his eyes like he was in pain, and when he opened them, the full intensity of his blue gaze zeroed in on me. "I know we don't know each other very well yet, but if it's okay with you, I really feel like I need to hold onto you for a minute. If you're willing to let me, I mean."

Everything inside me softened and warmed as I moved unconsciously toward him, sliding my arms around his waist without hesitation. He encircled me with his own, warm and strong, like they were shoring up my defenses.

Except for once it felt like someone else was inside those walls, helping me from within.

God, it felt good to be held like this, I realized, a bit dazed. Sturdy and solid, with his heart beating steadily under my ear, Jake ran his hands slowly up and down my back while his chin came to rest against the top of my head. I sighed and all the tension in my back and shoulders drained away until I felt almost limp with relief.

"Is this okay?" he murmured into my hair.

I laughed against his sternum. "This is more than okay, I think."

"Good, because it feels damn near heavenly to me."

It was a long time before I finally drew back and I missed his embrace immediately. Reluctant to fracture the soft sense of peace surrounding us, I touched my fingers tentatively to the line of his jaw, the caress so light that he shivered at the sensation. Jake held as still as he could, his arms at his sides, and waited for me to speak.

"I should probably try to get some sleep. Thank you, Jake. I hope I didn't screw anything up for your business tonight."

"You didn't screw up anything, period. Go to bed and try to relax, okay?"

I nodded, then watched as he reached into his wallet for a business card with a golden mermaid tail across the front. When he held it out, I took it and ran my fingertip over the embossed print.

"Here, so you have my number if you need me. Night, Nora."

He caught my hands in his and squeezed lightly. I closed my eyes for a second, doubting his reassurances but letting them fill me up nonetheless, crystallizing into something like a fragile sense of hope. Even with the aftereffects of the confrontation still skittering through my veins, something had changed between us tonight. Accepting comfort from Jake had melted the remainder of my resistance.

"Goodnight, Jake," I whispered.

Releasing his hands, I took a tiny step back, then another. I turned and trudged up the stairs, all the while feeling his eyes on my back like a brand.

Something had definitely changed.

Chapter Six

JAKE

S TANDING AT THE BOTTOM of the stairs until she was safely inside the apartment, I waited until I heard the lock turn and saw the kitchen light go off, then strode to my truck to drive back to The Mermaid. If that drunken idiot hadn't gotten the picture and left already, I was fully prepared to educate him on just who had screwed things up tonight.

I could still feel the ghost of her hands in mine, those fine bones of hers impossibly delicate under my fingers. The memory of her bringing that son of a bitch to his knees flashed before my eyes and I had to admit that Nora was far from the breakable little thing I'd first imagined her to be.

Another wave of fury washed over me, just as it had when I saw the man grab her. But shit, the way she'd taken the sucker down...I was impressed beyond belief. I'd seen Casey perform a similar move once, but she had a good six inches on Nora and the body of an athlete, thanks to a lifetime of playing rugby.

Casey's warning about stepping in echoed in my mind. I couldn't say I would ever be glad that I was too late to intercept the guy, but if she was right, if Nora would've been more pissed at my interference than she was at my attempt to comfort her afterward, then maybe it had been for the best in some ways.

Besides, she'd accepted that comfort barely two minutes later. Trembled under my palm as she fought for breath, clung to my hand all the way home, burrowed into my chest like she was made to be there.

And as much as I'd wanted to kiss her while we were standing at the bottom of the stairs, that had seemed like tempting fate a little too far after so much success. By the time she went inside, I was relieved to see her looking only a little sheepish instead of traumatized.

Tonight was a turning point, though I wasn't sure exactly what that might mean for us going forward.

By the time I turned into the lot at The Mermaid, I was able to pull a veneer of calm around me in order to deal with things—not as Nora's friend, which was probably the highest label I could claim at that point, but as a business owner.

Sam would back me up, I knew that without a doubt. Hell, my dad would probably be proud of my actions, and I could already imagine the heart-eyes my mom would throw in my direction when she heard.

The Lincoln family would *never* choose the money that events could bring in over keeping our customers safe, and I intended to make that perfectly clear tonight.

Nora wasn't the only one willing to throw down with assholes.

MY RELIEF WHEN NORA showed up the next afternoon vanished as soon as my sister swept in through the front doors. I had to bite back a groan, wishing she'd waited another day or two to pounce after I'd texted her and my parents about the incident last night.

As expected, they'd all been outraged and supported my reaction—and Nora's. I should have known that would only amp up Sam's desire to meet my new neighbor.

"Jakey boy," Sam sang out as she slid onto a stool at the bar. "How's business?"

Like a ghost of sensation, I felt Nora's dark, curious gaze on us and wondered for a brief moment if she thought Sam was my girlfriend. It was juvenile of me to experience a quick burst of warmth at the idea that she might be jealous. I knew that, but I basked in it all the same.

"Hi, Sammo," I replied lightly. "You know exactly how business is, since I send you regular updates. Want a drink?"

"Something girly, if you don't mind." She leaned close and whispered, "Is she here? Your new neighbor? Jesus, Casey told me exactly how she took that asshole down last night. I want to meet her. Introduce me? Pleeeease?"

Rolling my eyes, I mixed her up a Blue Lagoon and topped it with a tiny umbrella. I slid it across the counter and served another patron a beer before coming out from behind the bar. Sam trailed behind me like an eager puppy. Nora had turned her focus back to her computer and didn't notice our approach.

"Nora," I said cautiously. There was a lightning-quick flash of alarm in her eyes at the interruption, but it was gone before I could be sure I'd seen it. "If you have a minute, my sister would like to meet you. Samantha Lincoln, Nora Cassidy. Nora, Sam."

Nora's features eased into an expression of polite interest. When she immediately held out her hand to Sam, I frowned a little, but Sam shook it quickly and settled into the bench across from Nora, leaving me no time to ponder. My sister launched straight into the kind of chatter that had driven me up the wall when we were teenagers, so I shot Nora an apologetic grimace before I went back to the bar.

Sam laid claim to the same color hair as mine, though hers was highlighted with a pale golden blonde, and her eyes were more gray than blue. As always, my twin spoke at a startling speed; from behind the bar, I watched as Nora closed her laptop and tried to follow along. Just when I started to feel like I ought to rescue her from my chatterbox sister, a rush of customers crowded around the bar and my opportunity was lost.

By the time they moved on, Nora sat alone at the booth once more, looking utterly bewildered. She rubbed her temples and was staring blankly at the laptop screen when I finally managed to return. I slid into the seat my sister had vacated, setting a fresh glass of root beer before her as a token of penance.

"Sorry about that. She's like a force of nature. I've learned to just let her roll on through, because it's easier than trying to contain her. I hope she didn't say anything too outrageous."

Nora snorted, a gloriously unladylike sound that made me grin. "It's fine. I haven't been forced into anything resembling girl talk in a long time. She was very...nice."

I raised a brow. "Nice. Huh. I'm not sure I've ever heard anyone call Samantha 'nice' before."

"Ouch," she said with a laugh, a hint of teasing in her tone that drew my focus straight to her face.

I couldn't take my eyes off her expression, animated now in her amusement instead of so carefully controlled. Her laughter was as captivating as it was unexpected. For once, my presence didn't seem to dampen her reaction. I took that as a good sign.

With a mischievous smirk, Nora added, "Then I guess I won't tell you all the flattering things she said about you."

At that, I leaned forward and smiled in an attempt to cajole her. "Aw, c'mon, now you *have* to tell me."

For a heartbeat, Nora seemed frozen in her seat, like she was battling the instinct to lean toward me in response. I hoped she found me as magnetic as I found her, anyway. In the end, she sat back against the vinyl of the booth instead and let her gaze wander over me before she replied.

"According to your sister, you're quite a catch. Thirty-three years old, fit, smart, most definitely single—she made sure to mention that fact at least seventeen times in the course of three minutes—handy around the house and good with cars."

"Why, Nora, you're making me blush," I drawled.

She rolled her eyes, then held up her fingers to tick off each point as she listed the rest. "You don't smoke, don't drink to excess, have a good head for numbers, and you're respectful with the ladies, though she mentioned you keep yourself too busy to date much. I didn't catch if you're a religious man, but it does seem like you're in the running for sainthood."

Sam might have said those things, but hearing Nora recount them sent tendrils of heat along my veins.

I covered my face with my hands and groaned to hide my reaction. "Oh my god. Now I'm *really* sorry I sent her over here, especially after last night. Please, let me make it up to you."

Nora's eyes widened a little, though whether in anxiety or excitement, I wasn't sure. "That's really not necessary," she replied.

The protest sounded weak, so I gathered she was too curious about what I might lay out in reparation to put any force behind it. There'd be time enough for her to shoot me down afterward, I'd make sure of it. Still, it felt like the perfect opportunity to make the offer without her feeling pressured to accept.

"Please consider it, Nora," I said as my hands dropped to the table. "Lady's choice: I can fix up that fan belt that makes your little car sound like a baby werewolf howling at the moon every time you start the engine, or I can take you out to dinner. Someplace that isn't here."

This was a risk and I knew it, but if she gave any sign that she wanted me to back off, I would. I was intrigued by her calculating expression as she weighed the options. In truth, I wasn't sure which one sounded better to me—either would be a step forward, however small.

"That sounds like you're offering manual labor versus an actual date. What part do I play in this little scenario if I choose the car repair?"

A slow smile crept across my face. "Well, I suppose you might have to bring me a cold bottle of soda while I'm working. Maybe hang out, pass me a few tools, that kind of thing. You'd be doing *me* a favor, really. I've been itching to get under the hood since you pulled up."

The unintentional innuendo had her dark gaze jerking to meet mine, and I was temporarily distracted by the rising flush in her cheeks. Her lips parted but no words came out. My stomach bottomed out as I realized what I'd said.

"The hood of your car, I mean. Because of the noise," I fumbled.

Despite the blush rapidly spreading under her skin, Nora choked back a laugh at my attempt to smooth things over. Before replying, she tapped her chin thoughtfully for a minute.

Unlike my sister's long, always-painted nails, Nora's were un-polished, trimmed short and neat. Like the rest of her, they struck me as refreshingly natural, effortlessly beautiful.

"I would have to pick the car, mostly because I'm actually afraid it's going to die a dramatic death the next time I hit the highway, but you really don't owe me anything, Jake. We can just forget about payment and you can accept that I'm perfectly able to handle polite conversation with strangers, even if you haven't seen much proof of that so far."

The last part came out sounding rueful instead of snarky, so I simply grinned. "Car it is. I'm off tomorrow, I'll grab the parts in the morning and be over around noon. Finish your root beer, I'm closing up in ten. Can I convince you to walk home with me? We're heading in the same direction anyway."

Ah, there it is, I thought when her jaw tightened almost imperceptibly, but to my surprise, she nodded anyway.

"Okay," she said softly.

I bit my lip to try to keep my idiotic smile in check. "Okay."

Chapter Seven

NORA

His eyes lit up like a kid on Christmas and my entire traitorous body responded to that flash of joy. It was adorable and aggravating, the way it made my insides flutter, but I couldn't hold back another smile as he left the table to finish up at the bar.

While I waited, I drank the rest of my soda and reflected on everything that had happened since I arrived in Spruce Hill.

I didn't want to be beholden to anyone, especially not Jake, who'd seen me at my lowest already, but the offer of a place to work in peace was simply too good to pass up. The Mermaid was clean, noisy enough without the chaotic energy of a dive bar—or the constant hassle of drunken frat boys who didn't like to take no for an answer—and this little corner spot kept me from drawing too much attention to myself.

Last night had been an anomaly, and shockingly, I still felt safe there.

Each time I came in, I completed more work than I would have expected *and* consumed another delicious meal.

Tonight had been another aberration, thanks to Sam's whirlwind conversation, but I could resist the temptation that was Jake Lincoln, especially if it meant getting my assignments done ahead of schedule. It would be well worth it for the productivity alone.

And if he felt guilty enough about his talkative sister to fix up my car, so be it. I wasn't so shortsighted as to turn down that offer.

By the time Jake locked the doors of The Mermaid behind us, my nerves had taken that flutter in my belly almost all the way to nausea. We'd walked this same path together last night, but it was different now, wasn't it?

We'd held hands, hugged as we said goodnight. What if he expected that again?

I had no reason to assume any ulterior motive behind his offer, but that didn't soothe so many years of caution. There was pepper spray in the front pocket of my bag, if I needed it. I knew how to defend myself—and Jake was well aware of that fact now.

Right. No need to overreact. This man had been nothing but kind so far.

I was sure Jake felt the tension thrumming through me the minute he turned away from the door. Without apparent effort, he set out to soothe me—subtle, intuitive choices that most people wouldn't even have noticed, but I was hyper-aware of his every movement.

Before we started down the street, he slipped his hands straight into his pockets and my shoulders relaxed ever so slightly, no longer worrying about whether he expected me to hold his hand. Along the widest part of the sidewalk, he stayed a good foot away from me. Once we turned onto our street, we had no choice except to shift closer together, but it seemed like he made sure not to brush against me, even accidentally.

Jake told stories about Sam to lighten the mood. As I laughed, most of my remaining tension evaporated and I found myself actually enjoying his company during the walk. When we reached the end of Mr. Jenkins' driveway, he kept his hands in his pockets while he nodded to my car.

"You sure must love that hunk of junk," he said with a grin.

I sighed and patted the little blue car affectionately—or at least, I patted one of the few sections of metal that was still blue instead of ravaged by rust. "She's my baby," I replied simply.

"Love conquers all," he joked. "We'll get her fixed up right tomorrow. Goodnight, Nora."

He was already backing away toward his own driveway when I finally said, "Goodnight, Jake."

Though I wasn't quite sure how it had happened, I felt lighter, almost buoyant. For the first time since meeting Jake Lincoln, I stopped feeling like Spruce Hill was a mistake and had to admit that maybe, just maybe, it was the best decision I'd made in years.

S ATURDAY MORNING DAWNED BRIGHT and hot, with the forecast promising a scorching summer day. I stood in front of the low dresser in my bedroom as I tried to decide what to wear. Shorts? The thought of standing in close proximity to him in my favorite cutoffs felt a little too dangerous, a little too much like tempting fate. I could wear jeans—and sweat to death standing out there.

I cringed at the thought of Jake having to resuscitate me when I passed out from heat exhaustion, coming to my rescue yet again.

The inner war waged for another three minutes before I swore loudly and colorfully and grabbed a pair of cropped leggings off the pile I'd tossed onto the bed.

"Problem solved," I muttered.

Outraged that I was debating what to wear like a god-damn teenager preparing for a date, I threw on the rattiest t-shirt I owned, an oversized tie dyed number I usually reserved for use as pajamas, and shoved my hair into a messy bun. I'd put a six-pack of colas in the fridge when I got home last night, so I grabbed two bottles before heading outside.

When Jake's truck pulled into his driveway a few minutes later, I was seated on the hood of my car with both hands clutching one bottle of soda and the other one beside me. Jake, curse the man, didn't so much as glance at my clothes, simply flashed that dimpled smile of his.

"Morning, neighbor," he called as he sauntered over. "You might be a tiny little thing, but I'm surprised the old girl hasn't dumped you right onto the driveway."

I narrowed my eyes at him and wondered if Jake could see the steam rising from the top of my head. "First off, I am not tiny by any stretch of the imagination, so we don't need to pretend otherwise. You just happen to be ridiculously tall. Second, if you continue insulting my baby, I'll shove that fan belt right up your ass and drink this soda all by myself."

He let out a low whistle as he grabbed the other bottle off the hood before I could confiscate it, then swept a cheeky little bow. "My, aren't we touchy, and on such a beautiful day. Please allow me to offer my most humble apologies."

Those pretty blue eyes of his were dancing with mischief, however, which basically rendered his apology moot. I narrowed mine at him until he laughed.

"Very well, I'll keep my mouth shut about this fine vehicle *and* her lovely mistress. Thanks for the soda."

Though I muttered something uncomplimentary beneath my breath, a grudging smile tugged at my lips when I slanted a glance in his direction. "Apology accepted, this time at least. Baby's a sensitive old girl, and in my experience, saying mean things about her tends to lead to breaking down on the side of a deserted stretch of road in the middle of the night."

"How often are you out on a deserted road in the middle of the night?"

"More than once, let's just say." I paused to raise a quizzical brow at him as something occurred to me. "You have a bit of an accent, almost like...a hint of a southern drawl. Why is that?"

"Probably because I'm not from around here," Jake said with a shrug. "I'm surprised you caught that. We moved here when Sam and I were fourteen, so it's mostly faded since then."

"Language and word usage are a huge part of my job. I tend to notice that kind of thing. Where are you from?"

His delight in the fact that I was asking questions about him was obvious. Even when he tried to hide a smile, that dimple peeped at me like a beacon.

"We grew up near Atlanta. My mom got transferred out here for her job before we started high school. Dad opened The Mermaid a couple years later. This town kind of grows on you, I guess. Both of us went away for college, but somehow Spruce Hill ended up reeling us back in. When my dad asked us to take over The Mermaid for him, that was that."

Curiosity overtook my annoyance. "You two are twins?"

Jake heaved a dramatic sigh, though he seemed pleased I'd come around to actually engaging in a conversation. "Unfortunately, yes. I'm twelve minutes older, which is obviously the source of my superior wisdom."

I laughed, but Jake didn't take offense. In fact, he smiled at me like my laughter was a gift—then that smile warmed as his gaze traveled over me, like he saw right through my ridiculous outfit choice and still appreciated what was hiding underneath. With all the force of a thunderbolt, I realized that maybe those two things were one and the same.

He liked me. Whether I was reserved or chatty, it didn't seem to matter.

I met his eyes, glittering blue in the sunlight and soft with some unidentifiable emotion, then swallowed hard. He cleared his throat and straightened away from the car to grab a toolbox from the bed of his truck.

I hopped down off the hood, sidling a few feet away while Jake popped it open and started to work. When he asked for specific tools, I handed them to him without commentary.

"I'm impressed," he said after the third or fourth time. "My only experience with an assistant is my sister, who would've taken ten minutes to rifle through the toolbox with every request, more to fuck with me than because she's actually clueless."

"That doesn't shock me. She's a trip."

He shook his head at me and all my annoyance from that morning evaporated. We fell into companionable silence, punctuated here and there when I'd lean over to ask a question or two about the inner workings of the engine, eager to learn.

My father would've been proud.

I felt a twinge, missing the sound of his voice. We were due for a catch-up call, but he was enjoying his retirement boating along the Atlantic and was out of cell service range until he came back to shore.

After one particularly long string of questions, Jake grinned up at me. "Ah, Nora, I see that insatiable curiosity is another of your more intriguing traits."

I flushed and turned away to put a wrench back in the toolbox. What the hell else did he find intriguing about me? I couldn't quite decide if that was flattering or frightening, so I set it aside and made no further comment as he worked on the engine.

It was approaching dinner time when Jake dropped the hood and had me get in to start the car. When the engine turned over with a low rumble instead of a howl, I gave a delighted cry.

"There she is," Jake said, clapping a hand on the roof of the car. "I knew we could do it."

"You are a god among men, Jake Lincoln."

The words tumbled out before I could stop them, but Jake's satisfied expression almost made the slip-up worth it, despite the heat rising in my cheeks.

"She's got heart, I'll give her that. Just like her owner," he said when I turned the ignition off and stepped out of the car. My breath caught in my throat, but he simply smiled at me in that sweet, friendly way of his and continued, "I'm starving. How about a pizza?"

"Jake," I began.

He held up his hands and flashed another disarming smile. "I'm not trying to sneak a two-fer out of you, Nora, I'm just hungry. I'll be up all night puking if I eat a whole pizza on my own. We can sit out on the deck if you're afraid to be alone with me. I am, after all, a god among men."

Though I laughed at that comment, my pulse leapt as I considered. After a moment, I nodded. "Okay. But I will have you know that I am definitely not afraid to be alone with you," I said, the statement coming out a little too defensive.

Jake regarded me steadily. "No?"

"Of course not," I huffed. "I'm just not interested in . . ." The words trailed off and I waved a frustrated hand between us.

His eyebrows shot upward. "In what, exactly?" he asked, leaning his hip against the car. He tucked his thumbs in his belt loops and watched me with a maddeningly patient air.

Damn him. "Anything romantic. At all."

"Okay, I'll scrap the poetry I planned to recite and we'll just stick to pizza. Is beer too romantic? I might have some powdered lemonade."

When he rocked back and forth on his heels a little, I almost snapped. The sweet, small town boy act was much less convincing now that I knew he was from Atlanta instead of the middle of nowhere.

"Thank you for replacing the fan belt, Jake. I'll get my own dinner," I said, a little more sharply than I'd intended, and turned quickly toward the stairs to my apartment. Embarrassment flooded my veins, hot and uncomfortable.

"Nora, wait," he implored, catching my hand in his. I jerked it away like I'd been scalded and his teasing façade dropped instantly. He ran a hand through his curls, leaving them adorably tousled. "I'm sorry. Shit, I'm really sorry, Nora. I swear I'm not actually an asshole. I'm just prone to speaking before I think sometimes. Most of the time, probably."

My lips quirked at that. "It's fine, Jake. I really do appreciate your help with my car."

"I can't bear for you to walk away angry, not even a little. I'm not like him."

"Not like who?" I asked, startled by the vehemence in his voice.

"Like the guy who grabbed you."

I huffed a laugh. "Believe me, I'm very aware you're nothing like that guy."

"Please, let me make up for being an idiot. I'll order a pizza, mix up some lemonade. I might even have ice cream in the freezer. I solemnly swear to you that I am not trying to get in your pants. Just dinner between friends. Cross my heart."

I made the mistake of looking over at him, at his gentle smile with the barest hint of dimple peeking out. His earnest expression drew a surprised laugh from my chest, but the pleading look in his guileless blue eyes was what did me in.

"Okay," I said finally, mature enough to acknowledge defeat.

"Okay," he repeated. "Now, what do you want on your pizza?"

"I guess that depends on your feelings about mushrooms."

Jake laughed and said, "Love them. If you want to sit out on the deck, I'll go order and wash up."

While he went inside, I waited on one of the rocking chairs on his back deck. As I drew my knees up under my chin, my gaze wandered across the yard. It stretched back a fair distance from the house, the lawn a lush green dotted with mature trees. A sturdy wooden fence ran most of the way around, with a sea of forget-me-nots growing along it. At the back corner, beneath a hawthorn tree, there was a little koi pond nestled among some rocks.

It was peaceful back here, quiet in a way I didn't expect to appreciate as much as I did. Even with Jake gone, his presence lingered—and I didn't hate it.

There'd been no shortage of insincere men in my past, as quick with the charm as they were with a swift departure when they'd gotten what they wanted, but everything about Jake Lincoln felt distinctly genuine. Had I ever known a man who was so freaking *nice?*

Now dressed in a clean shirt and dark jeans, Jake interrupted my thoughts, stepping outside carrying a pair of glasses and a pitcher of lemonade.

"I'm sorry it's not fresh-squeezed," he said as he poured for us both.

"I assure you, I wouldn't know the difference. My bar is set pretty low," I replied, "though the food at your place has certainly upped the ante."

He clinked his glass against mine before settling into the seat beside me. "Cheers to that. I worked as a bartender after college, but I'm no chef. Bea does some amazing things in that kitchen.

I know enough about cooking to keep myself fed, that's about it."

When he flashed another brilliant smile, I knew there wasn't a chance in hell I'd be able to keep him at a distance.

No, I would just have to be ready for damage control.

Chapter Eight

JAKE

S HE HUMMED A LITTLE, then fell silent. I wondered if direct questions about her own past would cause her to bolt or clam up—I had no desire to watch those walls shoot up around her again, not when I finally seemed to be making some progress, even if I wanted desperately to know if there was something more behind her panic attack after the incident at The Mermaid.

"Hey," I said after a few minutes, still feeling more than a little chagrined, "I really am sorry about earlier. I shouldn't have teased you. I give you my word that I'm not pushing for anything romantic if you're not interested, but I would really like us to be friends."

Friends. How innocuous the word sounded, so sweet and uncomplicated.

"To be perfectly honest, I don't think I'm very good in the friendship department," she admitted quietly.

I shook my head as I took another sip of lemonade. "I don't believe that for a second. Seems more likely that you're afraid to take the risk."

"Why do you say that?"

Maybe she meant for the question to sound casual, but instead it came out in a terrified squeak. Her body had gone completely still, except for a tiny tremor in the hand holding her lemonade.

With my gaze on the hawthorn at the back of the yard instead of on the woman panicking by my side, I spoke as gently as possible. "You're not cold, Nora, or even unfriendly. Your commitment to that car out front shows you've got a loyal streak a mile wide. Not everyone is an open book like me." I shot her a smile. "Some folks are just slow to trust. There's nothing wrong with that. The best things in life are worth working for."

She eyed me cautiously for a second, then she smiled and my heart stuttered in my chest. "You're a very philosophical man, you know. If you're really sure you want to be friends with me, then I'll try. I can't promise more than that."

I was inordinately pleased with her answer, but the arrival of a gawky young delivery boy interrupted our conversation. When I presented Nora with a steaming slice of mushroom pizza, her sigh had my insides igniting. Even the sheepish little grin she sent in my direction before taking her first bite was appealing.

Get yourself under control, I told myself firmly as I sat back down beside her. *You just promised her friendship, you jackass.*

We ate in silence until I got up to fetch each of us another slice.

"Is that a koi pond?" she asked, gesturing toward the back corner of the yard with her plate.

"It is, yes, but there aren't any fish in there yet. I bought the house a few years back and it's been a work in progress ever since. It's easier to deal with messing up drywall than living things. I don't know the first thing about keeping fish alive. I guess I'll have to learn, or maybe turn it into a little water feature. Wouldn't a waterfall look nice back there?"

"It would."

I cocked my head thoughtfully. "Someday I'd love to adopt a dog, though."

"Me too," she said quietly. "And if my apartment is anything to go by, you're amazing at renovations. I'm sure the house will be up to snuff in no time."

"I do what I can," I replied, struggling not to preen at the compliment.

"How do you find the time along with running the restaurant? That seems like a full-time job in itself."

I shrugged. "Labor of love, I guess."

"Your sister was right about one thing," Nora mused.

"That I'm a truly excellent catch?"

She laughed, a rich, musical sound that I was beginning to find addictive. "That you're very handy," she corrected.

As much as my gut told me to resist asking personal questions, I grew more desperate to *know* her. "I'll take that as a
compliment. So," I said, as casually as possible, "what about
you? Small town or city girl?"

Though she went silent for a moment, I was delighted when
she didn't freeze up on me. "Little bit of everything, actually,"
she said softly. "I was a Navy brat. We moved around a lot."

I lifted a brow. "Wow. That must have been hard. Moving
here was a big adjustment for me and Sam, and that was only
the one time."

"I guess it is pretty tough for some kids. And for some adults,
obviously. Just about the time you settle in and make friends,
you pack up and move again. I always thought it was fun to see
so much of the world, though. This might come as a shock to
you," she added dryly, "but I wasn't the most sociable kid. Being
alone never really bothered me."

I laughed, imagining a miniature version of her prickly self.
"I'm sure you were adorable. So now you've got the travel bug?"

"Maybe that's what it is," she hedged, suddenly sounding
self-conscious.

"Or maybe you're just looking for a place to call home."
From the way her expression flashed with something soft and
vulnerable, I gathered that one struck a chord with her.

She gave a tiny shrug, her gaze on the back corner of the yard.
"Maybe."

From anybody else, I would've considered that a rebuff, but
I heard the longing in her voice, caught the wistful glint in her

eyes as she studied the pink tinge of the impending sunset over the trees. I bit back the urge to continue nudging, to ask if she thought Spruce Hill might fit the bill.

If I played my cards right, she'd open up when she was good and ready, not a second before. I carefully turned the conversation toward safer subjects, fully aware of the grateful smile she threw my way.

It was nearly dark when Nora said, "I better get going. This was . . ." She cleared her throat. "This was really nice, Jake. Thank you."

"It was my pleasure, Nora."

That much was completely true—I hadn't expected to enjoy the evening quite so much, but Nora was an exceptional companion, once I'd edged past those defenses. I stood when she did and held out a hand, grinning when she took it without a trace of her previous hesitation.

"Will I see you at The Mermaid tomorrow?"

The look she shot at me was both amused and annoyed. "Your sister bullied me into meeting her for coffee in the morning, so maybe not. I might need a night off from work to recover from that level of socialization."

I winced dramatically. "Ah, well, best of luck with that," I joked. "I can call your phone at a designated time so you can use it as an excuse to get the hell out of there, if you want."

Though she laughed, Nora kept her palm out and curled her fingers. "Give me your phone, I'll add my number to your contacts."

Simmer down, buddy, she's just playing along, I told my-self as I handed it over. Still, I felt a rush of pleasure when she gave it back. It was progress, no matter how small.

"Let me know if you need an escape call," I said with a wink.

The smile that curved her rosy lips caused a bolt of heat to streak its way through my insides, settling firmly some-where in my chest even as tiny sparks continued down my limbs. It took all of my willpower not to reach out and touch her. Instead, I dropped my gaze to the phone and sent her a text that said, *Friendly neighbor rescue service here.*

She smirked at the message and pocketed her phone. "Have a good night, Jake," she said softly.

"You too, Nora."

As she cut across the grass toward her apartment, I was left grinning like a fool and clutching my phone to my chest.

This woman was slow to warm, that had been obvious from the start, but she was quirky and clever and I'd give almost anything to earn her trust. I was dead certain the eventual thaw, however long it was in coming, would prove well worth the effort. The sound of her laughter captivated me, so much so that I struggled not to imagine the other ways she might be slow to warm up.

One thing was absolutely certain—Nora Cassidy needed a friend. First and foremost, I was determined to be that for her. And if anything else came of that friendship, I would definitely not complain.

I just hoped Sam would go easy on her tomorrow. My sister was not known for her subtlety, and I got the impression that any overt movements might send Nora fleeing from Spruce Hill altogether.

Chapter Nine

NORA

FOR THE FIRST TIME in years, I pulled my one and only dress from the closet to study it with a critical eye. My capsule wardrobe didn't really include anything overly fancy. When I met Sam the other night, though, she looked like a fashion plate, perfectly poised and put-together.

I was one hundred percent sure I couldn't come anywhere close to that, but I didn't want to sit across from her looking like a total slouch.

A choked laugh escaped me as I thought about the gross shirt I'd worn yesterday—if Jake minded associating with a slob, he certainly gave no indication. Something told me that his sister wouldn't care if I showed up in similar disarray, but my pride won out. With the dress clasped to my chest, I pawed through the rest of my limited options.

"It's probably time to update the wardrobe," I muttered. Then I followed the comment with the stern admonition, "For your own sake, not to impress the guy next door. No matter how obnoxiously attractive he might be."

The dress had been a consignment store whim, because it fit perfectly and made me feel girly as hell. With a flared cotton skirt that landed halfway down my thighs, it had an off-shoulder ruffle at the top and was a pretty shade of cornflower blue that reminded me of Jake's eyes. That thought garnered another irritated scowl.

Why couldn't I get him out of my head?

I left my hair down for once and slipped on a pair of sandals. As I pulled up the directions to the coffee shop on my phone and left the apartment, I forced myself not to so much as glance toward Jake's house.

Just meeting a friend for coffee, I reminded myself, trying to calm my frazzled nerves while I turned the key in the ignition. Baby's engine would probably never purr a day in her life, but the lack of that hideous screeching noise I'd gotten so used to made me smile. I patted the dashboard affectionately and sent up a silent word of thanks to Jake for charming me into a free repair.

I parked on the street a few shops down from the cafe, admiring yet another adorable block of Spruce Hill's main shopping drag. When I stepped onto the sidewalk, though, a chill scurried up my spine.

Like I was being watched.

Struggling to keep my expression blank, I glanced around at the scattered pedestrians picking up breakfast or hurrying off to work, but I didn't see anything out of the ordinary. No one was paying any attention to me, except a curvy redhead with paint splatters on her jeans who shot me a smile as she passed by.

No ghosts from the past, no glimpse of the man from the bachelor party. Nothing.

Forcing myself toward the coffee shop, I shook off the sense of foreboding when I spotted Sam at a table on the tiny patio. As expected, she was dressed to the nines in a pale pink blouse with a plunging neckline, a gray pencil skirt, and heels so high I would've broken an ankle the minute I took a step in them. When I offered a shy wave as I stepped onto the sidewalk, she beamed at me like I'd just made her day.

"Oh damn, girl, you look amazing," Sam gushed when I reached the table.

My cheeks heated at the compliment, but it made dressing up well worth the effort. She rose and wrapped me in a hug, ignoring the way I froze like I'd never been embraced before. God, I really needed to get used to being around people again.

Especially friendly, affectionate people like Sam and her brother.

"Been a long time since I had coffee with a friend," I admitted as she drew away. We took our seats and I glanced around. "This place is adorable. Did you order already?"

"No, I convinced one of the kids working here to come out to take our orders so we wouldn't have to wade through the crowd inside. There he is."

Sam leaned back and crossed her long, slender legs. She waved a perfectly manicured hand at the teenager, who flushed crimson as he rushed over to the table. Once he'd written down our orders on a small notepad, he disappeared back into the cafe.

I cocked a brow. "How exactly did you convince him?"

Though I wasn't entirely sure I wanted to know, Jake's sister was by far the most interesting woman I'd spent time with in years. I was curious about what wiles Samantha Lincoln would put into play to get what she wanted.

"I used to babysit the kid," she whispered, leaning forward in a way that displayed the upper swells of her breasts above her low-cut top. A tiny mermaid tail pendant hung just above her cleavage. "And I told him I'd tell his parents he likes to peek out his window at night to watch me undress if he wouldn't bring our coffees straight to the table."

"Does he really?" I asked, my mind drifting to my own neighbor.

"No. But I guess he thought they'd believe it, because he agreed."

I threw back my head and laughed. "Wow. You are a formidable foe."

"Don't I know it?" Sam replied with a wink. "Here he comes—show a little leg, he deserves a tip."

Instead of shifting the hem of my skirt upward, I sat back and struggled to keep a straight face while the boy set down a tray with our drinks and a couple pastries. He forced his gaze from Sam's cleavage with obvious effort and disappeared without another word.

"I think you've scarred him for life," I murmured, grinning.

"Speaking of scarred for life, how are you holding up?"

I huffed a laugh. She might seem disarmingly cheerful, but she was just as perceptive as her brother. "I'm okay. Really."

She studied my face so closely I had to fight not to squirm. "Sometimes things like that come back to bite you when you least expect it. If that happens, promise me you'll tell one of us? Me, Jake, even Casey. Isolation isn't always a good thing."

"I promise," I said around the lump in my throat.

"Good. You've got friends here now. Don't forget it."

It was such a simple statement, but even from a woman I suspected turned everyone she met into a friend—whether they liked it or not—it seeped into my chest, sinking deep and planting itself there.

Another point won in favor of Spruce Hill.

We chatted about lighthearted topics for nearly an hour before Sam ventured, "So, you live next door to Jake?" My smile dimmed ever so slightly, a fact which her sharp gray eyes caught immediately, then she leaned forward again and added brightly, "I'm also a realtor, did he tell you? If you decide you're looking to buy, let me know. Don't you just love that apartment? It doesn't look like much from the outside, but I couldn't believe how well it turned out."

"Your brother is very talented," I replied in a carefully neutral tone, sipping at my latte. Sam grinned and I saw the resemblance to Jake clearly, right down to the dimple.

"Okay, brushoff noted. I'll stand down. I like you, Nora. I haven't known too many women who didn't throw themselves at Jake's feet. Lord knows it's good for his big head for him to get rejected now and then. Unless you'd prefer the more feminine version of my brother, in which case I would quite happily steal you away from him." Sam arched a golden brow and gave me a wide smile.

Though my mind waged a brief internal war over which part of that to respond to first, I finally said, "I'm not rejecting him. I'm just not looking for a relationship. Or...well, anything else, really. For now, I'd just like to keep things uncomplicated, if that makes sense. And while I appreciate the offer to steal me away, there's nothing to steal. Jake and I are not an item."

"The fact that you didn't insist you're straight did not go unnoticed," she teased, her dimple peeping out against a broad smile.

"I was taught to never tell a lie," I deadpanned, sending Sam into stitches. A little smile tugged at my lips when I added, "But since I will admit to being stupidly attracted to your brother, it feels a little incestuous to consider it. No offense, because obviously you are gorgeous and fun and under different circumstances, I would absolutely be tempted to take you up on your offer."

"Interesting. Well, I was just checking. Can't let Jake have *all* the fun. I've got my eye on somebody special, anyway, just waiting for the right moment to pounce." Sam winked as she popped a piece of chocolate croissant into her mouth.

The flirtation dropped away as she launched into a discussion on local shopping options, cajoled me into agreeing to go to the nearby outlet mall with her someday soon, and finally proclaimed that she had to rush off for a house showing. Sam clasped both of my hands in hers before she rose from the table.

"Thank you for coming out with me today. You're a cool chick, Nora Cassidy. Don't be a stranger."

With that, she rose in a flurry of motion and fluttered off with a wave. I felt like a tornado had just blown past.

Quietly, I sat there for another moment, gathering my scattered thoughts in the wake of the force that was Samantha Lincoln, then I left the table and returned to the quiet bubble of peace inside my car.

The Lincoln twins posed a serious risk to the solitude I usually sought, but somehow, I wasn't even upset about it. In fact, I found it refreshing, energizing even. They made me feel like I could be part of something bigger than myself, maybe fit into some greater whole.

If anything, *that* should have been the real warning.

Chapter Ten

JAKE

WHEN NORA PULLED INTO the driveway, I'd just finished mowing Mr. Jenkins' lawn. I'd texted Sam earlier, warning her to take it easy on Nora—she wasn't like Sam's usual touchy-feely friends. My darling sister had replied simply enough: *I do have eyes, you know.*

Even if Sam was known as the bold twin, where I was the patient, subtle one, her eyes were probably even sharper than mine. It didn't take a rocket scientist to see that Nora was as reserved as they come. That snarky response from my sister reassured me that Sam was perfectly capable of adapting to the situation, but then she sent one more text.

Nora's headed my way. Holy shit, she looks HOT today!

I'd been stewing over that comment ever since. Throwing myself into manual labor and yard work had barely taken the edge off of my anticipation over seeing her when she arrived home.

I took a steadying breath before she stepped out of the car. There was a certain look of challenge in her dark eyes, like she was daring me to make a comment about her outfit. In response, I simply wiped a hand over my jaw and smiled at her.

"How was coffee with the whirlwind?" I asked.

She laughed at the very apt description of my sister and absently rubbed at her forehead. "It was good. Apparently I'm being dragged out to some outlet mall in a week or two."

It took a Herculean effort to force my eyes to stay on her face instead of wandering in leisurely appreciation from head to toe the way I desperately wanted to. My peripheral vision would have to suffice for now, and fuck me, from what I could see, my sister had been completely correct.

Smoking hot.

"Did she hit on you?" I asked, lifting a brow. I kept my tone deceptively casual as I pushed the lawnmower toward the garage.

"She did offer to steal me away from you, yes."

"Oh?" The thought that Nora was mine to be stolen sent a surge of something fierce and thrilling through me.

"And I told her I'm not looking for a relationship. From either of you. A heads up might have been nice, though," she muttered.

"You seem fully capable of holding your own. Besides, twins can be very competitive. Gotta let you make your own choice without coercion, right?"

Nora huffed. "I don't want anyone competing over me, and I hate to tell you, but my choice is that I just want to be friends. With both of you."

"Of course," I agreed easily, but I let my gaze brush over her as I passed.

Holy hell. I barely managed to contain a strangled groan.

The dress hit mid-thigh, revealing full, smooth legs above the delicate sandals on her feet. The generous flare of her hips gave the loose skirt a bit of swing, and though the neckline was disappointingly modest, my fingers itched to brush across the fine bones of her collar, to stroke over those pretty shoulders and trail down her arms.

Today, she looked wholly different—and I was fairly certain it wasn't just the dress. Everything about her seemed less guarded, her eyes a little brighter, those full lips a little more ready to smile.

I hoped that I'd had at least as much to do with that circumstance as my sister had.

After tucking the lawnmower back into the garage, I paused on my own driveway. A strip of grass a yard wide separated us, but I could have sworn I felt the warmth of her seeping into my skin. Trying not to gawk, I wiped my forehead with the back of my arm.

"You look nice," I said, tamping down on the litany of compliments whirling through my brain.

"You look hot," she replied absently.

My eyebrows shot up as a smile burst across my face. "Do I, now?"

Her features immediately arranged themselves into an expression of horror. "Oh my god. I meant sweaty. Hot in temperature. I have to go now. Oh, god. Goodbye, Jake."

Without another word, she spun on her heel and practically ran up the stairs to her apartment while my startled laughter rang out behind her.

"Just strike me dead right now, please," I heard her mutter as she dug in her purse for the key.

"Nora," I called, watching her fumble with the lock.

She covered her eyes with one hand for a minute, then finally peeked through her fingers to look down at me from the landing. "Yes?"

"You're looking pretty hot yourself." I grinned broadly and saluted. Before she could recover enough to tell me off, I winked and disappeared into the garage.

Just friends, my ass.

No friend of mine had ever turned quite that shade of red over a misspoken word or two. I was willing to bet that Nora Cassidy had already veered pretty far off of the friendship path.

I sure as hell had.

OVER THE FOLLOWING WEEK, any awkwardness I worried might develop between us after that slip up never materialized. It seemed like Nora expected me to tease her about it the next time I saw her, bracing when I brought her a refill of root beer, but I made no mention of it.

Then, once or twice, I caught her looking at me in a way that made my blood heat, a way that made me *want.*

Still, she didn't open the door to anything deeper and I didn't push.

Just friends, I told myself again and again. Eventually, maybe it would sink in. Until that point, however, I was stuck fighting the stupid desire to smile like a fool every time she was nearby.

We fell into the habit of walking home together from The Mermaid whenever Nora stayed until closing time. On the days in between, she tended to show up closer to lunchtime, as though to prove to us both that she wasn't rearranging her life to suit me.

It didn't matter—I'd take whatever I could get. Those quiet walks had become the highlight of my days.

Slowly but steadily, I peeled back my layers of "don't scare Nora away" protection: first by removing my hands from my pockets, then by gradually reducing the distance between our bodies on the sidewalk. I never touched her unnecessarily, though I had to catch her elbow once when she stumbled over a crack in the sidewalk. Even in the faint glow of the street lamps, I could see her blush, but when she didn't immediately yank her arm from my grasp, I considered that progress.

By the time we were walking close enough for me to catch a whiff of her shampoo or lotion—something fresh and fruity, like peaches or pears—I was hooked.

"So," Nora said one evening, "you and Sam own The Mermaid, but you're also a bartender-slash-handyman and she's also a realtor? Is this a family trait, being such over-achievers?"

I laughed, but I was always pleased when she initiated an actual conversation. "Well, our full-time bartender broke his wrist playing kickball with his buddies, and my part-timer is taking some evening classes this summer. Normally, I only do a shift or two each week to keep my foot in the door. I like getting to know our customers."

"I've noticed," she muttered, but she flashed me a smile.

Winking at her, I added, "Some more than others. Anyway, Sam does our marketing, but you've seen her energy level—she thrives on being busy all the time. Like, really busy. Plus, she loves what she does. She's a good judge of character and gets a kick out of pairing people up with the house of their dreams. It's like matchmaking, but with real estate."

She hummed in response. "Being a good judge of character seems to run in the family, too."

"Why, Ms. Cassidy, was that a compliment?" When her hand shot out to give me a playful shove, I grinned. Conversation, compliment, and physical contact? Seemed like my lucky day.

"No, but I'm not oblivious," she said tartly.

I waited patiently for her to continue, but the silence stretched. Finally, I said, "No, you're not oblivious, but you were wrong."

"About what?"

We had reached the stairs to her apartment, so she turned and lifted a brow. I didn't touch her, but I let my gaze whisper across her features like a caress.

"When you said you weren't good at being friends. You're doing just fine in the friendship department." I gave her a little salute. "Have a good night, Nora."

She blinked at me in surprise before murmuring, "Goodnight, Jake."

Our gazes locked, held, and I barely managed to keep myself from reaching out to tuck a wisp of hair behind her ear. Her lips parted, her breath hitched, then she turned to jog up the stairs, leaving me staring after her in the quiet night.

One step closer, I told myself, but damn. It felt like a big one.

Chapter Eleven

JAKE

THOUGH I WAS DISAPPOINTED, I wasn't particularly surprised when Nora didn't show up to The Mermaid for a few days. Maybe she just needed time to fortify her defenses.

I decided to give her space the first day, sent a friendly text that went unanswered on the second, and began to worry—soul-deep, heart-pounding worry that seemed a little excessive when I thought about it logically, but which I couldn't deny—by the third.

When Sam called to ask if I'd done something to make Nora ignore her texts, I was unable to quell the rush of fear pulsing through my veins.

"I haven't heard from her either," I admitted. "She doesn't always come in every day, though."

"I'm worried. I asked how she was holding up after the incident with that guy, and she brushed it off like it was no big deal."

Fuck. It was a big deal and Sam knew it, even if I hadn't given my family the details on Nora's reaction during our walk home. What if Nora started having flashbacks and avoiding the restaurant completely?

With the reassurance that I'd check in on her, I hung up with Sam and left The Mermaid immediately. Thankfully, I'd brought the truck to work, so I could get home quickly to figure out just what the hell was going on. Nora's car was parked in the driveway, exactly where it had been for the last few days.

I jogged up the stairs, my gaze catching on a bundle of tiny flowers in front of her door. They lay in a loose clump, withered and dry, shifting in the breeze.

Had she picked them herself and dropped them here? Why wasn't she answering?

Ignoring the flowers as I stood outside the apartment, I texted her one more time and waited to see if she would answer. When that proved fruitless, I called her phone, though she'd told me how much she hated talking on it. Faint ringing drifted to my ears from inside the apartment.

The sheer curtains were just opaque enough to prevent me from seeing inside, so I knocked lightly at the door, pressing my ear to the glass.

"Nora?" I called, then knocked again, louder this time.

The apartment wasn't that big; she should have heard me. Unless she was asleep in the middle of the day. Or unless she'd fallen and cracked her head open. Christ, what if I found her lying in a pool of blood?

My heart clenched painfully in my chest. It had been stupid not to try harder to reach her these last few days. Regret and fear warred within me.

"Nora, I'm going to get the spare key from Mr. Jenkins' house. I'll be right back."

Fortunately, Mr. Jenkins had plants that needed watering in his absence and the old man had left me with his house key. The spare apartment key was in one of his desk drawers, in case of emergencies.

This was definitely an emergency.

I jogged to the side door and let myself into the house, fighting down the panic rising at the back of my throat while I rifled through the drawers. When I finally found the key, I sprinted back through the house, across the driveway, and up the stairs.

A twinge of guilt broke through the fog of my anxiety. Nora was an intensely private woman—forcing my way into the apartment felt wrong on a number of levels, but not as wrong as leaving her in there alone, hurt or bleeding or who knew what else.

I leaned my forehead against the door, called out, "Nora, I'm coming in," and turned the key in the lock.

My gaze traveled frantically across the kitchen, anticipating blood splatters or signs of a struggle, but everything was tidy and undisturbed. That didn't stop my imagination from running wild. I tossed the key onto the counter and moved to the living room, where I froze.

Nora's phone was there on the low coffee table, along with a box of tissues, a half-empty mug of tea, and a bottle of cough syrup.

I took another step and located the woman herself, curled up on the loveseat.

All of my breath rushed out in a sigh of relief, until I saw that she was wrapped in a heavy blanket despite the heat of the day, her face ghostly pale except for brightly flushed cheeks that practically glowed in the afternoon sunlight.

"Oh, Christ. Nora? Can you hear me?"

I crouched down beside the loveseat to set a hand gently against her forehead. Her skin was burning hot, searing my palm. As I swore under my breath, wondering what the hell to do, her eyelids lifted drowsily and she blinked up at me, her dark gaze glassy and disoriented.

"Jake?" she whispered, squinting at the brightness of the room as she tried to focus her eyes on me.

"Yeah, it's me. I'm sorry to barge in on you here, but you weren't answering your phone. I was afraid you'd fallen or something."

Gently, I smoothed her hair back from her face and smiled. She was in rough shape, but she was alive and uninjured. I stroked my palm over her fevered skin, silently berating myself for not checking on her sooner.

"I'm okay."

"I mean this in the nicest possible way, Nora, but you look like hell and you're burning up. There's a clinic in town, I think maybe I should take you over there."

"No!" The hoarse exclamation burst from her lips so quickly it surprised us both. She shook her head, burrowing deeper into her blanket, and mumbled, "No, I'm okay. I don't need a doctor. Please, Jake, I just want to sleep. I'll feel better in the morning, I'm sure."

I studied her for a moment, then nodded. "Okay. I'm going to carry you to your bed then, all right? Just relax, I've got you," I murmured as I slid one arm beneath her knees and the other under her back to lift her, blanket and all. Her eyes drifted closed and didn't open again even after I laid her on the bed, though she rolled onto her side and curled into a tight ball.

"I'm sorry." Her voice was muffled by the blanket she'd drawn up around her chin. "I couldn't reach the phone."

I eased down onto the bed beside her. *If she were feeling better, she'd be kicking your ass,* I warned myself, but it was no use. Seeing her like this tore me apart inside. Even when she was still twitchy around me after first moving in, she'd always been so vibrant, shining like a lantern in the dark.

This Nora seemed more like the faint flicker of a candle flame, weak and vulnerable.

"Nothing to be sorry about," I said gently. "Can I get you more tea, or some broth maybe? Something for the fever?"

The questions went unanswered, and I realized she'd fallen back asleep. I could hardly bear to leave her side, but I forced myself to go into the kitchen and rifle through her cupboards, looking for soup but finding little more than dry cereal and packaged snacks. I drew my phone from my pocket and fired off a text to Sam.

Even if all I could do right now was keep an eye on Nora while she slept, I'd make damn sure I was ready to take care of her properly once she woke up.

An hour later, Sam dropped off several large containers of soup from The Mermaid and an assortment of cold medicine. The flowers had blown off the porch by the time I met her at the door, and I left Nora's side only long enough to stick the containers in the fridge and set the medicine options out on the counter. Then I lay carefully back down on the bed, close but not quite touching her.

It took all of my willpower to resist the urge to gather her into my arms.

Just after midnight, Nora mumbled something that broke through my light doze. I reached out to stroke her hair, noting with relief that the fever didn't seem to be running quite so high anymore, and she repeated it a bit more clearly.

"You should go. Might get you sick."

I scoffed. "I'm healthy as a horse, Ms. Cassidy. I'll pop some extra vitamin C, if it makes you happy, but I'm not leaving until you're feeling better. Sam dropped off some soup from The Mermaid, do you think you could eat something?"

Though the bedside lamp was on, her eyes looked nearly black in the dim light. "I can try," she whispered.

Her focus still seemed hazy, but I smiled at her before her eyes drifted closed again, then rolled off the bed, careful not to jar her. When I returned with the soup, I set it on one of the bedside tables and helped her sit up against the pillows.

"This might be easier if you weren't wrapped up like a burrito," I said with a grin.

"Blanket burritos are the best thing for illness. Where did you go to med school?" she grumbled.

I laughed, relieved at the return of her wit. "I'll remember that for the future. Must be a regional thing. Do you need me to feed you?"

"Not if you value your life." Nora scowled at me as she struggled to withdraw her arms from her wrappings.

I lifted the bowl with one hand and wrapped the other arm around her shoulders for support while she managed to swallow a few spoonfuls of soup. Though part of me waited for her to send me away so she could wallow in her misery, I rejoiced in the fact that she simply leaned against my shoulder and seemed to take comfort in my presence.

After I set the bowl aside, I helped to tuck the blanket around her body once more and lowered her back down to rest, though I regretted not nestling her into my arms when I had the chance.

"How long have you been sick?" I asked when her eyes didn't immediately fall closed again. I reached over to lay my palm against her forehead. Her skin still felt heated, but I was confident that the fever had come down at least a few degrees.

Nora blinked a little and I wondered if she even knew what day it was. "I was feeling a little off the morning after I saw you last. It was just a headache at first, so I thought it was probably stress-related. The fever started that night, I think. I woke up shivering a few times."

"I hate the thought of you here alone and miserable. You could have called me, you know. That's what friends are for," I said gently.

She flinched, just slightly, though I didn't mean it as an admonition or an accusation. I might not have readily used the word *wistful* to describe myself, but at that moment, it seemed fitting. Concern for her flooded my body and I saw her reading my furrowed brow, taking in the downturn of my lips.

"I didn't want to bother you," she mumbled.

"I'm guessing you didn't want to need help. When you've survived on your own so long, I imagine it must be pretty hard to ask."

She didn't contradict me. After a moment, she whispered, "You're a good friend, Jake."

"So are you, Nora. So are you."

We both fell silent, but her eyelids looked heavy again, those long lashes sweeping drowsily downward before she forced them back up. Her complexion was still deathly pale, but the crimson flush of fever was finally fading.

I decided to risk a swift rejection and reached out to trace a finger over her cheek. Instead of pulling away, she leaned into my touch as I smoothed back the hair at her temple.

"Close your eyes and rest, Nora. I'll be right here if you need me."

She didn't need to be told twice. With my fingers sifting lightly through her hair, she drifted off to sleep.

Chapter Twelve

NORA

I AWOKE SLOWLY, BLINKING against the brilliant sunshine streaming through the bedroom window as the blur of the last few days drifted in and out of focus. When I rolled my head on the pillow, I saw Jake's long, lean form stretched out beside me. The fever must have broken, because sometime during the night I'd torn off layers of sweat-soaked clothing and thrown my burrito blanket onto the floor. My skin still felt sticky, my eyes gritty, but I seemed to be back to a normal temperature.

Shower.

The urge spurred me into action as I sat up slowly and lowered my feet to the floor. I was relieved when the room didn't spin drunkenly as it had before I finally collapsed onto the couch the day before, but my entire body ached as though I'd run a marathon.

"Careful," Jake warned, his voice husky with sleep. "Sometimes your muscles are weak after a fever."

Though I didn't glance back at him, I felt his eyes on my back as memories of the night filtered into my mind in foggy glimpses. A few hours earlier, I dimly recalled that he'd helped me to pull off the tangled blankets, then later the gray sweatpants and oversized hoodie. The fever must have broken at that point and I was now down to a t-shirt—*only* a t-shirt.

I'd already been in pajamas when I started feeling too ill to care about something as unimportant as underwear. My spine stiffened under his gaze.

"Oh, god," I whispered. "Oh. My. God."

My hands were resting on my bare thighs and I suddenly recognized the coolness of the sheets against my ass. Even though I was sure he couldn't see anything incriminating from his current position, he'd spent the entire night six inches away from me. It was too much to hope that he was unaware of my current state of undress.

"Steady, Cassidy," he said, his even tone belying his amusement.

I glanced back, annoyed that my pathetic situation didn't stop a smile from spreading across his face as I threw out a few choice expletives under my breath. In fact, his dimple only deepened. I closed my eyes as humiliation swept over me.

To my profound irritation, his comment about weak muscles was spot on. There was no way I could stand up on my own right now. My legs felt like jelly, and I would *not* risk falling on my face, bare ass in the air, with Jake watching me. No matter how comforting his presence had been last night, I was beginning to wish I could send him on his way and crawl to the bathroom alone.

Logic waged a swift battle with emotion for a minute before I sighed and accepted my fate.

"I need to shower," I said tightly, "but I think I'm going to need your help getting there."

"I'd be happy to act as your spotter," he said with a broad, innocent smile as he came around the foot of the bed.

The glare I shot him would've warned off a lesser man, but he still reached out and set his palm against my forehead, which was blessedly cool for the first time in days. Relief softened his features as he tucked a strand of sticky hair behind my ear.

"Seems like you're on the mend, at least. You scared the hell out of me, Cassidy."

The glow that sparked in my chest at his admission gave me enough of a boost to accept the hand he offered. As he helped me to my feet, I gritted my teeth and prayed that the shirt covered my lower half adequately. Jake, to his credit, didn't so much as glance toward any bare skin. When we reached the bathroom, he turned on the shower for me and stepped back, studying my face carefully as I leaned back against the sink.

"Not to sound indelicate here, but are you sure you can manage this on your own?" His lips twitched when I glared at him. "I promise I'm not going to hit on you while you're this weak, Nora, but if you slip and crack your head open, I'm going to see a whole lot more when I have to rush you to the emergency room."

"I won't fall," I ground out. *If sheer determination alone was enough to keep me upright, anyway.*

"You're the boss. I'll stand out in the hall, *if* you'll leave the door open."

At my sharp nod, he winked and moved to the hallway. Before he rounded the corner, though, he held up his hands and flexed those long fingers.

"Yell if you need any help."

I relied on my own stubborn pride to steady myself as I pulled off the shirt and stepped into the shower. As much as I wanted to linger under the soothing spray of hot water, Jake was right—I felt like I might topple over at any moment. I washed my hair quickly and used my favorite pear body wash to rid my skin of the layer of grime that had accumulated during my illness, then turned off the water and reached for the towel hanging on the bar.

That was the precise moment when I realized I'd now have to face him almost completely naked, instead of just half, as I twisted the towel into a tight knot across my chest.

Jake appeared to be thinking about that exact same thing when I appeared in the doorway, upright but swaying slightly. So swiftly I might have missed it if I hadn't been focused on his expression, his gaze flitted across my bare shoulders, stroking over my skin so tenderly I almost felt it. He offered his arm like a gentleman and, without any other option aside from collapsing onto him, I took it.

Once we reached the bedroom, Jake gently pushed me down until I was sitting on the bed. "Tell me what you need and where to find it. No sense using up all your strength going through drawers, unless you want me to have to dress you at the end of it."

My eyes narrowed, but I did as he suggested, even though my cheeks flamed when he pulled a pair of plain cotton underwear and my favorite bra from the dresser with a nonchalance that contrasted vividly with the heat in his blue eyes. When he handed me the stack of clothes, he gave me a dimpled smile and I was forced to forgive him the sin of being so helpful.

"I'm going to heat up some soup, if you think you can eat a bit more?"

With both hands clasping the towel above my breasts, I nodded. "Yes, thank you. My appetite seems to have returned with a vengeance."

Jake grinned and left me there in the bedroom with the door not quite fully closed. After dressing myself with slow, sluggish motions, I walked into the kitchen—not with any degree of grace, but steadily enough—and dropped into one of the chairs at the tiny table. He'd rummaged through the cabinets to find a pot for the soup and buttered some of the rolls Sam had included in her delivery.

The sight of those rolls alone made my empty stomach rumble in anticipation.

"That smells amazing. Jake...thank you. For everything. I know I'm not the easiest person to try to take care of."

"You're welcome," he said as he set two bowls of soup and the plate of rolls on the table, then he sat down across from me. "I would've come sooner if I'd known you were sick. I just thought you needed some space and I didn't want to push it."

I nodded, grimacing contritely. "I'm sorry you were worried. It's been a long time since I've gotten sick. I figured it would turn into a cold and I'd be right back on my feet."

"I'm just glad you're feeling better now."

The words were soft and heartfelt enough that my breath caught for a moment as a blush heated my cheeks and I dropped my gaze back to my meal. Unconsciously, my tongue ran across my lower lip and I heard Jake fumble his spoon. I took perverse pleasure in it after being the one at a disadvantage for so long. Still, I'd never liked being fawned over and no matter how sweet he was, I wasn't about to start now.

"You don't have to babysit me, Jake. I know you're busy, so please don't feel like you have to stick around if you have other things to do. I promise I'll keep my phone close at hand so I can call you if I fall down."

"I have nowhere to be right now," he countered, "so if it's okay with you, I'll stay at least a little longer. Just to make sure you don't have a relapse. I'm tending the bar tonight, but if you need *anything*, Nora, I want you to text me right away. Please."

"Scout's honor," I said, realizing I'd finished the entire bowl of soup and polished off two of the heavenly rolls that had become one of my favorite things from The Mermaid, second only to the strawberry shortcake from that first visit.

Jake insisted I continue to take it easy while I recovered my strength, so we ended up on the loveseat together to watch a baking competition on the small television. I curled up at one end with Jake at the other, his long legs stretched out before him. Somehow, my frozen bare feet ended up tucked against his thigh. At some point, he set his palm over my ankles and I was too grateful for his warmth to complain, especially when his thumb hooked around to gently rub my arches. I had to bite back a moan, embarrassed by my response to that simple touch.

When it was time for him to head to the restaurant, he found a spare blanket in the linen closet and tucked it around me on the loveseat.

"Remember, you need to rest," he said. "Text me if you need anything, even if it's a glass of water, got it? I'll take the truck so I can get back here quickly."

"That seems like overkill, but okay." I squeezed his hand before he released the blanket. "And Jake, thank you again."

He cupped his other palm over my cheek, brushing his thumb across the skin that no longer felt flushed with fever. "You're welcome. Text me if you're going to bed, so I don't panic again over radio silence, deal?"

I couldn't remember the last time someone had worried so much about my wellbeing. I let the glow of it surround me and nodded. "Deal."

After Jake left, locking the door behind him, I rested my head against the arm of the loveseat and let out a soft sigh. Even my embarrassment over being helped to the shower was slowly evaporating under the soothing blanket of contentment he had left in his wake.

As the evening wore on, I fought back my exhaustion long enough to exchange a series of texts with Jake. As requested, I let him know when I finally caved and went to bed, hours earlier than usual.

Jake wished me goodnight and sweet dreams, then insisted I keep my phone with me in case of emergencies.

I felt a little silly, but tucking the phone under my pillow made me feel that same glow as I had under his tender care, giving a tangible connection to him to comfort me until sleep overtook me at last.

Chapter Thirteen

JAKE

TWO DAYS AND A near constant string of texts later, I was working under the hood of my truck again when Nora trotted down the stairs and approached me. I glanced over my shoulder, then straightened and gave her my full attention. Though she wasn't wearing the blue dress that had haunted my fantasies for days, she looked damned good in denim cutoff shorts that made her sculpted legs seem a mile long.

For a swift second, I let myself appreciate the stretch of skin that I'd felt too guilty to ponder during her illness.

"Howdy, neighbor," I drawled.

This time, her beautiful eyes danced in response to the greeting. My gaze traveled over her features. I expected to find dark circles under her eyes, a lingering pallor maybe, but she looked well-rested and heart-stoppingly beautiful.

"Howdy yourself," she said, peeking under the hood. "I'd make some casual comment about engines if I had any idea what wouldn't make me sound like an idiot."

I cocked one hip against the front bumper. "Might take a few lessons to get you up to speed, but you're a quick study." My head tilted as I looked at her. "How are you feeling?"

"I feel totally fine, no relapse. All of my muscles seem to have returned to full strength. I even managed to bathe and dress myself without your assistance."

I smirked at that and bit back a flirty retort. The way she shrugged one shoulder, the wry smile, the light in her eyes—it all made me want to wrap my arms around her again, but the ball was now in her court.

"In any case, I'm completely recovered."

"Good," I said softly. "That's good."

"Actually, I wondered if you were interested in another pizza night? My treat this time, to thank you for taking care of me while I was sick. And I'll bring dessert." The words flowed out in a rush, like she needed to say them quickly, before she lost her courage.

Hopefully, my answering smile was warm enough to soothe her nerves. "I can't think of anything I'd like better. Tonight?"

She nodded, a little shyly. "Or whenever you're free," she added quickly. "I don't want to cause any more issues with your work."

Though I had, in fact, skipped out on the restaurant to stay by her side during her illness, I had a feeling she was referring more to the drunk who'd grabbed her. That was the opening I'd been waiting for; I reached out and cupped her cheek in my hand. My heart lifted when she shifted ever so slightly, nuzzling her face into my palm.

"Let's get one thing perfectly straight," I said, my voice gentle but firm. "You haven't caused a single issue at my work. I swear to you that what happened that night will *never* happen again in my restaurant—not to you, not to anyone else. Okay?"

"Yeah," she replied softly.

"And you'll break my heart if you stop coming to The Mermaid to work. As for pizza, I'm free tonight, if that fits into your schedule."

Nora's breath hitched, stalling for a long moment before she let it out in a quiet whoosh, then she nodded. "Okay. Five?"

I reluctantly dropped my hand, but I held her gaze. "It's a date," I said.

The word was very deliberately spoken and I waited to see if she would shy away from it, but she simply gave me a sweet, beautiful smile and jogged back up the stairs to her apartment.

A T FIVE O'CLOCK SHARP, Nora walked up the stairs to the deck. To my absolute delight, she was wearing the blue dress again, with those deep brown curls tumbling about her bare shoulders, and she held a box from my favorite local bakery in her arms. I unfolded from my chair to take the box, but this time I let appreciation show as my gaze traveled over her.

Fucking hell. She was stunning.

"I ordered the same pizza we had last time, I hope that's okay," she said, clutching the fabric of her skirt like she was trying to keep her hands steady.

"That sounds perfect. I'll put this in the kitchen until we're ready for dessert. Want a tour of the house?"

Though her lips parted slightly in surprise, she nodded and followed me through the French doors that connected the deck to a spacious kitchen I'd spent a great deal of time fixing up after I moved in.

"This is the size of my whole apartment," she said, impressed. "Did you renovate all of this yourself?"

I nodded, both pleased with the admiration in her tone and ridiculously turned on by the way she ran her fingertips over the edge of the granite countertop. "It was the first project I took on after buying the house. The whole first floor looked like something from the seventies. It was pretty horrific," I said with a grin.

"So, you own a restaurant but on the side you're a bartender, contractor, mechanic, *and* nursemaid." One delicate brow arched upward in amusement. "That's a pretty wide range of skills, even for an overachiever like yourself."

As much as I wanted to offer her some insight into my other more intimate skillset, I swallowed back the reply and simply inclined my head. "I am a renaissance man, what can I say?"

"Look, Lincoln, I think we need to get something straight before this goes any further."

My muscles locked, gaze riveted on the flush in her cheeks. "What's that?"

Nora narrowed her eyes at me and my brows shot up when she poked the center of my chest for emphasis. "I am not made of glass."

"No, you're definitely not."

"You're not going to offend me or scare me off by being flirty or dirty or whatever causes that steamy look in your eyes."

I sucked in a sharp breath, but she wasn't finished.

"I don't want you to censor yourself because you're afraid I'm going to crumble or run away. I'm not. I know you caught me in a moment of weakness while I was sick, but that's over. Say what you want to say, all right?"

With a slow perusal of her ferocious expression, I said, "Well, Cassidy, I know good and well that you're tough as nails, so let's put that aside for a minute. You do have to admit that *this* is a far cry from the woman who moved in all those weeks ago, peeking out through the curtains before she'd venture outside."

I gestured to her, a sweep of my hand from her head to her feet. She looked fierce and fiery and so very *alive* that I wanted nothing more than to kiss her breathless. Her cheeks flushed darker but she didn't break eye contact, like we were locked in a silent battle of wills.

"Okay, you're right. I'll give you that much," she conceded. "But that was then, this is now."

Gently, I replied, "I wasn't born yesterday, Nora. I know what it looks like when a woman's running from something. Or someone. You can't blame me for wanting to go easy on you. I'm not asking any questions—your business is your business, and I'm not planning to pry—but I'd have to be blind not to see that even if you're not afraid right this very minute, you damn well *were* afraid of something."

At that, she jerked as if I'd slapped her and I was immediately filled with remorse. When I opened my mouth to apologize, though, she held up a hand to stop me.

"Fair enough," she said evenly. "I admit that I was...nervous. Moving around the way I have, it's not all rainbows and adventures. Sometimes it's hard and scary, but dammit, I *like* it here. And I like you, and I like the way you make me feel, and I didn't want to screw up my chances here in town if that feeling wasn't mutual."

She stepped forward and laid her hand on my chest, my heart thumping under her palm. Even now, I knew she was nervous, but I sincerely hoped it was an entirely different variety of nerves than when she first moved in.

I covered her hand with mine, my brain focused on the part of her speech that sent heat streaking through my limbs.

"Oh, it's mutual, all right. Humor me, though, with a little clarification. How exactly do I look at you?" I asked, my voice low and just gravelly enough to send a visible tremor up her spine.

"Like you can't stop thinking about kissing me."

"Probably because I haven't stopped thinking about kissing you since the day you got here."

Her lips quirked. "Then hurry up and kiss me already."

There it was, the invitation I'd been longing for. It lay not just in the words, but in the gleam of her dark eyes, the way her tongue darted out across her bottom lip. I set my other hand at her hip and bent my head, brushing my lips across hers in a teasing caress. A shuddering breath escaped her, then she pressed closer, drew my mouth deeper.

God, she was sweet. So impossibly sweet. As her hands snaked upward to my shoulders, mine went to the small of her back, drawing her body flush against me. She tasted like summertime, warm and welcoming.

I angled my mouth against hers, experiencing a ripple of fierce satisfaction when a low hum of pleasure vibrated deep in her throat. This wasn't how I'd imagined things between us, not by a long shot. How many times had I warned myself I'd have to take it slow, measure every reaction carefully, keep things gentle and unhurried? Instead, she was clinging to me for dear life and clearly succumbing to the same inferno of desire that raged inside me.

The doorbell startled us both into flying apart like teenagers caught necking. Nora slapped a hand over her chest as if to slow the galloping pace of her heart and blinked up at me until I was able to shake myself out of my reverie.

"The pizza," I croaked finally.

Nora giggled—actually giggled, like I'd heard Sam and her friends do at sleepovers all those years ago—and I found myself laughing along with her until we were both doubled over with tears in our eyes. I hadn't laughed until I cried in as long as I could remember.

"I paid over the phone," she gasped, "but you'll have to go get the door. Oh shit, my mascara is probably everywhere."

In fact, she looked even more outrageously beautiful than before, dark eyes aglow, face flushed and animated. I put my hands on either side of her body, bracing myself against the countertop she had so admired, and kissed her again. This one was hard and fast, but no less combustible. When I pulled back to go answer the door, her lips were a deep, rosy pink, and she sagged against the counter while she caught her breath.

I returned with the pizza and set it on the countertop beside her. "Now, where were we?" I murmured, but Nora held up a hand.

"Easy, cowboy. I think maybe we should probably eat dinner first, before...anything else. I could use some fortification."

I cocked my head at her, wondering if she'd changed her mind, but that enticing glow of desire hadn't faded from her features. "You're saying we need sustenance," I replied slow-ly. "Fuel. Energy."

She snorted, which brought a wide grin to my face. "Yes, to all those things. Eat up while it's hot."

My blood simmered at those words. "Oh, I intend to," I said softly, trailing my thumb across her lower lip. Nora's breath hitched a little and I felt it sear through me.

As we ate, I found frequent excuses to touch her—a brush of my fingers along the back of her neck, a hand at her knee. Each caress started a tingle that spread along my limbs like wildfire. If the flush under her skin was any indication, it was doing the same for her.

"Does it bother you, the fact that I saw your reaction to me those weeks ago?" I asked when she paused to dab at her lips with a napkin.

"Only because it's embarrassing."

I lifted a brow. "A single woman alone in a new town can't be nervous about it? Makes sense to me you'd need time to settle in."

"No, I know. I'm normally not quite so jumpy, though."

"Was that because of me?" I hated that, but she shook her head before I finished the question.

"No. I mean, not directly. Just...it was very clear that you saw it, and usually I'm better at hiding those things."

"You don't ever have to hide from me. You know that now, right?"

She bit her lip, though it couldn't quite hide the tiny smile curving at the edges. "I know."

Slowly, determined not to spook her now that we'd moved past another hurdle, I lifted my hand to cup her jaw and brushed my thumb across that full lower lip. "Good."

Fuck me, but the look in her eyes at that simple caress had me ready to throw caution to the wind and carry her straight to my bed.

Instead, I summoned every ounce of self-control and we finished dinner. When I rose to clear away our plates, I peeked into the box she'd brought with her and let out a groan, leaning down to draw in a whiff of carrot cake from Carmello's Bakery.

"Oh, shit," I murmured. "This is my favorite."

Nora watched me with amusement. "I know. I asked. There are certain benefits to being everyone's favorite business owner, apparently. Everyone in town knows everything about you."

"Not everything," I said as I closed the box and reached out to pull her to her feet.

I framed her face with my hands and kissed her, soft and sweet, without a trace of our earlier urgency. A breathless laugh slipped from her just before my mouth met hers again, deeper, more insistent this time. Her hands tangled in the front of my shirt as my mouth shifted to trail along her jawline and nuzzle her ear.

Nora clung to me like she would evaporate into mist if I stopped touching her, like the sheer force of our desire was holding her together.

"Promise me something?" I murmured, letting my breath tickle her earlobe.

"Yes?" The word came out on a strangled gasp as she tipped her head back to give me room to explore.

"I want you to tell me what you want, what you need, if you want to stop or back up or slow down. I don't want anything between us to make you uncomfortable. And before you accuse me of treating you like you're breakable," I added as my teeth grazed her throat, "this has nothing to do with that. I just want to know that you're enjoying yourself as much as I am. There's no rush. You've got nothing to prove here. Deal?"

Her fingers threaded into my hair. "Yeah, deal. But Jake?"

"Yes, Nora?" The words rumbled along her collarbone, raising goosebumps across her skin that I traced with my lips.

"I think you should stop talking now."

I laughed softly, but I obeyed. Her nails skimmed along my scalp until I groaned against her neck. It was true, she wasn't as fragile as I first thought, not by a long shot. I was beginning to wonder instead if she had surrounded her true self with walls of spun glass. It felt like the Nora in my arms had burst forth and let those barriers crumble to dust behind her.

This Nora was eager and enthusiastic and driving me up the wall with those soft purring sounds in her throat.

Still, I was determined not to rush things, no matter how tempted I was to take her right there on the kitchen table. When my palm slipped under the hem of her skirt, stroking a path along the outside of her thigh, she tightened her fingers in my hair to tug my head away from her collarbone.

"Time to continue the tour," she told me. I blinked at her, uncomprehending, so she nipped lightly at my jaw. "Do you have a bedroom around here, or just a fancy kitchen? I think we should take this somewhere more comfortable."

My lips curved upward at that. "Oh, yes, as a matter of fact, I do. Let's go."

But first, I kissed her again, letting my mouth convey every dark desire I hoped to explore, then I took her hand and led her upstairs.

Chapter Fourteen

JAKE

When Nora stopped dead at the bedroom door, a flash of concern chipped through the haze of need surrounding my brain. I glanced quickly at her face and the worry evaporated. She was simply studying the room: the king-sized bed, the midnight blue walls. A tiny smile played across her lips and a fascinating twinkle lit her eyes.

"Oh, this is lovely," she murmured, entering the room and running her fingers over the rich oak of the bed frame.

The motion, especially combined with her expression, was intensely erotic. I wanted to feel those fingertips drifting along my skin.

"I'm glad you like it. You're welcome to join me here any time," I replied, watching her closely.

Patience. I wanted her so badly I ached, but still I waited. Once her eyes met mine again, I took a slow step toward her, then another. When I was at last standing before her, she ran her hands over my chest.

"I think . . ." She drew a breath. "Would you mind taking this off? I want to see you."

I did as she asked, tossing the shirt onto the dresser. Nora's sigh floated through the room. "Better?" I asked, grinning at her expression of appreciation.

"You're beautiful," she said. Her palms lifted to glide over my skin, molding to the muscles of my chest and shoulders, smoothing the rough golden hair she found there.

"That's my line," I said, my voice low and husky as I set my hands at her waist. "You are so, so beautiful, Nora. Do you have any idea how much I want you?"

In answer, she lifted her face for another deep, earth-shaking kiss. I was certain I could get lost in a woman like her, a woman whose every touch, every glance, set my soul aflame. Each nerve ending was starved for her touch, burning for her. Had I ever desired anything else with this depth, with such intensity?

If I had, the memory of it was swept away in a stroke of her tongue.

Without releasing my mouth, Nora twined one arm around my neck and used the other to tug my hand upward from her waist until I was cupping one perfect breast in my palm. My thumb brushed slowly back and forth across her nipple until it tightened and peaked against my hand. She sighed into my mouth as heat shot straight to my cock.

Encouraged by her reaction, I rolled the bud between my fingers until she gave a frantic little cry that I felt more than heard. Then she yanked at the ruffled neckline of the dress, pushing the bodice down past her hips until the garment fell straight to the floor, and kicked off her sandals, never breaking the contact between our lips.

"God, you are so soft," I whispered as I slid one hand across her bare skin until I reached the clasp of her strapless bra.

She shimmied until it dropped away and my hands immediately took the place of the pale gray satin. While my fingers plucked and teased, guided by the sweet little sounds she made, Nora fumbled with the zipper of my jeans.

"Do you want to slow down?" I asked, nuzzling my nose along her jaw.

"Not on your life," she whispered. A growl of satisfaction escaped her when she finally managed to tug the zipper down.

I released her just long enough to shove the jeans over my hips and step out of them. In a movement so swift that she let out a little gasp of surprise, I lifted her, my hands curving around her ass, squeezing gently. She wrapped her legs around my waist and I carried her around to the side of the bed, then lowered us both until she was lying across the deep blue comforter and I was stretched out along the length of her body.

When my mouth closed over the peak of one breast, she arched upward against me with a guttural cry. My fingers continued to torment her other nipple as my blood reached a rolling boil, spurred ever onward by the soft, breathless gasps that escaped her.

I adjusted my position to grant each breast equal attention, smiling wickedly against her delicate flesh when my name fell from her lips like a prayer. Her hips shifted restlessly beneath mine, driving us both rapidly toward fever pitch. One of her hands grasped at the bedding while the other tangled in my hair, clutching me tight to her body.

I drew back, swirling my tongue around one rosy nipple and then the other, drawing another desperate whimper from her as I kissed a burning trail along her collarbone and up her throat before settling on her lips.

"What do you want, Nora?" I asked against her mouth. "Tell me."

"Naked! Time to get naked," she gasped as my hips rolled against hers, the heat between her legs searing me through the remaining layers of fabric.

I drew her lower lip lightly between my teeth, basking in the way her thighs tightened around my hips, then reared back onto my knees so I could hook my thumbs around the waistband of her panties and draw them slowly down her bare legs. They were the same pale gray satin as her bra, and I let the lacy edges tease her skin so I could watch her eyelids flutter at the sensation. When I started to crawl back up her body, she shook her head.

"I said naked. That means you, too."

I bowed my head and grinned as I pushed my boxers down, noting the way she rose up on her elbows to watch my cock spring free.

"Satisfied?" I asked, running my palms along her legs from ankle to knee.

"Not yet," she muttered.

I laughed as I stretched out alongside her again. "You're a truly incredible woman, did you know that?"

My hand curled around her hip and paused there when she shivered slightly at my touch. After a heartbeat, I felt her muscles relax, so I let my palm run over the lush curve of her ass. She tensed, clearly ticklish, when I stroked down the back of her thigh, but she offered no resistance when I caught her knees to spread her legs wider.

Her eyes locked on my face as she waited for me to continue. "Did we come up here to make small talk all night, Lincoln?" she demanded when I simply smiled down at her.

"I'm appreciating all of your numerous virtues and you want me to cut to the chase? Not a chance, Cassidy. You are exquisitely beautiful. Deliciously sensitive. Perfectly responsive." I punctuated each statement with soft nips and kisses from her neck to her breasts. "I can't get enough. I want to touch you. Yes?" My hand lifted, hovering a fraction of an inch above the soft, dark curls between her legs.

"Yes. About time," she grumbled, opening further for me.

My soft laughter caressed her heated skin as I finally touched her where she wanted. Her head fell back as my fingers parted her folds, stroking, circling, learning every inch of her. She was slick with desire, lifting eagerly to meet me, and hot, so hot. I would gladly risk being seared by that heat, branded by it.

When I plunged one finger deep inside, she gave a soft cry that nearly unraveled my remaining control. Another finger joined it, curling inside of her in a way that had her writhing underneath me. I let her responses guide me as I teased and toyed, drawing her closer, relishing the way her hips lifted to meet my hand, the way her eyes fell shut and her lips parted. There was something intensely erotic about watching her, seeing her shift and squirm and gasp.

I couldn't get enough.

When the orgasm burst over her, I leaned down and kissed her, drinking in each quiet sound of pleasure that passed her lips. Once her eyelids fluttered open again, she caught my self-satisfied smirk and cupped one hand around the back of my neck while the other wrapped snugly around the base of my cock.

"You're good, I'll give you that," she teased, kissing me even as her grip slid along my length and made me groan against her mouth. "Let's see just how good, hmm?"

I was ready for the challenge. "Oh, I look forward to showing you, Cassidy."

Still firmly in her grasp, I reached across her body to pull a condom from the drawer of the nightstand. Nora released me and watched as I drew it on, her tongue brushing across her lips in a way that made me more than a little desperate to be inside of her at last. Still, I paused as I positioned myself between her legs, studying her face for a long moment before I dropped down and kissed her.

I kept my lower body perfectly still, poised at the ready, waiting for her to make the final move. Her eyes flared with impatience when she realized what I was doing.

With a low, unutterably sexy growl, she gripped my hips and arched her own upward, drawing me deep within her. Once there, her eyelids fell closed and I struggled to keep my own open so I didn't miss a second of that expression on her face. I'd imagined this, the two of us coming together, in so many different ways.

Not a single fantasy could possibly compare to reality.

Scorching heat, wet and welcoming and so fucking tight, I had to freeze right there, buried to the hilt, until I was sure I wasn't going to lose control and embarrass myself.

When I got a handle on it, I started to move, watching her intently as I drew slowly back and sank deep once more. Her lips parted on a gasp and her eyes flew open, then she locked her legs around my waist, making a strangled little sound with each slow thrust.

"Good?" I asked, waiting until she nodded and dug her fingers into my shoulders.

I thought I'd already made it clear to Nora that I was a man of infinite patience, but given the heat we seemed to generate just from kissing downstairs, her impatient wriggling implied she expected me to act with that same desperate passion. Instead, I kept up the infuriatingly slow pace until she was inching toward another explosive climax, whimpering frantically until my teeth scraped across her nipple and she arched upward with a sharp cry as she came around my cock.

Heaven, pure and simple.

As her limbs tightened around me, I finally started moving faster, striking the very core of her with each thrust, capturing her mouth with mine in a rhythm that mimicked the movement of our bodies. She clung to me, ankles linked at the small of my back, meeting me stroke for stroke.

When my name burst from her lips in a breathless cry, I reached between us to press my thumb against her clit, and the final eruption left us both quaking in the aftermath.

With what little energy I had left, I rolled away to throw out the condom. I was back at her side before her breathing had even slowed. She was still limp as I drew her into my arms, and when I cocked a brow down at her, she gave a breathless laugh.

"Good doesn't even begin to cut it," she said, tucking her head into the hollow of my shoulder. "I think I called you a god among men once before. I guess I was right."

I kissed the top of her head as I trailed my fingers up and down along her spine. "I'm glad I passed muster, because I might never move again. At least we'll have these memories to keep us warm at night."

Her laughter floated over me and a different kind of warmth settled deep in my chest. This Nora was such a bold contrast against the prickly little thing she had seemed at first. Lying here with her felt as natural as breathing. In boneless languor, we stayed curled up together in my bed for a long time afterward, a tangle of limbs and blissful satisfaction.

I wasn't in any way opposed to cuddling after sex, but I'd certainly never enjoyed it as much as I did with Nora. Each of her sweet curves fit perfectly against the planes of my body, so achingly soft that I wanted to stay like that for the rest of my natural life.

"Thank you," she murmured into my skin.

"Believe me when I say it was my pleasure."

"Hmm. Mine too."

I laughed against the top of her head and tightened my arm around her as she snuggled close. It came as no surprise that she wasn't one for pillow talk, but as evening fell outside the bedroom window, it seemed like words came more readily to her lips, little questions and conversational tidbits as she drowsed there, draped against my chest. I wondered if she felt more secure in the growing dark or if it was simply an effect of our coming together.

Whatever the reason, I was more than willing to enjoy the shifting dynamic. This was more than just casual sex for me.

I only hoped she felt the same.

Chapter Fifteen

NORA

"WHAT DID YOU STUDY in college?" I asked, barely able to open my eyes.

Jake's fingers toyed with my hair, sending little waves of pleasure over my loose, exhausted muscles. He pressed a kiss to the top of my head before he answered.

"Business. I dabbled with accounting, and medieval history one semester. You?"

My soft laugh ruffled the hairs on his chest. "So you're not a Renaissance man, but a medieval warrior?" I mused. For a moment, I was too lulled by his fingers in my hair to form the words, then I said, "I have a degree in world languages."

"Makes sense," he replied, the tenor of his voice rumbling under my ear. "How many do you know?"

"A few. It helped that my dad is fluent in several foreign languages, so I was able to practice speaking with a real human when he was around, or by writing letters when he wasn't."

"That is unbearably sexy, you know."

When I laughed again, his fingers trailed down the length of my arm, raising goosebumps in their wake.

"What's your favorite language?" he asked.

I struggled to focus on the question instead of his fingertips, but I found his touch terribly distracting, especially now that I knew what those digits were capable of.

"Um. French, I'd have to say. It was the first language I learned after English. My dad taught me that one when he was around, from the time I was a toddler I guess, and then he made sure I had tutors lined up when he was deployed. Sometimes it was just a teenager on base who would quiz me while babysitting, sometimes they were actual French teachers who'd fit me in after school."

This was followed by an exchange of silly getting-to-know-you questions that had somehow never seemed important between us until this point, things like favorite color (mine: purple, his: the light blue of my dress tonight) and birthday (mine: September third, his: June tenth).

Jake was careful in what he asked, tentative almost, but I participated willingly, even when the questions turned more personal.

When our favorite foods came up, however, I yelped and propped myself up on one elbow to look down at him. From the spark of concern in his eyes when he saw my expression, he must have expected something tragic to come out of my mouth.

"Jake! We forgot about dessert!"

"Did we?" he asked, cocking a brow as a slow smile spread across his face.

The effect that smile had on my insides was instantaneous, but I shook my head. "Oh no, you're not getting any more of that until I try some of this famous carrot cake. I spent an hour thinking about how good it looked before I came over here and I'll have you know that I've now worked up an appetite."

"Sustenance again?" Jake pasted a look of pure innocence on his handsome face. "I can't deny you that, not when we've expended so much energy already—and hopefully will again as soon as I've recovered. If you want to wait here, I'll go get it and bring it up."

Eating cake in bed with this devastatingly attractive man was an offer simply too good to refuse. I watched him bend to pull on his jeans, unabashedly admiring the way those sleek muscles of his back blended into what had to be the nicest ass I'd ever seen up close.

When he caught me staring, he leaned over the bed to kiss me one last time before he winked and trotted downstairs shirt-less.

Without him, the room felt colder, so I slipped under the comforter and nestled deep into his pillows. They smelled like him, a faint trace of pine and fresh cut grass. Was it creepy to press my face against the pillowcase just to breathe it in?

Without him there to judge, I decided I didn't care and did it anyway.

The man was a walking aphrodisiac; I wanted him again already, missed the heat of his body, the way he filled me, the joint sensations of being both tenderly cared for and enthusiastically worshipped.

Jake returned quickly, clutching the box in one arm and a pair of forks in the other. The second his gaze landed on me snuggled up in his bed, there was a quick shift in his expression, a flare of his pupils—something that on another man might have been possessiveness, but that seemed too primitive for a man like Jake Lincoln.

Hunger? Need? Pure, blind lust? He set the cake and forks on the side table as I pondered it.

Then again, the look in his eyes when he removed his jeans seemed remarkably similar to what I was feeling. There was a blatant haze of desire gathering in those baby blues and I wondered if primitive might be just what I wanted right now, with him. He lifted a brow as he slid under the covers beside me.

"Dessert? Or *dessert?*" he asked, dropping his head for a light, teasing kiss.

"Cake first. Then Jake."

The teasing words made him laugh aloud, but he settled back against the pillows to cater to my demands. I grinned and leaned across him to grab a fork from the side table, intentionally letting my breasts graze his bare chest along the way. Despite proclaiming my need for food, I felt my body readying, tingling under his gaze just as it had under his skilled fingers.

With the bakery box balanced on his impressive abs and his free arm wrapped around me, we dug into the cake together. After a first tiny bite, I abandoned all pretense of dainty feminine manners and closed my eyes on a dramatic sigh.

"Oh, that is good," I moaned.

Jake nipped at my earlobe, grinning when he felt the shiver run through me. "Your repeated use of the word 'good' feels a tad insulting."

"You could do worse than being compared to this heavenly confection, Jake Lincoln."

My eyes lifted to his as I very deliberately licked the frosting from my fork. A vision of him lapping frosting off my nipples promptly filled my head, and from the molten heat in his eyes, I wondered if he was imagining it too.

"Temptress," he growled, but he took another bite of cake as I laughed.

Between the two of us, we made an impressive dent on the pretty cake, then I flopped back on the pillows as Jake set the box on the bedside table. When he turned back to me, I had the blanket pulled up to my chin, so he raised a questioning brow.

"Maybe I should go," I said quietly, though I made no move to leave the bed.

"If that's what you want, sure. Or, as an alternative, you could stay," Jake countered, watching me closely.

If he thought I was really spooked, I knew he'd back off immediately. That knowledge bolstered me against the uncertainty that had started creeping in. When I said nothing after a long, silent moment, he rolled onto his side, his face six inches from mine on the pillow.

"If you really want to go home, I won't insult you by trying to convince you to spend the night. We can get dressed right now and I'll walk you home, hopefully kiss you goodnight, and come back to bed alone. But I'd be honored if you would stay, Nora."

His tone was soft, somehow managing to sound reassuring without cajoling. My fingers twitched a little, tightening around the blanket and then opening again. Though I got the distinct impression he wanted to reach out and touch me, to clasp my hand in his own and offer comfort, he held perfectly still.

This decision needed to be mine alone, and the fact that he recognized that settled something deep in my chest.

"I don't usually . . ." I trailed off, my gaze shifting away briefly before returning to meet his. "It's just easier to be the one to walk away first."

"Love 'em and leave 'em," he replied, nodding. The words were gentle and entirely without bite.

"Something like that. You really want me to stay?"

He reached over and tucked a curl behind my ear. "I'd love for you to stay. And without expectations—if you want to sleep here next to me, that's fine. You want to cuddle, even better. And if you decide you want more than that, I am absolutely willing to work off that cake in a way that ought to satisfy us both."

From the way he looked at me, I knew he meant every word.

Even though I'd used the word *usually,* the truth was that I *never* spent the night with anyone, whether it was a one-night stand or any of the brief relationships I'd attempted not long after I first set out on my own. Audrey and Jamal had never tried to change my mind, they'd just accepted that I slept alone, end of story.

Still, with Jake's blue eyes watching me in that soft, warm way of his, I couldn't quite bring myself to walk away just yet.

"I'll stay," I whispered, reaching out to trace the sharp line of his jaw. "For tonight, anyway."

"Excellent decision. So, sleep?"

I narrowed my eyes at him. "Oh no, I choose what's behind door number three, thank you very much."

Without another word, he made good on his promise. It didn't take long before I seized the reins and rolled him onto his back. If he had any lingering doubts as to how I felt about elevating our relationship to a different level, I set about systematically erasing them, one by one, moment by moment, stroke by stroke.

By the time I collapsed against his chest, I wasn't sure I'd ever get enough of him. That thought was as beautiful as it was terrifying.

Just before I fell asleep, blanketing him with my body, the words *just friends* floated across my mind and I chuckled softly against his shoulder.

His only response was an unintelligible murmur, and I let go of consciousness with the knowledge that he, too, had clearly thrown that particular decree out the window.

Chapter Sixteen

JAKE

WHEN I AWOKE THE next morning, Nora was gone. The loss of her soft body beside me kicked off an ache inside my chest. It lingered even when I reminded myself she *had* spent the night.

And what a glorious night it had been.

Baby steps. She would need time to get used to things, get comfortable with this level of intimacy—something beyond the physical. Every time she opened up to me, she showed more and more of her true self, the one she'd hidden behind those thorns, like the blossoms on the hawthorn tree out back.

Eventually, with patience and kindness and trust, I was almost certain she'd show me the rest.

I swallowed my disappointment, then glanced at the clock and swore under my breath. It was almost eleven—I hadn't slept past eight in years. Of course, I hadn't had such a fascinating companion to keep me up half the night, either.

The thought had me grinning up at the ceiling as memories of Nora, naked and glorious and bold, danced before my eyes.

Even though I'd joked about my sister being a force of nature, coming together with Nora was like being caught in a hurricane. She was wonderfully intense, with every new height drawing me higher right alongside her. Everything about her made me want to learn more, experience more.

Had she really run away this morning?

It hit me like a bucket of frigid water. Disappointment wasn't the right word for what I was feeling—it was more a crushing sense of loss. Even though she'd warned me, made it sound like it wasn't personal, I still felt like I'd done something wrong. I wracked my brain, trying to think of a moment when I might have pushed too hard, rushed her too fast, but there was nothing. Everything felt so perfect, so natural.

Things seemed to be going so well between us, and she'd given every indication of enjoying the night as much as I did. Her admission about being the first to leave echoed in my head and made my chest ache again, because I recognized that she was speaking from experience.

How could I make it clear that I had no intention of walking away from her without scaring her off with the force of that admission?

I rubbed a hand over my face as I sat up. It was a moment before I noticed that the cake box was gone from the bedside table, replaced by a scrap of paper she'd pulled off the notepad from the kitchen. Leaning over, I grabbed it and reread the words several times before they sunk in.

You're cute when you sleep. Just couldn't bear to wake you. Cake's in the fridge. Leftovers make an excellent breakfast, FYI. ~N

I couldn't hold back the idiotic smile that spread across my face. This didn't feel like a "first one to leave" type of situation. This felt...good. It felt like a beginning, a promise of more to come, not like she considered things between us over and done with. I thought about texting her but forced myself to wait. Even if she'd warmed up to me—and fuck, had she warmed up—I still had the unsettling feeling that it wouldn't take much to scare her off.

Patience and continued reassurance seemed to be just the thing to coax Nora from behind her walls. I could provide both of those things, not just until she recognized I wasn't going anywhere, but for as long as she wanted me around.

If there was one thing I'd learned from being a twin, it was that I was the steady one in the face of Sam's animated exuberance. I was the one happy to wait for my pleasure, to work for my reward, no matter how long it took. Sam loved a challenge, yes, but she thrived on a continually changing routine that accommodated her flashes of interest and fits of whimsy.

Steadfast and steady, my father had always called me, usually after my sister went whirling through a room and left me blinking in her wake. Though I knew he'd meant it as a compliment, it hadn't felt like one back then, not when our class-mates flocked to my sister from the first day we started at a new high school and referred to me only as "Sam's brother."

Now, though? Now it was clear that those traits weren't second best, they were just me. And they were exactly what seemed to draw Nora to me in the first place, to ease my path beyond that prickly defense system she'd managed to keep in place for so long.

She hadn't run away.

The warmth twining through my chest was neither as simple as relief nor as basic as pleasure. It was...contentment. Joy. Nora hadn't replaced the barricade around her heart after last night. She'd let me in, and I'd be damned if I didn't fight to keep my place there.

With that in mind, I set about getting ready for work, still grinning from ear to ear. Just before I walked out the door, my phone rang with my twin's ringtone.

"Can't you ever use your psychic twin powers for good, instead of evil?" I demanded as I answered the call.

"Nope," Sam replied. "How's our girl?"

I held the phone away from my ear to glare at my sister's photo on the screen. "*Our* girl? I kind of hate that, Saman-tha. Why are you asking, anyway?"

A low whistle sounded from the other end of the line before Sam said, "Well, that was an answer in itself. Did you sleep with her yet?"

"For Christ's sake, that's none of your business," I muttered, but the words were without heat. I was more annoyed at her uncanny ability to sense when my love life took a turn than with the question.

"Someone is touchy this morning. I just need to assess whether she's loosened up a bit. Eased into the small town life, you know? Do you think she's in a good mood today?"

I tripped over my thoughts of Nora *loosening up* and heaved a sigh. "As far as I'm aware, yes, she's in a good mood."

"Good, then I'll strike while the iron's hot. Enjoy your day, brother!"

Before I could even ask what the hell that meant, she'd hung up. One thing was certain about my twin—nothing stayed under wraps for long. I'd give Nora a bit more time before checking in with her, and hopefully by that point I would know what Samantha Lincoln had up her sleeve.

"Strike while the iron's hot," I repeated, shaking my head.

Nora could certainly take care of herself, but I'd never let Sam hear the end of it if she pushed Nora into joining in on one of her crazy schemes.

I shoved the phone in my back pocket, grabbed my keys from the kitchen counter, and headed out to the truck. Though I didn't see any movement from those frilly curtains in Nora's door at the top of the stairs, I gave a little salute, just in case she was watching.

My sister might be a whirlwind, but thanks to my beautiful new neighbor, I was on cloud nine.

Chapter Seventeen

NORA

I WAS SITTING ON the little loveseat that had come with the apartment when I heard Jake's truck pull out of the driveway. Even back in my own comfortable surroundings, I felt oddly off-kilter, like my mind was telling me I ought to be a bundle of nerves right about now while my heart whispered soothing things in my ear that kept my muscles soft and loose.

Jake was like a balm for me, body and soul. I hadn't felt this good in years, physically or emotionally.

Once he was gone, I forced myself to get some work done, but before I hit any real groove in the translation, my phone chimed from the coffee table. A full minute passed before I reached for it. Instead of a text from Jake, as I'd expected, I found a message from his sister.

Shopping Friday? Pleeeeeeease?

I groaned and pinched the bridge of my nose as I thought about it. Going on Friday would give me the whole week to finish the project I was currently working on and to get some time in on other things, as well—whether or not I spent my nights with Sam's very sexy, very talented brother.

Would five days be enough time to train myself not to blush when Sam inevitably asked what was happening between me and Jake?

Though this was exactly the kind of entanglement I had so steadfastly avoided, I didn't feel bad about it, not even a little. Well, at least not about getting tangled up with Jake, which involved utterly mind-blowing pleasure unlike anything I'd ever experienced. Getting the third degree from his sister might lead to some small amount of discomfort, however.

I could handle it, I assured myself firmly, and texted Sam back to set a time for our shopping trip.

It wasn't until afternoon faded into evening that a text from Jake finally appeared. I'd just eaten a bowl of cold cereal for dinner and turned on some mindless television sitcom to keep me company in the quiet apartment, a move that baffled me even as I did it. Work was the only time when I appreciated so many sounds around me; normally I relished quiet time to myself when I wasn't busy translating.

Shit, was I...lonely? I'd barely been away from Jake for twelve hours. It was ridiculous to think that I was feeling that loss so keenly. Grumbling at my own idiocy, I grabbed my phone off the coffee table.

Busy tonight?

Only two little words, but heat flooded my body. I stared at the phone, my thumbs hovering over the keyboard.

Not busy at all. How's work?

Boring. The hot chick I usually scope out from behind the bar never showed. Had to entertain myself by counting tiny drink umbrellas the rest of the night.

A startled laugh burst from my lips, followed by a wide grin. *That's tragic. Did you have cake for breakfast?*

Though three little dots indicated he'd started typing, it was several minutes before his response came through. *Sorry, customers keep bugging me. Don't they know this is more important? I figured I'd save the leftovers for tonight, in case you were interested in joining me for dessert.*

"You should say no," I told myself, laying my head back against the cushioned loveseat. "You're going to make a habit of this, of him. It'd be better to just say no."

The words seemed to echo in the empty apartment, then I picked up the phone and typed, *I'm in.*

A nervous flutter rose from deep in my belly, even as anticipation edged into more sensitive parts of my anatomy. The phone chimed once more to say, *I'll pick you up on my way home, around ten.*

I laughed at that, then tossed the phone aside and drew myself a hot bath. The apartment's bathroom was tidy and perfectly adequate, but it wasn't nearly as luxurious as the master bath I'd tiptoed into this morning at Jake's house. I'd stood there for a solid minute, admiring the gigantic glass shower stall and impressive corner tub before finally remembering I had to pee.

"Fantasizing about a man's bathtub is a new low," I muttered as I sank down in the steaming water.

Instead, when I closed my eyes, I remembered the way his hands had stroked over my skin like he couldn't possibly get enough, that hot, hungry mouth that had performed unspeakably erotic acts and whispered words both dark and sweet. I forced my eyes open, staring at the gray tiled wall as I wondered what it was about Jake Lincoln that had made it so easy for him to slip through my defenses.

Once the water cooled, I washed my hair, braided it, and threw on jeans and a tank top. The dress had been a fit of whimsy on my part, brought on by the desire for him to look at me as he had after my coffee date with Sam, like I was a vision of beauty.

Or lust.

As I studied my reflection in the bathroom mirror, my fingers lifted thoughtfully to my lips. Was it my imagination, or did I still look like a woman who'd been well and thoroughly kissed?

My hand dropped just as Jake texted to tell me he was outside. I pocketed the phone and met him on the stairs, feeling strangely shy as I locked the door behind me. He was standing about halfway up the stairs with that beautifully crooked smile on his face.

"I didn't want to startle you by knocking," he said, watching as my eyes widened.

"That's very thoughtful of you," I replied even as I kicked myself for the stupid response. I stayed frozen for a moment until the wave of awkwardness passed, then came down the steps toward him. When I was two steps above his position, I paused, bringing the two of us very close to eye level. "You're an interesting man, you know."

"I'll take that as a compliment, coming from such a fascinating woman. I've got a hunk of carrot cake with our names on it, though I have to confess it does look like it was attacked by hungry badgers."

I laughed. "Badgers, huh? I'm sure they were extremely attractive and very naked badgers, at least. How was the rest of your shift?"

"Quiet and, like I said, boring."

He offered his hand and looked inordinately pleased when I immediately slipped mine into it. When we reached the driveway, he turned to look at me, his contented smile fading into an expression of concern.

"You didn't stay home because of me, right? Nothing between us changes my offer for you to come in to work, Nora."

"No, it wasn't that. I just needed some time to think." I broke off and shot him a horrified glance. "Oh god, that sounds maudlin. I don't regret a single minute of last night, Jake. I want that to be perfectly clear. I just didn't want to catch myself daydreaming about your insanely attractive naked body while I was sitting in a public place, how's that?"

"Daydreaming, huh?" He chewed on that, then his gaze sharpened on my face. "And what happened with that guy isn't going to keep you from coming back either, is it?"

I actually rolled my eyes at that and tugged his hand toward his house. "No, some drunken asshole isn't going to rob me of my favorite writing nook. I've never come to The Mermaid every single day, Jake. Today was just a home day. I told you I can take care of myself."

"Yes, you did. Where did you learn that move, by the way?"

"Self-defense classes. My dad insisted," I grumbled, tugging him harder when he paused again. "For god's sake, Lincoln, are we going to stand out here chatting all night? I want either cake or sex, in whichever order you choose, and I'm getting impatient."

Jake's heated glance gave me some idea which order of events he preferred. "Did I say fascinating? Because you are the most goddamn bewitching woman I've ever met."

With that, his intoxicating mouth settled on mine, drinking in the soft sigh that escaped my lips. We were nearly to the front door, but I wasn't convinced Jake could keep his hands off me long enough to fumble for the doorknob. I laughed against his jaw when he swore under his breath, attempting to open the door without letting go of his hold on me.

"You're killing me," he said hoarsely when my hands clenched the front of his shirt. "I feel like a teenager again, clumsy and so turned on I'm pretty sure there isn't enough blood reaching my brain."

"Open the door," I ordered, but I didn't release him. In fact, as soon as the key was in the lock, I kissed him again.

Jake barely managed to shut the door behind us and toss the keys in the vicinity of the hall table before sliding his hands under the hem of my tank top, pressing against the small of my back to fit me more closely against him. Pleasure hummed in my throat as his lips traveled across my jaw.

"Does this mean the cake has to wait?" I asked sweetly.

Jake threw back his head and laughed before cupping my face in his hands. "This means everything else on the planet has to wait."

The joyous smile that spread across my lips told him that was the right answer, and together we raced up the stairs.

Chapter Eighteen

Jake

WE SETTLED INTO A comfortable rhythm over the following days and, much to my delight, Nora also returned to her little booth in the corner several times that week. There was something intensely satisfying about being able to look over and speak a thousand words with just a glance. It was that same pleasure I'd felt when she first started coming in—multiplied by a thousand now that our connection strengthened day by day.

As a bonus, I started counting the number of times I was able to inspire a blush in her cheeks with nothing more than a raised eyebrow.

My current record was three in one evening, but the payback came when she held my gaze and popped a piece of strawberry between her lips. I almost abandoned the bar to drag her into my office then and there.

After we left The Mermaid, our nights were spent together, exploring one another and testing the limits of the hurricane forces between us. It was a perfect technique for drawing her out from behind her walls, because my intuition about when to press forward and when to back off seemed to reassure her more than words ever could.

Of course, the fact that she trusted me enough to be so responsive was why I was able to read her so well. As a result, I could barely remember a time when I'd been so happy and so fulfilled all at once.

Since I knew that Nora's shopping trip with Sam was weighing on her nerves, on Thursday night we left the restaurant early to go back to my place. I'd caught the way Nora eyed the huge bathtub at my house with something pretty damn close to longing, so I asked Sam to pick up some kind of girly bubble bath, which she'd sneakily delivered to me at work the previous day. Before heading to The Mermaid for my shift, I'd positioned candles around the master bathroom.

Nora cocked a suspicious brow when I told her to stay put downstairs, covered her eyes as instructed when I brought her up, and gave a girlish shriek of sheer delight when I revealed the candlelit bathroom and steaming tub filled with bubbles.

She turned and threw her arms around me, though not before I caught sight of her radiant smile—and, I thought, the sheen of tears in her eyes.

"Oh my god, Jake," she whispered, "I thought maybe you were leading me to a sex dungeon. Oh, this is beautiful, thank you, thank you, thank you!"

I burst out laughing as I clutched her tight to my chest. "Sex dungeon, huh? I mean, if the lady desires, I'm sure I can adjust my renovation plans. I'll just need a few extra supplies to make that happen."

She whacked my shoulder lightly and surreptitiously wiped at her eyes before turning back to survey the scene before us. "This is a pretty big tub," she mused. "Will you be joining me?"

I started pulling off my shirt before she even finished the question. "Hell yes, but the point of this exercise is relaxation, so don't go getting all handsy on me."

Nora's beautiful laughter echoed off the tiled walls, but when she sank chin-deep into the water, it was her sigh of pure bliss that wound its way around my heart with a gentle squeeze. I never even used the tub, nor had I really ever expected to, but we stayed in there for almost two hours with nothing more sexual than a game of footsy to accent our soft conversation.

Nora looked so at peace that I was just about willing to add this into our nightly routine. With her dark hair piled high, her eyes closed, and her head tipped back against the porcelain, I had a tantalizing view of her neck and shoulders. Only the upper swells of her breasts were visible until the bubbles at last began to collapse on themselves, then I caught the occasional glimpse of deep, rosy pink beneath the water and my mouth went dry.

A sheepish grin tugged at my lips when she caught me staring.

"I was told the point of this exercise was relaxation," she informed me primly, but the glint in her eye told me she was finished with that portion of the evening.

"I have a very delicate constitution and the water is freezing now," I protested. "I had to warm myself up somehow, didn't I? Do you want me to suffer from hypothermia?"

She crawled over to me, sweeping away bubbles with her hand until she was straddling my thighs. "You have a rock solid constitution—among other things, it feels like—so why don't you let me warm you up?"

With a wide smile, I enthusiastically agreed. Though I was always happy to take the lead whenever she wanted me to, letting Nora guide our lovemaking was a gift in itself. She was as inventive as she was playful, easily coaxing me into trying out whatever it was she had in mind.

So far, she'd never steered us wrong.

Sometimes I thought about her declaration that she wanted nothing from me beyond friendship—especially when she was doing wicked things with her mouth or when she was writhing underneath my own—and I had to keep myself from laughing and ruining the moment.

When we abandoned the tub, though, bubbles dripping down our bodies to join the puddles on the floor, Nora's limbs wrapped tightly around me, laughter was out of the question.

She was as likely as not to disappear before I awoke, but she lingered in bed with me on Friday morning, welcoming the soothing way my hands stroked over her hair and skin as I woke up to her in my arms. We lay there in the stillness of the morning, listening to the birdsong outside the window as I basked in the warmth of her soft body tucked against my side.

"You know you don't have to go, if you don't want to. Shopping with Sam, I mean," I mumbled sleepily.

Nora seemed to consider it as she traced abstract shapes across the muscles of my abdomen with one finger. I knew she liked to watch the way they rippled under her hands, to feel her effect on me in such a tangible way. In fact, she seemed to enjoy seeing my every reaction, just as I enjoyed hers—the woman held nothing back when it came to our time together.

"I do want to go. I think. I'm just even more out of practice with the girls' day kind of thing than I was with this." She waved her hand vaguely over our bodies.

"Jesus Christ, Nora, if you're this good *out* of practice, it's a good thing you weren't *in* practice. I probably would've died of a heart attack by now."

She laughed against my shoulder. "That's not what I meant, you jerk."

Tugging on a lock of her hair, I waited until she met my eyes and said, "Look, Sam might blow through a room like a tornado, but she's a good friend. She may talk your ear off or try to convince you to buy thigh high boots—which would be absolutely fine by me, in case you wondered—but she's not going to pry into your life. Not about us, and not about anything else you don't want to discuss."

"Thigh high boots, huh?" she mused, snuggling closer against me. "Well, now I'm looking forward to this shopping trip."

With a growl, I took her mind off of shopping for the remaining hour before she needed to get ready. Her peals of laughter bounced around us, dancing like the sunlight coming through the window, until the giggles faded into the soft, throaty moans that made me wish I were the one spending the entire day with her.

Since she insisted on going back to her apartment to shower and dress for the shopping trip, I decided I might as well get some yard work done. No way would I miss seeing whatever cute outfit she threw together for a day out with my sister, especially knowing how she'd dressed up just for their coffee date.

It was only fair that I get to see it too, or so I told myself as I worked at a snail's pace so I wouldn't be caught standing around doing nothing when she came out to meet Sam.

My sister's red Mustang pulled into Nora's driveway right on schedule. She gave me a jaunty wave, which I returned with a sardonic smile, then both of us caught sight of Nora coming down the stairs at the same time.

If I'd been able to photograph our matching reactions, I might have laughed at them in the future, but I was too busy trying not to embarrass myself with an epic erection in front of my twin.

"Holy shit," I whispered.

"Holy shit, indeed," Sam concurred through the lowered car window. "You are one lucky son of a bitch, no offense to our mother."

Nora was wearing a cropped, pumpkin-colored blouse with a flouncy floral skirt that made my palms itch to run along the back of her thighs, to hook around her knees the way she liked. Short black boots left a long stretch of bare leg visible—I was almost willing to rank them higher than the fantasy boots we'd discussed only hours ago. Her hair was pulled half up, the rest falling in loose, enticing curls around her shoulders.

Sam shot me a sideways glance as she bit back a grin. "If your mouth is watering like a garden hose even after spending all night with her, you must really have it bad, brother."

"Oh, believe me, I do."

I gave Nora a smile, one I hoped could convey all the things I had in mind for the minute I got her to myself again, and opened the passenger door of Sam's car for her. Before she slid into the seat, my hand sank deep into the hair at the nape of her neck and I bent down to kiss her. It was a deep, thorough, mind-numbing kiss that left her blushing brilliantly in front of my sister.

"Have fun," I murmured, winking at her dazed expression as she got in the car.

Sam's burst of laughter filled the air as I forced myself to back away. Still, I couldn't quite make my feet lead me into the garage until the Mustang finally disappeared from view at the end of the street.

"You are one lucky son of a bitch." I repeated my sister's words in a whisper, let them waft over me, and another tendril of warmth curled around my heart.

Hell, yes, I was.

Chapter Nineteen

NORA

"Damn, girl," Sam said as we pulled away. "First off, you look smoking hot. Second, he is absolutely infatuated with you, in case you didn't know that yet. And third, we are going to have a freaking fantastic day."

I laughed, feeling my anxiety evaporate as classic rock poured from the radio. Despite the differences in their personalities, the Lincoln twins both possessed that surprising talent of setting me at ease no matter how nervous I might be. It wasn't long before the two of us were chatting comfortably about a dozen different things, including Sam's love life, though somehow we carefully skirted around the topic of my own.

As it turned out, both Jake and Sam had been correct on all counts. Sam was a blast to shop with, despite the fact that she encouraged me to try on every sexy little outfit we came across.

She didn't pry, though she did give me a few knowing looks whenever Jake came up in conversation.

I didn't end up buying any boots, but I somehow let her talk me into purchasing a lacy black bra and matching thong.

Without thinking, I said, "I don't see the point, if I'll just end up naked anyway." Then, utterly mortified, I slapped a hand over my mouth while Sam roared with laughter.

Once she finally got control of herself, she gasped, "Oh, Nora. You are a treat. No wonder my brother is hooked on you." She saw my expression start to drop and shook her head quickly. "Oh, sweetie, it's not a bad thing, I promise you. He's a good guy and he's clearly crazy about you. And I can tell you right now he's going to be salivating when he sees you in those, no matter how quick he is to tear them off you."

I choked on a laugh, but I sobered quickly. "I didn't really mean to fall into a relationship right now," I admitted.

Why the words were tumbling out—and to my new lover's twin sister, no less—I had absolutely no idea, but Sam clucked sympathetically and looped her arm around my shoulders.

"Things don't always happen the way we expect them to," she said, "but sometimes the best things come along when we're not even looking for them. Now, let's buy these pretty little panties and get some grub, hmm?"

The restaurant Sam chose for lunch was an adorable, bustling Italian bistro at the edge of the strip mall. Though she carried the conversation, as she had for most of the day, that didn't bother me. Now that my brief moment of reflection had passed, I felt almost as at ease with Samantha Lincoln as I did with Jake.

In the back of my mind, I wondered if this was what it felt like to have a big, close-knit family. It quieted the echoing cavern inside me, cloaking me with warmth, as though their companionship might somehow fill the void.

When the bill arrived, I snatched it up off the table, insisting that it was the least I could do. Sam apparently knew a lost cause when she saw one, so she left me to pay while she ran to the restroom before the drive home.

The day was gorgeous and the sunshine too tempting to resist, so I decided to wander outside to wait. Big ceramic pots of flowers lined the sidewalk and I trailed my fingers along the smooth edges as I moved away from the busy entryway. A crowd of people brushed past me on the sidewalk and I was shoved hard against a man in dark sunglasses.

"Careful," he said with a smile, then he was swallowed up by the crowd.

Recognition hit me, stealing the breath from my lungs, and I had to wonder if I could even trust my eyes. For the second time since I arrived in Spruce Hill, icy tendrils of dread curled around my heart. That voice and the cold, arrogant smirk that accompanied it were like a ghost reaching straight into my chest and squeezing tight.

I suddenly felt like I was drowning, unable to draw air deep enough into my lungs. It was a hundred times worse than after the guy at The Mermaid grabbed me, and this time I didn't have Jake there to help.

By the time I saw Sam exit the restaurant, painful gasps choked me as I staggered away from the crowd, bracing my hands against my knees just to stay upright. Her mouth moved, but the harsh drag of each breath and the thunderous cadence of my pulse in my ears drowned out her words.

"Nora!" Sam called as she shoved through the group, my name finally cutting through the panic. Her eyes flew wide when she reached my side. "What the hell happened? Here, sit, tell me what's going on."

"No," I whispered. "No, we have to go. Please, can we just go?"

Sam took my arm, murmuring soothing words even as she glanced back at the bistro, searching for the source of my reaction. I tried to look, to explain what happened, but all I caught was a swift glimpse of the man in those dark sunglasses, then he was gone again.

"We're going, sweetie, everything is going to be fine," Sam said softly, wrapping her arm more snugly around me.

God, I hoped she was right.

By the time we arrived back at the apartment, I felt like I'd regained most of my composure. A quick glance in the visor mirror showed my complexion to be less ghostly, leaning more toward "Victorian lady who's never seen the sun." Oxygen was reaching my lungs again and I'd stopped trembling like a newborn lamb.

All in all, it was almost like nothing had ever happened.

Almost. Maybe. If it weren't for a swift undercurrent of terror that skittered along my nerve endings every few minutes.

I firmly refused Sam's offer to keep me company until Jake got home, insisting that I'd be perfectly fine and just needed to clear my head. Despite my attempt to brush off the incident as just a fluke, I was pretty sure Sam could tell it had affected me far beyond that brief panic attack outside the bistro.

I wanted to reassure her that I was okay, but after all her kindness, I didn't want to lie to her.

Soon, I hoped to be able to tell her I was fine and actually mean it.

Chapter Twenty

JAKE

I WAS CHECKING INVENTORY spreadsheets in my office when Sam came into the restaurant. As she gave a perfunctory knock and opened the door, I froze. We'd always been able to read one another easily; she looked spooked, her shoulders tight, like she was bracing for something.

The relative calm I held onto for the first fifteen seconds probably had to be attributed to Nora's effect on my general mood, but Sam's strained expression chipped through it quickly.

"What's wrong?" I asked, half rising from my seat before she motioned me back down.

For a moment, she didn't speak, gathering her thoughts in a very un-Sam-like way that sent my blood pressure skyrocketing.

"Sam, talk to me. What is it?"

"Maybe nothing," she said as she sat on the edge of the desk. "I don't like to snitch, especially not on my friends. Even more especially not on someone who obviously doesn't trust very easily. I really don't want to intrude on Nora's private life, and I probably have no right to make a big deal out of something if it actually wasn't, but if she isn't willing to let me help her through this, maybe she'll be more open with you. "

I rubbed a hand over my face, trying to brush away the sudden rush of fear that crashed over me when she started speaking. "I understand, Sam. Believe me, I do. But you wouldn't be here if you didn't plan to tell me what's got you looking like that. Is Nora okay?"

Sam's eyes, as familiar as my own, lifted and she gave a jerky nod. "She's fine, or at least she says she is. I'm pretty sure she had a good time shopping, then after we stopped for lunch, something freaked her right the hell out. Like, panic attack level freakout."

"Shit," I muttered. I'd told Sam about the bachelor party incident, but not about the panic attack on the sidewalk afterward. "What happened?"

"I was on my way back from the bathroom and she got jostled into some guy in the crowd. I don't know if she knew him or if he reminded her of someone, but she lost it. Completely lost it. Gasping for breath, shaking uncontrollably. She insisted we leave and she finally calmed down a bit once we got in the car, but it scared the shit out of me, Jake."

I stood then and came around the desk to wrap my arm around Sam's shoulders. "Did you see him? What did he look like?"

She shook her head miserably. "Not clearly. Tall guy, dark sunglasses. Maybe blond or light brown hair? It was really crowded."

"Okay. I'll take care of her. You did the right thing by coming to me." I sucked in a calming breath and squeezed her tight.

"I like her," she said, her voice still muffled against my chest.

I huffed out a laugh. "So do I."

Though I felt like there was an angry swarm of bees in my veins, I walked her out, gave her one last reassuring hug before she got into the Mustang, then forced myself not to sprint the entire way home. As I hurried down the sidewalk, I thought about Nora's swift, instinctive response to the drunk who'd grabbed her, the way she'd skirted my comment about running from something.

Not all rainbows and adventures.

Her words reverberated through my head again and again until I reached the stairs to her apartment, wondering at the source of her panic attacks.

Something had to have happened to cause them.

I paused halfway up, thinking again that I should text her instead of knocking, but the door opened before I could make a decision.

Nora propped her hip against the doorframe and gazed down at me. She looked a little worn out, but otherwise hale and hearty, which dramatically reduced my anxiety for her wellbeing. Her feet were bare and she'd changed into a pair of simple black leggings, which I had to admit was probably for the best, since that little skirt would've been a bit too distracting.

"I figured you'd show up sooner or later." The barest hint of a smile curved her lips, but it didn't quite reach her eyes.

"Please don't hold it against Sam," I said gently. "She was worried about you."

The silent admission that I was worried, too, was probably written all over my face. Nora watched me as I slowly mounted the stairs. I half expected her to send me away, to slam those fragile walls back in place, but she stayed right where she was.

"I'm not upset with her at all. I figured she'd head over to tell you as soon as she dropped me off. Are you coming in or are we standing on the porch all day?"

I bounded up the remaining steps and cupped her chin in one hand when I reached the top. Nora waited patiently as my gaze traveled over her features, drinking her in like we'd been apart for a matter of years instead of hours.

As much as I expected her to downplay the encounter at the bistro, I really hoped she would trust me with this. My careful inspection finally drew a tiny smile from her, along with a sigh of resignation. When her expression remained calm and open, not a shutter in sight, I almost sagged with relief.

I kissed her before I dropped my hand. It was a light, chaste kiss, barely brushing my lips past hers, but its effect seemed like just as much a balm as my gaze. Her posture relaxed slightly before she backed into the apartment. I followed, closing the door firmly behind us.

This place had been as familiar to me as my own a year ago, taking up most of my free time and every last drop of energy. With Nora here, everything felt different, softer. Instead of the bachelor pad Jenkins had commissioned, it had become something more intimate, more feminine. The light suited her.

Unbidden, the thought that she needed more light in her life sprang up within me.

Before I could reflect more on the changes she'd brought, both to the apartment and to my own life, Nora perched at the edge of the loveseat and patted the cushion beside her. I sat, stretching my arm along the back so my fingers could thread gently through the ends of her hair, and waited patiently for her to speak.

She stared down at her hands in her lap, clenching them into fists and then unclenching, so I reached over to cover them with my free hand. As my thumb stroked over her knuckles, I felt the instant when her muscles started to relax.

"If you don't want to talk about it, we can just sit here a bit," I offered.

Nora took a deep breath and let it out slowly. "I definitely don't want to talk about it, but I think we need to. *I* need to."

She fell silent again, but she turned both her hands so they were sandwiching mine between her palms, clasping my hand like a lifeline. I lifted them to press my lips against her knuckles and she squeezed tighter.

"First, I feel like I need to give you some background on… well, everything."

I recognized this moment for what it was—another wall crumbling between us, another thorny hedge set ablaze. "You can tell me anything, Nora, I hope you know that."

She nodded. "Like I mentioned, I was a Navy brat. We moved around a lot. I didn't mind so much, but for my mom, it was pretty lonely. As soon as I left for college, she split. Asked for a divorce, packed up her stuff, and moved out. My dad wasn't even in the country at the time."

"Ouch," I murmured.

"It gets worse," she said, sighing. "College was where I discovered I worked really well with noise around me, so I let my friends drag me to bars—they'd drink and flirt, I'd write papers in a corner. One night, though, this guy approached me, asked me out, didn't want to take no for an answer. His name was Shawn Milton. My friends noticed that he wasn't taking a hint and brought the guys they were talking to over to scare him off."

Anger simmered across my skin, but I kept it together and nodded for her to go on.

"Things escalated. He had his hand wrapped around my elbow, but when he saw the guys coming, he grabbed my wrist to try to yank me out of the bar. I fought him, but I had no training of any kind back then, and we were almost to the door when the group reached us."

"Christ," I whispered. "No wonder you reacted the way you did at The Mermaid."

She gave a weak smile. "Yeah. I thought my friends were going to be too late. I've never felt so helpless in my life, and I never wanted to feel that way again."

"I take it they made it in time?"

"Barely. He shoved me into a table and ran when they got close. Then he moved on...to my mom. I found out she'd hooked up with him a few months later. I have no idea if he sought her out because of me, or how he even found her. Maybe it was a coincidence."

My brows drew together. "Pretty big coincidence."

"Yeah. When I told her about that night, she brushed it off. She told me he made her feel young again. I got my own apartment at the end of freshman year and didn't make a lot of effort to see her—Shawn gave me the creeps, and my dad was devastated by the divorce. You'd think at nineteen, it wouldn't feel like you had to choose between your parents, you know? But maybe if I'd visited her more, I might've seen it sooner."

I lifted my hand from the cushions and stroked her hair. "Might have seen what?"

"The signs. The little ways he took control of her, the manipulations. We weren't all that close, but she'd always called or emailed a couple times a week when I first left for school. It slowly tapered off to a short email once a month, and eventually I started to think it was Shawn writing them instead of her."

My muscles tensed. "He was abusing her?"

"Physically, I don't think so, but I still don't know for sure. Something weird was definitely going on, though."

"Right." I forced my jaw to unclench. "Go on."

"One night when I spoke to her on the phone, he wasn't there, which almost never happened. She mentioned Shawn borrowing money and asking for joint bank accounts. I managed to convince her it wasn't a good idea. She had money socked away from the sale of the house after the divorce, not a ton, but enough to keep her afloat."

Dread weighed me down at the direction this story was taking, but I knew Nora needed to get it out. I pressed my lips to her temple and waited, listening to the way her breath trembled past her lips.

"I brought it up to my father when I went out to see him about a week later, but we were too late." When she paused, I squeezed her hand gently and she closed her eyes. "Shawn flew into a rage when she wouldn't give him access to her accounts. He trashed the apartment and disappeared with all of her cash and valuables. He tried to clean out her savings even though he wasn't added to the account, but the bank wouldn't let him make a withdrawal."

"Jesus Christ."

"She was devastated. She blamed me for 'upsetting him' and refused to speak to me for months. Even now, we barely talk."

"You saved her from being scammed and she blamed you for him being an asshole?"

"Pretty much."

I shifted to pull her onto my lap and wrapped my arms firmly around her. My own parents were recently retired and traveling the world together, but we were all so close. It was hard for me to imagine facing something like that, especially at such a young age.

"Holy hell," I muttered. "Oh Nora, I'm so sorry."

She nodded against my chest. "He's why I took the self-defense classes. And why I overreacted when that guy grabbed me at The Mermaid. It's hard to forget how the apartment looked when we got there. It was like a scene from a horror movie. I thought we were going to find her—"

Dead. The unspoken word hung in the air as my arms tightened around her. "She was okay though? He didn't hurt her?"

"She was terrified...and then she was pissed. My dad wanted to help sort out the apartment, at least, but she wouldn't let us do anything. Eventually, it seemed like our presence did more harm than good, so we left. It was almost a year before she spoke to me again, and that was to tell me she was marrying some other guy she'd just met. I wasn't invited to the wedding. I tried to keep in touch for a few years, but eventually I just gave up."

For a long time, I simply held her. My mind raced as I processed all she'd said, trying to piece together all the things I knew—and the things I *thought* I'd known about her. It had been clear from the start that she'd suffered some past trauma, but this was beyond anything I'd imagined.

"Is that who you saw today? This Shawn guy?"

A shudder wracked her body, but she shook her head firmly. "No. I don't think so, anyway. That guy at the bar that night, he looked so much like Shawn, it threw me a bit. He's been on my mind a lot more than usual since then."

"Understandably. Did the guy today look like them, too?"

She nodded. "In a generic sort of way, yes. Mousy brown hair, tall. Creepy. I didn't get a good enough look to really say."

My hand moved slowly up and down her back, the repetitive movement comforting us both as something fierce and protective ignited along my veins. "So there's no reason to think that guy is trying to find you? To settle a grudge?"

At that, she sighed heavily and buried her face against my neck. "No. I mean, I don't think so. I don't know why he would bother. After it happened, my dad called in some favors to dig into Shawn's past. It turned out he'd done something similar to half a dozen other women, and after my mom, he disappeared into thin air. He's probably drinking mai tais in Tahiti or something by now."

"You haven't seen him again since it all went down?"

"No," she hedged, but the word was unconvincing.

I cupped the back of her neck and tipped her head so she could see my raised brow. "No?"

"I don't know for sure. There have been a few instances over the years where I thought I saw him out of the corner of my eye in random places. When I'd look again, he'd be gone. I thought it was my mind playing tricks on me, because it happened more at the beginning."

"Does it still happen?"

She hesitated, then said, "The day I had coffee with Sam, I got that same feeling, like someone was watching me, but I didn't see anyone. Probably just my nerves."

So soon after the incident at the bar, I wouldn't be surprised if her imagination had run wild, but what if someone had actually been watching her? I didn't want to freak her out any more than she already was, so I kept that to myself for the time being.

"Is he the reason why you moved around so much?" I asked.

"Not directly. I just start to feel claustrophobic when I've been in one place too long. I guess I always blamed my childhood rather than that period of time, but...I don't know. I think I've been looking for somewhere I might finally feel safe."

"I hate that you've been dealing with this for so long." I kissed the top of her head and tucked her back under my arm, snug against my side.

"I just always wondered if I should have done something different, you know? Been more tactful or something so it didn't all come crashing down on my mom like that."

"Nora," I said, my voice firm, "not a single thing that happened was your fault. All of that is on him."

"I know. Logically, I know that."

I thought back to the scene at the bar, wondering if the fresh trauma from that night had colored her reaction to a chance encounter today. Not that I could blame her for it, even if that happened to be the case. The longer I thought about it, the more my gut twisted with that fiercely protective surge of emotion.

"Have you had panic attacks like that before?" I asked.

After the incident at The Mermaid, I'd chalked up her breakdown on the sidewalk to an adrenaline crash, but the thought of Nora struggling to breathe when I wasn't there to help her through it opened a gaping chasm in my chest.

A tiny sigh ghosted past her lips. "The year after it happened, I had a few of them. Maybe more than a few, I guess. My dad insisted I talk to a therapist and that helped. It helped a lot, really. The panic attacks tapered off, but I saw the therapist until I graduated and moved away. After that, I think...I think I started avoiding anything that might trigger one."

I chewed on that for a minute, reflecting on the way she'd moved around so often, avoided serious relationships, kept to herself as much as possible. It might have kept the anxiety at bay for a time, but I was beyond certain now that she wasn't cut out for such a lonely existence.

And as much as I wanted to wrap her in my arms and protect her from the rest of the world, I was also pretty sure she'd never agree to that.

Instead of offering something she might refuse, I pressed my lips to her temple. "Where's your dad now?"

"I think he's docked off the Chesapeake Bay at the moment. He retired and bought a houseboat. We keep in touch, when he has cell service, anyway. "

"I'd like to meet him someday," I said softly. "He must be a hell of a guy to have ended up with a daughter as special as you, Nora."

Though she had held herself together all through the sad tale of her mother's withdrawal, my gentle comment somehow opened the floodgates. I held her as she cried, stroked her hair and soothed her, hoping she understood just how precious she was to me already. Having witnessed the true depths of Nora's strength made her sorrow all the more heartbreaking for me to watch.

It was a long time before either of us spoke.

"My friend Casey is in town and she's going to take over bartending for a couple weeks until my full time guy comes back," I said, my voice low. "I wondered if you'd like to go away with me for a few days?"

The tears had dried and her breathing finally evened out, so she tipped her head back to look at me. "Away where?"

With my fingertips, I traced the curve of her cheekbone, the arch of her eyebrow. "Not far. There's this little bed and breakfast on the water, the Lakeside Inn. I think you'd like it. It's usually booked solid all summer, but my friend Henry is the manager there. I got an inside tip that they had a cancellation this week and he's holding it for us. I told him I'd let him know by tonight."

Slowly, Nora nodded. "Okay. On one condition."

I cocked a brow and waited, watching the way she first bit her lip and then offered a cheeky little grin.

She leaned close to my ear and whispered, "Give me enough warning before you do that thing that makes me scream, so I can muffle it with a pillow. I can't handle the thought of your friend overhearing that."

I let out a joyous laugh and kissed her soundly. "I solemnly swear I will warn you before I do that," I said, then added with a wink, "Like...how about right now?"

Chapter Twenty-One

NORA

As a result of my many travels, both as a child and an adult, I developed a longstanding love affair with maps. Paper maps, online maps, globes, phone maps—it didn't matter the format, as long as I could study them to my heart's content, tracing the lines of the rivers, hopping from one city dot to another, tracking my own path or sometimes my father's as they zig-zagged across the continent.

Maybe it was a childish exercise, but it never ceased to center me when I started to feel that itch beneath my skin that told me it was time to move on.

Before settling on Spruce Hill, the maps had shown me the wealth of waterways nearby: Great Lakes, Finger Lakes, rivers, canals. They all played a part in my choice of location this time around. I'd been landlocked for too long, and after I mentioned that fact to my father in one of our semi-frequent phone calls, he'd sent me a picture of Mr. Jenkins' apartment ad.

Everything had fallen into place after that, but all that water around sealed the decision for me.

Maybe you're just looking for a place to call home.

Now, with Jake at my side and Lake Ontario spreading before us, the words he'd spoken as we gazed out across his backyard echoed in my head. My fingers tightened on his for a moment and a soft, sweet ache in my chest receded as something else slipped into place, settling comfortably inside me.

"This is absolutely incredible," I whispered. The deep blue stretched as far as I could see, bobbing with gentle waves under a beautiful, flawless sky.

Jake kissed my temple and tightened the arm he'd slipped around my waist, tucking me firmly against his side. "I thought you'd like it here."

"I love it here, but I think we should go back in," I purred against his ear a few minutes later. "I have something to show you."

When his eyes widened, I simply gave him a sultry smile and tugged at his hand. Jake stumbled along behind me as we made our way back to the room, following willingly, his blue eyes sparking with heat every time I glanced at him.

Once we were safely ensconced in our charming little suite, he cupped his hand around the back of my neck and kissed me until I was wiggling impatiently against him.

"What is it you wanted to show me?" he asked hoarsely. "If it doesn't involve you getting naked, I'm not sure I'll survive to appreciate whatever it is."

I stepped back and pulled my t-shirt over my head, revealing the lacy black bra I'd bought with Sam. As I tossed the shirt aside, his breath hissed through his teeth and he dipped his head for a closer look. The fabric was sheer, giving a glimpse of what hid underneath the swirling lace pattern.

"Oh, this is nice," he drawled, straightening to kiss me again while his hands wandered.

His thumbs teased my nipples through the material until they hardened into tight buds, until I considered begging for his mouth to replace his fingers, but when he slid one hand behind my back to unfasten it, I remembered my plan and shook my head.

Jake groaned, but it was clear my teasing had him intrigued—and, pressed so close, I knew he was already hard as a rock. Still, the big reveal required a little more torment.

"Uh-uh," I replied, the sing-song words a direct contrast to the husky note in my voice. There was no way *not* to respond to the raw desire darkening his expression. "There's more to see. You used to be so patient. What's the rush?"

Jake tore off his own shirt and then pulled me snug against him, rolling his hips into mine and growling at the little gasp that slipped past my lips. After I unbuckled his belt, he returned the favor and slid down the zipper of my jeans. When he pushed the denim past my hips and brushed his hands over the curve of my ass, however, his fingers met bare skin.

I almost burst out laughing as his eyebrows shot up before he turned me around, leaving the jeans tangled halfway down my legs.

"Holy shit," he whispered when he saw the thong. "If my sister had a hand in this, I don't need to know. Fuck, Nora, you are . . ." He trailed off as I turned back toward him and lifted a brow in challenge.

"What am I?" I asked. Slowly, so slowly I saw his fists clench at his sides to keep from reaching for me, I wriggled out of the jeans and kicked them aside.

"You are so fucking hot, I might just lose my mind."

Jake hooked a finger in the front of the flimsy underwear and tugged me toward him. With one hand tangled in my hair, he kissed me until the fire burning inside of us both became all-encompassing. He tossed aside his own jeans and boxers, then swept me into his arms before I could protest—though I doubted I would have, not when he was looking at me like that.

Like I was the only thing in the world he wanted.

The laughter that bubbled from my lips made him smile with a different kind of warmth, softer and more tender, then he laid me on the bed and I turned my attention toward showing him just how I felt about his presence in my life. Before this trip was over, I wanted to be sure he understood.

And I was certain we'd both enjoy the process along the way.

Though I knew Jake had intended our little getaway primarily to take my mind off of recent events, it turned into something even more precious. Now that I'd told him about what happened with my mother, the murmured conversations we shared while snuggled in bed became deeper and more personal.

For the first time, I told him about the places I'd lived, the choices I'd made to avoid getting close to anyone, the aching sense of loss that had colored my final years of college.

Through it all, he stroked my hair or my skin, pressed kisses to the top of my head, made it clear he understood how big a deal it was that I was opening up. When I told him about my time with Audrey and Jamal, however, I felt his lips curve against my bare shoulder.

"You know, my sister and Casey both commented on you being bi, but I didn't want to push it by asking. I know straight guys can be idiots about that stuff—believe me, the two of them have told me that a hundred times."

I laughed. "I might have forgiven your faux pas," I teased, "or I might have made you do penance by providing orgasms. I don't know how Sam even guessed. I hadn't said anything remotely sexual about literally anyone."

"She's got a knack for reading people," he replied with a shrug. "Small town, you know how it is."

At that, I laughed. "Nosy neighbors, lightning speed gossip? If I didn't know before, I do now."

With his fingers sifting lightly through my hair, he asked, "Were you trying to avoid me, when you first moved in? You wouldn't even let me jump your car for you."

"Like the devil. Fat lot of good it did me," I muttered.

Jake grinned. "Must be my animal magnetism. You obviously can't keep your hands off me. Sorry if I ruined your solitary plans for Spruce Hill."

I propped myself up on one elbow and narrowed my eyes at him. "Do you object to my hands on you, Jake Lincoln?"

"Hell no. Your hands are perfect. Beautiful. Clever. Torturous. Absolutely mind-blowingly amazing."

"Then I guess it worked out well for both of us, didn't it?" I drawled.

Quiet laughter rumbled in his chest when I dipped my head to kiss him, but that shift remained.

Our final morning at the inn was spent in much the same way as the rest of the trip: in bed, naked, tangled up in each other's arms. Now that Jake knew pretty much everything about my background, I felt a hundred pounds lighter. It was humbling to realize just how bogged down I'd been by those secrets and half-truths. Jake, true to his word, really wasn't one to pry, but his calm acceptance gave me the confidence to finally stop hiding from my past.

"Should we be packing?" I asked, though I had no inclination to get out of bed.

As we lay there, Jake traced lazy swirls over my shoulder blades in a way that made it hard for me to keep my eyes open. My face was pressed into his chest and my lips brushed his skin as I spoke. I grinned when he fidgeted, then he playfully pinched my hip in retaliation and I yelped when he rolled us so he was smiling down at me, a mischievous glint in his eye.

"We've barely worn any clothes," he pointed out helpfully, "so most of it's still packed. Besides, I have a better idea."

I feigned a yawn, then burst out laughing when he blew a raspberry right between my breasts. "What is this grand idea you have?"

"Oh, I think I'd like to make love to you one more time before we go. Nice and easy, so don't go demanding I speed up, hmm?"

His lips trailed along my sternum, settling against my throat as I sighed softly and tipped my head back to give him room to explore. After a slow trek upward, his mouth paused at my ear while his hands stroked slowly down the length of my body. Every nerve ending stood at rapt attention, waiting for his command.

"Slow and gentle," he murmured. "The way I imagined our first time would be."

"That's what you imagined?" I asked, the question punctuated with a gasp. I was already arching against him, responding as he knew I would to both his touch and his low, seductive words. He'd learned that lesson well in our time together.

"Oh, yes. You were so nervous every time I touched your hand—you'll have to forgive me for not expecting that things would be quite so explosive between us, at least not at first. So today, I'm taking my sweet time. Not that I'm complaining about the other," he added casually, even as I wondered how on earth he could continue talking, especially since I felt his growing hardness pressing snugly into my hip, "but every time I touch you, I feel like I'm going to burst into flames."

He glanced up at my face just in time to see me cock an amused brow at his little speech, then he captured my nipple in his mouth and my head dropped back against the pillow.

Slow and gentle, I thought distractedly as he grazed the peak with his teeth. Before long, I began to whimper and urge him faster, but he was undeterred.

"Today, my sweet Nora, we are going to practice delayed gratification. Slow," he said against my skin, "and gentle."

I gave up trying to change his mind. His patience was truly fathomless, and once he set his mind to a task, there was no swaying him. With his hands and lips and—sweet heaven—his tongue, he explored, teased, tantalized until every inch of my body was burning with need. I'd forgotten all about his insistence on not hurrying until he was at long last poised over me, looking down at me with a tenderness that made my chest ache. Then he kissed me with such exquisite dedication that I remembered in a rush of sensation.

While I'd often felt cared for, worshipped even, in my time with Jake, this soft, slow, sweet kiss made me feel *loved*.

Even when a tiny sliver of panic invaded my mind over the realization, Jake's commitment to *slow and gentle* drew me deep enough to wash away any trace of fear or doubt. His lips didn't leave mine as he pressed into me with painstaking care, gliding forward so very slowly, until he was fully sheathed within me.

Maybe you're just looking for a place to call home.

The words echoed again in my head, spurred by the way he made me feel whole just by sinking into me. Without speaking, he showed me all he had to offer, poured every heartfelt emotion into making love to me. With slow, gentle strokes, he filled me again and again, his lips brushing mine in a caress as sweet as nectar.

Instead of a frantic climb toward release, I felt like I was floating upward, lifted by Jake's careful control and measured strokes. The resulting climax left me quivering beneath him as he slowed even more, just to start the process again.

"Hurricane Nora," he whispered into my skin. "You are everything."

When at last the world shattered around us both, he lowered himself against me and together we trembled in the powerful aftermath of what had washed over us. Those last words replaced the echo in my head, wrapping around me like a blanket as my arms clasped him tightly against my heart.

Because he, too, was everything.

Chapter Twenty-Two

NORA

THOUGH I STAYED QUIET as we loaded our bags back into Jake's truck, a soft, satisfied smile lingered on my lips as I blew a kiss toward the lake. I wrapped my arms around Jake's waist before hopping up into the passenger seat, still smiling even as we headed home. He linked his fingers with mine during the short drive, looking rather satisfied himself, and hummed along with the radio.

I caught him gazing over at me and realized I was absurdly, glowingly happy.

When we pulled into the driveway, I glanced over and gave a rueful grin. "It's probably a good thing that wasn't how our first time actually went, you know."

His brows lifted in amusement. "Oh? Why is that?"

"I don't think I would've survived it."

"Well, I might have imagined things slow and gentle, but I'm sure as hell not complaining about the way it turned out. I clearly hadn't calculated our chemistry correctly at that point."

His dimple peeked at me as he reached out to brush his thumb along my lower lip. After his eyes flitted to the heat rising in my cheeks, he leaned over to kiss me.

I couldn't help but laugh when he drew away. "Chemistry, is that what we're calling it?"

"What else would you like to call it?" he asked, his voice low, like he was tempting me to throw out the word he wanted me to use.

"Combustibility?"

Jake grinned. "That works," he agreed, then gave me one more swift kiss before opening his door. "We do seem to be pretty damn combustible together, Nora Cassidy."

"Yes," I replied, the blush rising further into my cheeks. "Yes, we do."

Jake lifted my small suitcase from the truck bed, then followed me up the stairs to the apartment. I heard him swearing as one wheel got caught on the planks halfway up, but by the time he'd wiggled it free, I stood frozen in front of the door.

It took only a second for him to reach my side, his gaze locked on my face.

"Talk to me, Nora." His voice came out gruff, strained, as fear rioted within me, but the tone was enough to snap me out of my fog.

"The door is open. You watched me lock it when we left," I said numbly, staring at the inch of space between the door and its frame.

When my gaze lifted to the door itself, Jake's followed, focusing on the shattered pane of glass above the deadbolt. My body jolted, my shoulder striking him in the sternum.

"Oh my god," I whispered.

"Don't touch anything."

Even if I'd wanted to, I could barely move, trapped beneath frothing waves of memory—walking up to my mom's apartment with my father at my side, the chaos within, the paralyzing fear that we were about to find her body at any moment.

Jake slid the suitcase onto the landing and clasped me to his chest as he dialed the police. Calmly and clearly, he relayed our location and a description of the situation to the person on the other end of the line.

My eyes stayed caught on the door: the tiny gap where it hung open, the glass shards at our feet, the realization that someone had broken into my little haven here.

All the while, my mind whirled with possibilities, each one more dire than the last. In the midst of it all, I held myself completely still in his arms, like that stillness might keep me from crumbling. As soon as the call ended, Jake shoved his phone into his pocket and rubbed my back until my breath came more easily.

"An officer will be here soon. Come on, we'll wait downstairs."

I let him lead me back down to the driveway, where he wrapped his arms around me while we waited. I wasn't accustomed to letting someone else take control in an emergency, but if there was one thing I knew about Jake by this point, it was that he could stay calm under any circumstances. Even if I were to break down and fall apart, he'd be there to keep me upright.

As we stood there, I leaned into him and Jake took his job in supporting me seriously.

The police cruiser showed up within minutes. Fortunately, Jake knew the woman who stepped out of the car, an old classmate he introduced as Detective Rose Hanson. She was beautiful and nearly as tall as Jake, with skin the same dark brown as my eyes. Her sharp gaze swept over us both, then she clasped my hand, listened to Jake's quick explanation, and told us to stay put while she checked the premises.

"No one's inside," she called back to us several minutes later. "Would you two come on up so you can tell me if anything is missing? I've got a team on their way out here, so don't touch anything, if you don't mind."

Though my imagination immediately summoned a scene of carnage, something even worse than when we walked into the wreckage of my mother's home with Shawn, the apartment didn't look any different than when we left. My meager belongings were just where they should be.

At least, it appeared that way as we walked slowly through the kitchen and living room, then we headed toward the bedroom.

"I really don't have anything of value, nothing worth stealing," I murmured, but finding the apartment undisturbed made me sag against Jake in relief. There was no mess, no destruction, nothing broken but that single pane of glass.

When we reached the bedroom, though, the ruffled skirt I'd worn during my shopping trip with Sam was laid out in the middle of the bed, a bundle of shriveled forget-me-nots resting atop it. They looked like they'd been torn straight from the ground, each blossom crumpled in death, the roots still clinging to clumps of soil.

My breath stalled as panic washed through me anew.

"What the hell?" Jake whispered.

He'd been standing right there in the doorway while I finished packing my suitcase, had watched me smirk at him as I zipped it closed, thinking about the underwear reveal I had planned. The bed had been neatly made for once and the skirt tucked away in a drawer.

"You were here when I packed up. You asked about the skirt making the cut—it wasn't there when we left. Right?" My voice trembled as hysteria rose in my chest, threatening to choke me.

"No, it wasn't there."

"Forget-me-nots," I said shakily. "Are they from your yard?"

"They might be. Nora, look at me."

Frozen, I stared at the flowers. The skirt was bad enough, but those withered blossoms felt like a harbinger of doom.

He turned me toward him, tearing my horrified gaze from the bed, and cupped my face in his hands. "You're staying with me for a while, okay? Is there anything else here you need, once the police are done?"

I shook my head, not in answer but in an attempt to force my brain to function again. It felt like my insides were vibrating, threatening to shake right out of my skin.

"No, I brought my laptop to the inn, just in case I had a chance to do some work. My notebook should be on the coffee table but I don't need it right away if the police want me to leave it here. Other than that, I'll just need some extra clothes, I guess."

With his hand wrapped firmly around my elbow, Jake led me back through the living room, but we both paused when I looked toward the low coffee table in front of the loveseat.

"No notebook," Jake said quietly.

I frowned at that, but by then, the rest of the police officers had arrived. Jake spoke in low tones to Detective Hanson, then lifted my suitcase again and led me downstairs.

"I told her we'll be out on the deck. Someone will be over to take our statements soon."

I nodded, letting him steer me along like an errant duckling. "Why would anyone do that? What was the point?"

Jake's fingers tightened around mine and he said, "I don't know. Maybe kids screwing around, a game of truth or dare gone wrong?"

"But the skirt," I whispered. "And the flowers."

He paused for a second. "When you were sick, there were flowers outside your door. Forget-me-nots. I thought maybe you'd picked them from my yard and dropped them at the door when something happened, but then you were sick and it slipped my mind."

"It wasn't me. Someone was on my porch." My lungs felt too tight to draw a deep breath.

Whoever it was I bumped into that day with Sam, I had a hard time believing that the break-in wasn't related, not with the skirt front and center. After talking it through with Jake, I didn't really think it was Shawn, but who else would've seen the skirt I barely ever wore except for whoever the guy in the crowd was?

And why the flowers? Was it a warning? A cruel prank? How the hell would anyone even know where to find my apartment? The uncertainty rattled me.

"Hey," Jake said, unlocking his door to set my suitcase inside before cupping his hands on either side of my face. "Whatever it is, we'll figure it out. In the meantime, I'll keep you safe. Trust me?"

"Yes," I replied, covering his hands with my own.

"Then it'll all be okay. I promise."

It was late in the afternoon by the time we finished speaking to the police. Every time panic spiraled upward from my stomach, Jake managed to ground me again. I absorbed his calm, let his steadiness settle my racing thoughts.

Sam stopped over to deliver bags upon bags of takeout. She hugged both of us tightly before she left. "You let me know if you need anything, got it?" she demanded.

I managed a faint smile as I promised that I would. Jake's house seemed even quieter than usual after Sam departed.

"So, now what?" I asked.

Jake laced his fingers with mine. "Now we let the police do their jobs. I have an alarm system here, we'll be safe." He cocked his head at me. "Do you want to get in touch with your dad, let him know about the break-in?"

For a long time, I didn't respond. Even without mentioning recent events, especially that panic attack, the fact that my apartment had been broken into would likely have him rushing to my rescue. I loved my father, but I didn't particularly want him intruding on the bubble of contentment that had formed around us—even if that bubble might already be on the verge of popping.

"Not yet," I said finally. "I don't want to worry him. Nothing was missing from the apartment, except my notebook, which cost eighty-nine cents during back to school sales last year. There's not even much written in there. It could've just been some kids messing around?"

"Yes, it definitely could have been," Jake replied, but his reassuring smile looked forced. "You hungry? Sam brought enough to feed an army."

"You do know the way to a lady's heart," I said, but first I leaned into him, drawing comfort from his sturdy, steady presence.

For once in my life, I wanted to trust that things weren't as bad as they might seem. I'd been doing everything alone for a long time. It felt good to accept reassurance from somebody else, especially if that someone was Jake. Even now, his hands stroked through my hair, soothing, establishing a connection that was reciprocated in how my fingers tightened in the sides of his shirt, the way I nuzzled my face into his chest.

A sudden, overwhelming flood of emotion washed over us both. I felt it ripple through my limbs, and Jake tightened his arms around me.

"I didn't realize how boring life was around here until you showed up," he said gently.

I gave a short laugh. "I think you must be a little twisted to enjoy all this."

He drew back just enough to give me a knowing look. "Well, I'm not enjoying *this*, per se. But sometimes being twisted can be fun," he murmured. "I think even you would have to agree with that."

With my cheeks rapidly heating under his gaze, I smirked. "Truer words have never been spoken." Then both of our phones signaled an incoming text. I got to mine first and laughed. "Sam says there's a *Princess Bride* marathon on TV tonight and that it would take our minds off things if we need a distraction."

Jake groaned in mock horror. "I had other distractions in mind, but I guess I could handle a movie night instead. It is a classic, after all."

"You didn't get enough 'distraction' over the last few days? I'm impressed, Mr. Lincoln." I batted his hand away as he reached for me. "I would've thought you'd be looking forward to some actual sleep. Your stamina is truly impressive."

"What can I say? I can't get enough of you," he said, lowering his voice to a seductive growl.

I shrieked with laughter when he lunged forward and slung me over his shoulder. Instead of heading toward the stairs, however, he brought me into the small lounge tucked on the opposite side of the kitchen, then bent to lay me on a worn leather sofa.

"Welcome to my Dude Lair."

I laughed even harder at that. "Really? Man cave is too trendy for you?"

It was a nice little room, cozy and welcoming, with dark wood paneling and built-in shelves lining the wall on either side of the television. There was a recliner that matched the sofa, a tattered coffee table, and gleaming hardwood floors. Despite my teasing, my eyes widened with appreciation. Aside from his bedroom, the Dude Lair showed the most evidence of Jake's personality.

"You better stop laughing at me, Cassidy, or I'm going to get a complex." He caught my wrists in one hand and stretched them over my head, then leaned down and blew a raspberry against the strip of skin visible above my jeans.

"Oh, you will pay for that, Lincoln," I warned, but he winked as he stood up and tossed me the remote.

"Lady's choice on dinnertime entertainment. Dessert, however, is my domain."

Chapter Twenty-Three

JAKE

I F I HAD TO choose between our previous nightly sleep-over routine, an intimate lakeside getaway, or simply hanging out on the couch watching old movies, I was a little shocked to realize that the couch was pulling slowly into the lead. Something about eating Chinese food from takeout cartons and cuddling up with Nora in my favorite room of the house had me thinking about the future.

More specifically, about my desire for Nora to be a part of that future.

Still, no matter how the walls around her had crumbled, I was wary of saying anything that might cause her to pull away after the stress of the day. It was nearly midnight when we ended up lying spooned together along the faded brown leather, Nora's head resting on my bicep, slowly cutting off my circulation.

"I could stay here forever," she murmured.

Though my muscles jolted in surprise, I forced myself to relax when I realized she was very nearly asleep. She might just as likely have been referring to the couch itself, rather than the more general *here* that could mean Spruce Hill, my house, or my arms.

Still, the quiet words filled me with hope and I tucked her closer against my chest.

My lips feathered along the shell of her ear as I whispered, "Then stay."

Her breathing grew slow and steady, and I found myself drifting right along with her. I was comforted by that sleepy confession, whether or not it meant what I hoped it did.

Sometime during the night, my phone vibrated against the coffee table. The buzzing sound was loud enough for me to jerk awake, but Nora didn't stir. I lay there for another minute, wondering what had woken me, until another short buzz indicated a missed text message. I reached carefully over Nora's soft, still form for the phone and blinked a few times to clear the sleep from my eyes. It was just after three in the morning and the preview showed only that it came from a private number. I swiped at the screen to open the message.

She'll pay. You'll both pay.

For a moment, I stared blindly at the words, then I swore under my breath, powered down the phone, and tossed it onto the floor next to the couch.

Nora shifted in her sleep but didn't wake, causing a swift rush of relief to course through me. I would wait until morning to get in touch with the police. God knew Nora had been through enough already and needed a good night's sleep. I reached over to pull down the folded blanket from the back of the couch, spread it awkwardly over us both, and tried desperately to forget those ominous words.

MORNING CAME TOO QUICKLY for Nora's taste, if her sleepy grumbles were any indication, and too slowly for mine—I'd lain awake for the rest of the night, staring up at the dark ceiling as I considered the possibilities behind the text.

A moment later, Nora rolled toward me, almost kneeing me right in the balls. Her eyes flew open when I flinched away.

"Oh crap, I'm sorry," she whispered, cupping her hand over my crotch.

I gave a strangled groan and lifted her hand away to press a kiss to her palm. "The family jewels are safe," I said dryly, "but we have something else that needs attention before those, I'm afraid."

Her gaze shot to my face, swept over my features, and her expression fell. The sight of her sleep-flushed cheeks and mess of chestnut curls made me want to kiss her, but we needed to get the bizarre text out of the way first. She sat up more carefully to avoid kneeing me again and spotted my phone on the floor. When she bent to pick it up, I rubbed my hands over my jaw.

"Someone texted me around three," I said quietly. "No phone number came up, but the message was...threatening."

Nora nodded slowly, as though this was a perfectly normal occurrence. Then again, it was starting to feel a little too familiar for my liking.

"Right. Okay. What did it say?"

Wishing I could shield her from this but recognizing that was impossible, I turned on the phone to show her. A frown appeared between her eyes as she read it. She picked up her own phone to check for anything strange, but there were no incoming texts or phone calls after Sam's message about the movie.

"Why would they send something like that to your phone instead of mine? I mean, obviously the second part applies to us both, but it seems a little odd for a threat directed at me to come through you."

"I don't know. My phone number is probably easier to find than yours—plenty of people in town have it, for personal and business reasons. I'm going out on a limb here, but I assume you don't give yours out quite so willingly."

Nora gave a choked laugh, but she didn't deny it. "No, I think you and Sam are the only people I've given it to since I moved here."

"Then that probably gives us the answer to why they sent it to me. I'm thinking we should go over to the police station, if you're up for it."

"You could have woken me up, Jake," she said softly, laying a hand on my stubbled cheek. "You look like you didn't sleep very much."

I leaned into her caress, then turned my head to press a kiss to her palm. "You needed a break. This is a small town, so I don't even know who's at the police station overnight. It didn't seem worth getting anybody out of bed for, least of all you. Besides, now we can show up with donuts and look like superheroes while *also* having donuts for breakfast."

Her soft laughter eased some of my tension and within half an hour, we were on our way to the station with a large box of donuts. Nora held them on her lap and shot me a suspicious look.

"Just how many police are on this small town force? This seems like an awful lot of donuts."

I winked at her. "Speak for yourself. I intend to eat at least half of those."

Even though my lighthearted comments were for her benefit alone, they seemed to help keep both of us from tipping toward panic. I knew she'd been on the verge of it as soon as I mentioned the text, and worrying about her safety was what had kept me awake most of the night.

You'll both pay.

I pondered the words again. Pay for what?

When we pulled into a parking spot outside the tiny police station, I jogged around to help her with the box, lingering to kiss her lightly on the lips before she slid down from the seat. Nora followed me inside and rolled her eyes when I cranked up the charm as I delivered donuts to the few officers out front. Even the police chief, a man named Roberts who I didn't think Nora had met yet, strolled out of his office to partake.

She hung back while I murmured to the older man, then I tipped my head toward the chief's office and we followed him there.

"Nora, this is Chief Roberts. Chief Roberts, Nora Cassidy," I said.

The chief smiled kindly at her as we sat before his desk, folding his hands over his round belly. "Been having a bit of trouble, I hear."

With a tight smile, Nora said, "Yes, sir." She glared at me when my eyebrows shot up. "Navy brat, remember?" she muttered.

"A Navy brat named Cassidy, huh? Your daddy wouldn't happen to be Captain John Cassidy, would he?" the chief asked, rubbing his chin.

Now it was Nora whose eyebrows lifted in surprise. "Yes, sir, that would be him. You two know each other?"

My eyes narrowed on the chief's face—something in his smile looked a little too innocent, a little too benign, like he'd already known very well who Nora's dad was. Though I hadn't realized her father had any ties to Spruce Hill, I wondered now if that was how she'd found the apartment. Mr. Jenkins' odd behavior surrounding the provenance of his new tenant might just have something to do with this tangled web that was only now starting to unravel.

The chief shot me a subtle wink and I shook my head in resignation.

Chief Roberts leaned back in his chair with an affectionate smile. "Your daddy and I went to basic training together. We kept in touch a bit over the years. Does your father know about the break-in?"

Nora shook her head. "No, sir, not yet. I didn't want to worry him if it all amounted to local kids making trouble. And please, call me Nora."

The chief nodded, folding his hands over his midsection. "Well, Nora, tell him I say hello next time you talk to him. As for the break-in, we talked to all the neighbors, but no one saw or heard anything unusual during the time you were away. We'll keep poking around, but with nothing stolen, I'm afraid it might not amount to much."

I pulled up the text from that morning and passed my phone across the desk. "There is one more thing, Chief. This came through around three this morning."

Pursing his lips, the chief nodded. "Mind if I have Detective Hanson check into this? She's our unofficial tech specialist, and she should be getting in just about now."

"By all means," I said.

"She's gonna be pissed if all the Boston cream donuts are gone," he muttered.

While the chief rose and took the phone out to Detective Hanson, I threaded my fingers through Nora's and pressed a kiss to her knuckles. She still looked blown over by the knowledge that her father was personally connected to Spruce Hill, so I decided to take her mind off it, however briefly.

"Kind of sexy hearing you all 'yes sir' and 'no sir,' Cassidy," I murmured with a devilish grin.

She wrinkled her nose at me. "Oh, you like that, do you?"

Laughter rumbled in my chest. "Well, I like just about everything you do, so I guess it's only natural. I can't believe the chief knows your father, though. Talk about a small world."

"No kidding. I was afraid he was going to offer to call him for me when I said I hadn't told him about this yet. You know, I should have known there was something fishy when my dad suggested this town. I assumed he'd passed through at some point. Next time I talk to him, he's going to get an earful for not mentioning this."

I just grinned. What I wouldn't give to be a fly on the wall during that conversation. I'd seen Nora go from feisty to sweet, aggravated to subdued—it made me wonder how her father responded to her spirit. Was the man stoic and cold to counter her flames, or did he give as good as he got?

With her free hand, Nora rubbed at her forehead. Though she tried to drop my hand when the chief returned, I kept my fingers entwined with hers. If the chief noticed, he gave no indication that he was anything but pleased.

"While Hanson's working on that, why don't you tell me about what happened down at The Mermaid a few weeks ago," he suggested as he sat back down behind his desk. "I heard you two had a spot of trouble."

His smile was friendly, his tone casual, but it was hard to miss the sharpness of his green gaze as it moved between us. My mind raced with the possibilities. I could practically see the gears turning in Nora's mind, too, and squeezed her fingers reassuringly.

"Nora comes to The Mermaid a few times a week to work on her laptop. We had a bachelor party that night, half a dozen guys from Oakville. They were already pretty rowdy when they showed up. One of them decided to make a play for Nora, then refused to take no for an answer. She defended herself after he laid hands on her."

The chief's eyes shifted to Nora, so she continued the tale. "He grabbed my wrist. As you can imagine, my father took self-defense pretty seriously, so I turned it around and brought the guy to his knees. I might have overreacted, but I didn't injure him. He went back to the bar and Jake walked me home."

"Nora, I wasn't asking because I think you did something wrong by defending yourself," the chief said calmly, though his gaze slanted back toward me, "only because I wondered if the man might have held a grudge after that. Especially since the gossip around town says that you came back to The Mermaid after walking Nora home, Jake, and had words with the man."

Nora's head whipped around in surprise. "You did?"

I puffed my cheeks as I blew out a breath. "I did. I *wanted* to break his nose, but all I did was tell him in no uncertain terms that no one lays a hand on a woman in my place of business. And I might have added that if I ever saw him near Nora or The Mermaid again, I'd make sure he came to regret it. I didn't touch him, not even to kick his ass out of my restaurant. His friends dragged him off the stool and practically carried him out, kicking and screaming. If they hadn't, I would've called you in to assist, Chief."

Though I was watching the police chief, who nodded his head with grudging admiration, I saw Nora's eyes roll toward the ceiling. Both of us looked at her, though my innocence was completely feigned.

"Men," she muttered. "I told you I could take care of myself, Lincoln. Did you really need to go all macho after that?"

"Macho or not, I told you that what happened that night would never happen again to you or anyone else in my restaurant, Cassidy," I countered calmly. Nora looked ready to scream, her brows drawn tight together and her eyes flashing, so I added, "I would've done the same for any woman who was assaulted in front of my eyes—or any man, for that matter. I'll admit that wanting to break his nose was maybe a little more personal, but since I refrained, the point is moot."

Chief Roberts glanced back and forth between us before chuckling. "Well, if that's settled, I'll just ask if you happen to recall the assailant's name?"

I shook my head. "Unfortunately, no. I know for sure that I had every one of them show identification when they got there, but I don't remember each of the names. I'll ask Casey, she was helping me out at the bar that night, and I definitely have a record of the one who called me to arrange it. I don't think that was the guy who grabbed her, but I'll get the information to you."

The chief nodded and rose to shake both of our hands. "I'll let you know if we find anything on the break-in. In the meantime, you're welcome to go in, fix that door, replace the lock, get whatever you need." He gave me a long look that conveyed the sort of manly warning I knew Nora would have a field day dissecting, if given half a chance. "Hanson will give you your phone back. I want to know right away if anything else like that shows up, got me?"

"Absolutely. Thanks, Chief," I said.

We stopped by Detective Hanson's desk to grab the phone on our way out and walked back into the morning sunlight.

Chapter Twenty-Four

NORA

"**Y**OU DIDN'T EAT A single donut," I pointed out when we were back in the truck.

Jake groaned. "You're right. Do you mind swinging by The Mermaid on our way home? I want to check my records for the bachelor party booking and Casey wants an official introduction bad enough that she offered to meet us there," he said.

Curious to meet one of Jake's friends, I agreed. I'd noticed Casey behind the bar with him that night and felt a twinge of self-consciousness, knowing she'd witnessed my probable overreaction and almost certainly heard more about it from Jake afterward.

Oh god—the whole town of Spruce Hill had probably heard about it.

"Would you believe me if I told you I've never been embroiled in this much drama before in my entire life?" I asked dryly.

"I believe that with every ounce of my being, Nora," Jake replied with a grin. "I'd go so far as to guess you wouldn't have spoken a word to me when you first moved in if you'd had it your way."

"Hmm. I suppose that's accurate. That howdy thing really was a turnoff, you know."

Jake laughed, but he shot me a pointed glance. "I say this only because I am utterly infatuated with you, Nora, but I have definitely noticed that you can be a little prickly."

"Infatuated," I repeated, cocking a brow. He wasn't wrong.

"Hopelessly devoted?" His lips tipped upward, clearly pleased that I'd chosen to question that particular word, rather than *prickly*.

We'd get to that later.

I laughed. "Does that mean we're going steady, Jake Lincoln?"

"Hell yes, it does."

"Good, I do appreciate knowing exactly where things stand," I said primly.

Jake's arm stretched out along the back of the seat so he could toy with my hair. When I relaxed my head into his palm and closed my eyes, he said, "You're like a cat, the way you lean in and purr every time I touch you. It's terribly sexy, you know."

I didn't open my eyes, but I smiled. "Well, I guess being compared to a sexy cat is better than a porcupine."

"I should have known you wouldn't let that comment slide," he replied with a laugh. "You're too soft for a porcupine, anyway, but you've sure as hell got claws. It's one of my favorite things about you."

He parked outside the restaurant but didn't make any move to leave the truck, just kept playing with my hair. With a soft sigh, I opened my eyes and rolled my head toward him so that his hand cupped my cheek.

"I appreciate you sticking around long enough to get past my prickly side. I'm not sure what you saw in me to make you think it was worth the trouble, but I'm very glad that you did."

"Well, I'm sure my position on ignoring a woman's signals has been made pretty clear by now, but I would've backed off in a heartbeat if you'd wanted me to, Nora. I do hope you know that."

His gaze was as soft as the way his thumb brushed over my cheek in a tiny, hypnotic arc. I swallowed the sudden lump in my throat and nodded.

"I know you would have. That's probably why I couldn't bring myself to give you the boot. No matter how many hurdles I threw out there, you cleared every one of them."

"And I'll clear any more that come my way."

I sucked in a shaky breath. "You see me in a way no one else ever has."

"I like what I see," he whispered, then leaned over and kissed me. By the time he drew away, I was dazed and a little bit ruffled, which was probably exactly what he intended. "There's more where that came from when we get back to my place."

My lips twitched up into a smile. "So your plan is to just hole up at your house and fool around all day until the police solve this mystery?"

"Well, I was planning to replace the door at your apartment and set you up with a security camera somewhere along the way, but as for the rest of the time, I'm not opposed to your plan."

There were definitely worse things than hiding away with Jake Lincoln, at least until we knew what was going on. The break-in by itself would've been easy enough to explain away, but the text?

That was intentional.

Just like the bar and the shopping incident, my thoughts had immediately gone to Shawn Milton when we found the apartment door open, even though I'd already decided it was highly unlikely that he was the one at the bistro.

Now I was thinking about the guy from The Mermaid, the way his eyes slithered over me, the way he shrieked when I twisted his arm. After learning that Jake had gone back to threaten him, it was obvious that guy had a reason to want revenge on both of us.

In truth, I wasn't sure what bothered me more—Jake getting tangled up in something because of me, or the niggling feeling that whoever was behind all this would be more than happy for me to continue my usual pattern of moving on after a few months.

What would it be like to stay for once, to put down roots instead of running away? To rely on someone else and be relied upon, to weave my existence into a tapestry of others?

Those questions echoed through my mind until I realized Jake was still watching me, quiet and patient as ever.

I shook myself from my tangled thoughts, keeping my tone intentionally light as I said, "Let's get this over with so we can hole up at your house."

"Excellent plan."

With a wink and that beautiful dimpled grin, he opened his door and led the way into the restaurant.

The Mermaid was eerily quiet at this hour of the morning, but Jake's friend Casey was waiting for us at one of the tables near the door. Her short hair was dyed a brilliant shade of red that bordered on burgundy, and she had bright hazel eyes and an easy smile that somehow made me feel immediately at ease.

And she was beautiful in a sharp, edgy way that made me wonder if this was who held Sam's heart.

"This must be the infamous Nora Cassidy," Casey said as she stood to offer her hand.

I shook it and shot Jake a look. "I don't know about infamous, but yes. It's nice to meet you, Casey."

"I'm going to go check the booking information. I'll be as quick as I can," Jake told us. "Sit, chat, give Casey the third degree about my background. Casey, you have my permission to tell her anything, unless it makes me look bad. Do *not* mention that birthday party junior year."

He winked at me and I laughed, grateful to him for not abandoning us to awkward silence. Casey returned to her seat across the table while I pulled out a chair. Though her lingering smile was friendly, her gaze was razor sharp on my face.

"He's crazy about you," she said.

"Sam said the same thing," I replied evenly.

I got the impression that Casey wasn't being possessive of Jake, only protective. It struck me much the same as Sam's attitude, a fact which I filed away to think more about at a later time.

Casey nodded and relaxed into her chair. "I had dinner with Sam last night. She might have mentioned it a few dozen times, but I've seen it for myself."

"You caught me on a bad night," I said, grimacing.

"To be perfectly frank, I thought I was going to be posting bail for him when that guy grabbed you. Not only was I pretty impressed with the way you brought the sucker down, I was also grateful that you took care of it before Jake could get involved. He's not a violent man, but he's got a protective streak a mile wide. Maybe two miles now, with you in the picture."

A wry smile curled my lip. "Glad I could help out."

"Are you as crazy about him as he is about you?" Casey asked. My eyes narrowed on her face and she gave a small, unapologetic shrug. "I'm not trying to force any declarations out of you, I just want to know he's not going to get his heart broken. Sam doesn't think you'll hurt him, but she tends to be an eternal optimist."

"I have no intention of breaking his heart," I replied quietly. Part of me was annoyed by the probing, but the other part was pleased to know Jake had friends who were willing to put themselves in uncomfortable positions in order to watch his back. "I've never really been known for making declarations of any kind, so I'll just say that I've never wanted something to work as much as I want this to. Does that answer your question?"

Casey's smile was swift and satisfied. "That's what I was hoping to hear."

"Good. I promise I'm not the enemy here, Casey. I—I'm happy. For the first time in a long time, and Jake is the reason for that."

The expression on Casey's face softened, but instead of speaking, she reached out and squeezed my hand on top of the table. As my throat clogged with emotion, I gave a quick nod and squeezed back.

It seemed that my friend count in Spruce Hill was slowly increasing.

Once I'd gained control of my voice again, I refocused on Casey with a flare of interest. Maybe it wasn't my place to question, but I was intensely curious—and desperate to shift the conversation away from myself.

"So, you and Sam seem to be very good...friends?"

"Hmm," Casey replied thoughtfully, but her eyes narrowed for a second before she grinned. "Good friends, yes. We all grew up together."

It was a very careful non-answer, but I smiled back at her. "Okay then, new subject. Junior year birthday party?"

Apparently, that was the opening Casey had been waiting for, because she launched into a hilarious recollection of Sam and Jake's seventeenth birthday party. Jake had been dared to chug a half gallon of blue raspberry snow cone syrup and ended up vomiting all over the cake. As a result, his twin gave him a black eye and the guests were all sent home early.

Damn, I wished I could have been there to see it.

Jake reappeared a few minutes later and shot a glare at Casey. From the way I was trying to muffle helpless laughter with my hand, he must have known the subject came up. Unfortunately for him, he could barely muster up even fake outrage and I saw that dimple peeking out at me beneath his scowl.

"Dammit, McDonald. I asked one thing. One thing!"

Casey gave an unrepentant shrug. "Sorry, Jakey boy. She asked. How could I refuse when she turned those big brown eyes on me?"

He grumbled under his breath, sliding into the chair between us. "Yeah, yeah. You get a pass this time, I guess. She's pretty irresistible."

I preened for a moment, but my smile quickly dropped. "Did you get the names?"

"I found the host's name on the booking and sent it over to Chief Roberts. He'll follow up with them to figure out who else was there. I need to hit the hardware store, Nora. I could have Sam come hang with you at the house, if you want?"

Casey choked back a laugh when I turned my narrow-eyed glare in his direction. "That's my cue, folks. Nora, it was a pleasure meeting you. Jake, I'll see you around, if you survive the next ten minutes." With that, she pushed out of her chair and left the restaurant with her hands in her pockets, whistling a jaunty tune.

Jake blinked at me in confusion. "What did I do?"

"I don't need a babysitter, Jake. Your sister doesn't need to keep me company and I really don't think I even *need* security cameras. I'm not helpless or a child or some kind of weakling."

My voice rose toward the end as my careful composure began to crack, and I covered my face with my hands.

"Nora," Jake said gently. He didn't touch me, just leaned his elbows on his knees and waited until I finally dropped my hands to look at him again. "Believe me, I know all of that. You know I do. I'm sorry if I made it sound like I thought you needed a babysitter, but I promise it was not my intention. Sam has been texting me nonstop all day, that's what made me think of it. That's *all* that made me think of it. You're the strongest person I know. I have absolute faith in you, okay?"

"I'm sorry I'm such a mess," I whispered, suddenly feeling so sad, so lost. If only I'd built a stronger foundation before it started crumbling under my feet.

He opened his arms in invitation. I stayed quiet for a long moment before I stood and wrapped my arms around his neck. The position placed his head level with my sternum, and he pressed a warm, sweet kiss to my collarbone.

"You are an absolute badass. A smoking hot badass, at that. Wanna come pick out a new door for your badass apartment with me? Letting me loose in a hardware store alone is a dangerous and generally expensive prospect, so you'd be doing me a favor, really."

"Yes. Let's go hardware shopping."

"I've never been more turned on in my life," he said lightly, blue eyes lighting up at my laughter as he stood and took my hand.

I dropped my head to his shoulder as we left the restaurant. When we reached the truck, Jake sighed softly.

"I wish I could shield you from the world."

I could see in his expression that he knew, even as the thought crossed his mind and slipped past his lips, that I didn't want someone to shield me. I wanted someone to fight by my side, to have my back, someone who respected just how strong I was and wouldn't try to shove me into the background for the sake of chivalry or macho pride or whatever happened to be at stake.

Before I could respond, though, he hugged me tight to his chest and shook his head.

"I know. Believe me, I know that isn't what you need from me, Nora. Whatever you do need, I'll give it to you, be that for you. No matter what."

Chapter Twenty-Five

JAKE

A S IT TURNED OUT, Nora was the best hardware store shopping partner I could have asked for. We picked out her new front door first, one with a peephole instead of a window. When I teased her gently about it being more difficult to peek out at me in my driveway, Nora simply cocked a brow and asked what I thought the security cameras were for if not to spy on me.

After that, we wandered the store side by side, her hand tucked around my elbow as I pushed the cart. We admired light fixtures and flooring samples, paint colors and power tools. Nora not only knew her stuff, she also had some amazing design ideas.

"Well, that does it, Cassidy. I'm putting you in charge of remodeling the rest of the second floor," I told her, then kissed her there in the plumbing aisle.

She laughed. "As long as you're funding my grandiose plans and providing the manual labor, I'm in."

We left with the new door, some security cameras, new locks, and an area rug that Nora insisted I needed in the Dude Lair. The fact that she used my term for the room sold me on it immediately and led to another dramatic kiss, old Hollywood style, in the middle of the store. A few bystanders even applauded when I swung a flushing, flustered Nora back onto her feet.

I executed a tidy little bow to the onlookers and then added the rug to the cart. Nora might have been more interested in the color scheme, all streaks of blues and greens, but it was also thick and impossibly soft—all I could imagine was Nora's lush body sprawled across it as I teased and tasted her.

All in good time.

I forced those graphic images from my mind in order to quash my immediate reaction to that particular fantasy. While I loaded our haul into the bed of the truck, Nora returned the heavy lumber cart to the corral. As she started back toward the truck, squinting toward me in the sunlight, she froze.

I followed her line of sight over my shoulder and saw a tall, fair-haired man in dark sunglasses staring straight at her from a couple rows over. In that instant, I had to make a choice—run toward him and risk the bastard circling toward Nora before I could get there, or get my ass directly to her side.

Images of a panic attack striking, of Nora struggling for breath, made the decision for me.

As fast as I could, I took off toward her, calling her name, but she was still rooted in place, her lips parted without any words coming out. Just before I reached her side, she pulled her phone from her pocket and snapped a picture. I glanced back to see the man turn and vanish between vehicles in the parking lot.

By the time I grabbed her shoulders, Nora blinked up at me, staring numbly even as her hands clenched in my shirt.

My voice low and urgent, I said, "Talk to me, Nora. Was that him?"

"It was him," she confirmed hoarsely, pointing now as she couldn't before. "The guy from the outlet mall. By that white Toyota."

I gave her a squeeze. "Get in the truck and lock the door. Go!"

Before she could protest, I was gone, running between rows of cars and peering in windows. There was no way for the guy to reach her without going through me, but a whoosh of relief washed over me when I heard Nora slam the door behind her and hit the locks.

The guy was a ghost. I wove in and out of the parked cars in that row, then the next, listening for another car door, an engine, a footstep—but there was nothing.

I rubbed a hand over my face and decided it was more important to get back to Nora than to chase aimlessly after the man. By the time I returned to the truck, I was breathing hard and cursing.

"Did you get a photo?" I asked after she unlocked the door for me. Nora stared back at me for a moment, so I said, "Nora, honey, you had your phone out to take a picture of him. Did you get it?"

"I didn't even realize I was doing it." Frowning, she pulled out her phone, swiped over to her camera roll, and opened up the picture. As she zoomed in on the figure from the parking lot, she grimaced. "This is a shit photo, but that's definitely the same guy that I ran into at the bistro. I recognize the glasses."

I studied it closely. "And it looks an awful lot like our friend from The Mermaid," I said grimly. "I'm going to send this over to the chief. We're making one more stop on the way home."

Nora nodded and slipped the phone back into her pocket. For some reason, she didn't look afraid so much as resigned. I reached over and touched her cheek with my fingertips. Even as the rush of adrenaline faded, the relief I felt in knowing she was safe made me dizzy.

"What's going on in that beautiful head of yours?" I asked, shifting the truck into gear.

"If it's the guy from The Mermaid, then it's not Shawn," she said simply.

A rush of breath left my lungs. "Oh, honey."

As we pulled out of the parking lot, I found her hand on the seat between us and clasped it tight. After she told me Milton wasn't the reason she moved around so much, I'd all but dismissed any chance of the man's involvement in this, especially when Chief Roberts voiced his assumption about the guy from the bar.

"I didn't realize that was still weighing on you. I'm sorry."

She offered a rueful smile in response. "Logically, I knew it wasn't him. Or that it didn't make sense for it to be him, at least. But I must have still thought, in the back of my mind, that it might be. Shawn Milton is a monster, Jake. That guy from the bar, whoever he is, he's just a man."

A man with a grudge, I wanted to point out, but I simply squeezed her hand.

When I pulled into another small plaza halfway to the house, I leaned over, kissed her swiftly, and said, "I'll be right back. Lock the doors behind me, I'll leave the engine running."

She nodded and I waited for the locks to click before I jogged into a storefront that looked more than a little questionable. If I didn't know better, I would've assumed it was the kind of adult video store one might find along a desolate highway.

A few minutes later, I came back out with an unmarked brown paper bag and passed it to her as I climbed in. From the expression on her face, she'd had the same thought about the store. The anonymity of the bag did nothing to contradict those assumptions.

"What is this?" she asked, looking almost afraid to peek inside. "Surely calm, steady Jake Lincoln wouldn't react to a surprise run-in with a stalker by buying sex toys, right?"

I shot her a quick wink, relieved that she was joking again. "A few cans of pepper spray, a rape whistle, a couple pocket knives, and an air horn."

Nora stared at me, her lips parted in shock. Apparently the sex toys would have surprised her less—a fact which I filed away for the future. "You've got to be kidding."

"Nope. I don't own a gun, so we're going to err on the side of caution. Your kung fu skills are impressive, Nora, but I don't want that son of a bitch getting close enough to grab you again. We need some things you can use from a distance."

"I already have pepper spray," she said calmly, finally rifling through the bag. "The can is much smaller than these, though."

"Why does that not surprise me in the least?"

A giggle welled up and bubbled out of her. "I kept it in the bag with my laptop once I started walking back and forth to The Mermaid. I was afraid I might have to use it on you, actually, when you walked me home the next time after my panic attack. God, you made me so nervous, you and your damn combustibility."

I looked over to see her shoulders shaking with silent mirth, her fist pressed to her lips to try to stem the laughter. "Did I, now? Here I thought I behaved like the perfect gentleman. I even kept my hands in my pockets so you'd relax."

That only made her laugh harder, until eventually she was wiping tears from her eyes. "Oh, believe me, I noticed. I think I fell a little bit in love with you right then and there."

Silence descended over us both as soon as the words left her mouth, broken only by the catch in Nora's breath. I was sure she'd spoken the thought without realizing its implications, but now that it had been said, we were both tangled up in the revelation.

A rush of tenderness made my chest ache as I reached over to touch her cheek, a light sweep of my fingertips that she immediately leaned into.

"Is that so?" I whispered.

Nora didn't respond—not in words, not yet. I didn't need verbal confirmation, however, so I just slid closer along the bench seat and captured her mouth, pouring my every emotion into the kiss and slowly, carefully drawing them from her in return.

The words she had accidentally uttered blended with all the words still unspoken, but we both understood.

When I drew back, I pressed my forehead to hers for a long, quiet moment. Then, when she offered a sweet, dazzling smile, I brushed the tip of my nose against hers and murmured, "Let's go home."

Chapter Twenty-Six

NORA

WE DROVE THE REST of the way in silence, but Jake kept hold of my hand the entire time, occasionally lifting it to his lips. How was it this man could convey so much with a single glance, a simple brush of his mouth over my skin? Though I suspected I knew the answer, I forced myself to set emotional declarations aside for the time being and tried to reflect instead on my relief that I wasn't being stalked by a ghost from my past.

It was stupid to be so grateful, I was fully willing to admit that, since I knew next to nothing about the man from the bar. Getting cocky because I'd taken him down once in a thirty second altercation would be a mistake. He could very well be even more dangerous than Shawn Milton.

There had to be a reason people said the devil you know is better than the one you don't, but the devil I knew was utterly terrifying.

What were the chances that this guy was worse?

Putting a face to the recent incidents had sapped the fear right out of me and left behind a sharp edge of anger. By the time we pulled into Jake's driveway, I'd replayed that scene at the bar in my mind a dozen times, struggling to recall as much about the man as possible.

Spiked light brown hair, wiry frame, clean-shaven. Almost as tall as Jake, but not as broad or well-muscled. I couldn't remember the color of his eyes, only the slimy feeling they'd left on my skin as he looked me up and down. The keening sound he made when he dropped to his knees reverberated inside my skull, along with his friends' taunting laughter when he returned to the bar.

At the time, my only concern had been getting the hell away from him, but now I recalled the furious humiliation sparking from his frame as he slunk away. Was that why he wanted to scare me now? Would he ever make a direct move, or was he satisfied with dancing around in the shadows?

Part of me had undoubtedly been annoyed to learn Jake had gone back to confront the man, even as I tried to look at the situation objectively. Jake's interest in me had been perfectly clear almost from the start, but there'd been nothing really between us when it happened. He hadn't reacted to the situation under the guise of *lover* or *boyfriend* or whatever it was he might be by this point in time; he'd responded as a business owner who had every right to tell a guy off for hassling women in his restaurant.

My reverie was interrupted when Jake opened my door and raised a quizzical brow. "Daydreaming?" he asked.

"What did you see in me when we first met?" I leaned my head back against the seat, studying his features.

"You mean besides the obvious fact that you're drop dead gorgeous?"

My cheeks heated a little, just as I was sure he'd intended, but I continued to stare at him until he coughed up a real answer. With a pensive look, he set one hand on my knee and braced his other forearm against the doorframe.

"I saw a beautiful woman who looked so lonely it made my chest ache, who seemed afraid to even shake my hand. And then, underneath that bristling exterior, I saw a woman who was clever and curious and so full of life, it practically broke my heart to think about what might have caused her to be so skittish."

My eyes widened slightly. Though I hadn't been sure exactly what his answer would be, it was far more insightful than I ever would've guessed.

"You're a perceptive man, Jake Lincoln," I replied, my chest tight with emotion.

He bent down to brush his lips across mine. "I'm a patient man. And you, Nora Cassidy, are most definitely worth the wait."

Before he could draw back, my arms shot around him and I buried my face against his neck. Jake clasped me tight and we stayed there in the driveway for several long minutes. For someone who'd been insisting I could take care of myself barely an hour ago at the police station, I was profoundly glad that for once, I didn't have to.

"Thank you," I murmured finally. "I needed that."

Jake kissed my forehead before lifting me down from the truck. "I am more than happy to hold you anytime you need it. Day or night, Nora, I'm here for you. You're not going to scare me away. Got it?"

That simple affirmation caused my breath to catch in my throat. It took a moment before I could nod and whisper, "Got it."

"Good. Ready to install your brand-spanking-new front door?"

Hand in hand, we went up and checked over the interior of the apartment again. The broken pane on the door had been boarded over and the glass swept tidily away, but everything else looked exactly as we'd left it. Jake eased his way around me to enter the bedroom and toss the skirt into the bottom dresser drawer.

"Now that is a crying shame," he grumbled. "I liked that skirt almost as much as the blue dress."

I laughed, and suddenly those threads of tension winding their way up the back of my neck and into the base of my skull began to loosen their hold. "Fortunately, your sister is an expert shopper. I'm sure she'd be happy to help me find a replacement."

Jake gave an exaggerated groan. "Great, now I'll be thinking about what you brought home from the last shopping trip while I'm trying to frame in the door."

"Well, if you work real hard and get all your chores done, maybe there will be a reward for you later." I batted my eyes at him and slid my hand seductively across his chest as I walked past.

While I sashayed back toward the front door, he muttered, "Okay, just gotta talk myself down from this hard-on. If I don't get blood flowing back toward my head, I'll probably end up drilling through my own hand."

"We can't have that. I quite like a number of things that require the use of your hands, so an injury would definitely interrupt my future plans," I teased over my shoulder.

When he finally walked into the kitchen, I handed him a cold bottle of Coke. Jake flashed a smile of thanks and we sipped in silence for a few minutes before he planted a hard kiss on my lips and got to work. As with the car repairs, I stood by to hand him tools, hold the flashlight when needed, and generally keep him company.

"Renovating is a lot more fun with you around. Not even an unhinged stalker can dampen your spirit and, shit, I really love that about you," he said when we had successfully installed the new door and locks.

I flushed scarlet at the casual way he said it, but he just opened and closed the door a few times before peeking out the peephole.

"You definitely can't see my driveway."

"Considering I haven't slept here much, I guess I can just look out the window from your front hall if I want to spy on you out in the driveway," I replied.

While he put his tools away, I slid a new key onto each of our keychains. It wasn't really meant to be a statement, but when I handed his keys back, he gave a slow smile, unfettered and sweet in a way that made my heart trip a little faster.

"I didn't think it was lonely when I was working on this place by myself, but now . . ." He trailed off, watching me for a moment. "I sure like having you around, Nora."

"I sure like being around, Jake," I replied.

The simplicity of the statements seemed to underscore the depth of our feelings rather than gloss over them.

"Now that your door is fixed, will you be staying here again?" he asked. His tone was light, but I caught the look in his eye that said he was hoping for a particular answer—and I knew exactly what it was.

I leaned my hip against the porch railing and studied him. "Why don't you tell me what you're really trying to say?"

Jake grinned a little. "I can always trust you to cut right to the chase. I'd like it if you'd keep staying over at my place."

"Because...you want to keep an eye on me? Because you'd feel safer knowing I'm protected by your security system? Because you like snuggling with me every night?" I arched a brow ever so slightly in challenge.

"Because, Nora Cassidy," he said softly, placing his hands on my waist, "I fell a little bit in love with *you* that very same day."

The words coasted over my skin, warm as the summer sun. Emotion clogged my throat and I had to take a moment to bask in the way he made me feel—treasured, protected, impossibly happy—so I could respond without letting tears of pure joy mar this moment.

"Is that so?" I breathed, echoing his earlier response.

His blue eyes glowed with pleasure and I couldn't stop myself from leaning forward to kiss him. With his fingers digging into my hips, he tugged my body against his, surrounding me with every beautiful thing that made up the man I was falling in love with.

"Now, let's get these cameras installed so I can take you home and claim my reward for getting my chores done," he growled against my lips.

Once the cameras were up, we sat on the loveseat with our heads together as we connected an app on my phone to the feed. There on my screen was a clear view of the landing at the top of the stairs. To test it out, Jake jogged over and went outside, causing an alert to chirp. The tiny black and white image of him waved up at the camera and offered a goofy smile.

The other camera was focused on a side door leading into the garage, even though there was no access from there to the apartment. Jake didn't want to risk anyone lying in wait for me to venture out, either.

He had just joined me back on the loveseat, where I was still admiring the system, when my phone rang, startling us both into a chorus of expletives.

"Oh, crap. It's my dad," I said, pressing a hand to my chest to slow my pounding heart. Clearly, my father had some kind of sixth sense for knowing the worst possible moment to call.

"Go ahead and talk to him. I'll go take the rug inside and be back in a few minutes." Jake kissed the side of my head and left me alone.

I waited through one more ring before I answered the call. "Hey, Dad," I said, hoping my voice sounded steady as I rose and walked over to the window to watch Jake heft the area rug over one shoulder.

Like Jake, my father was a perceptive man, and I was fairly certain I was still not very good at concealing my emotions from either one of them.

"Hey, Bear," he said brightly. I rolled my eyes at the nickname, grateful he couldn't see me. "I had no service for a while so I just got your email. You make it to Spruce Hill okay? An old buddy of mine is the police chief there, did I tell you that?"

"Yes, I'm here," I said, "and no, as a matter of fact, you didn't. You could have mentioned it when you sent me the apartment ad, Father Dearest."

"Didn't I? I could have sworn I told you about Roberts. That's why I even thought of Spruce Hill when you were looking for somewhere near the water. Maybe you'll run into him around town."

With a sigh, I replied, "Actually, I've met him."

My mouth snapped shut when I realized what I'd just said, distracted as I was by ogling Jake. Though I could have met the chief of police on any number of occasions in a small town like this, my father apparently caught something in my tone that sharpened his attention.

"Oh? Where exactly did you run into him?" he asked.

His voice was deceptively even, a sure sign that I was completely screwed. I closed my eyes, recognizing a trap when I heard one. John Cassidy knew very well that I couldn't lie to him without cracking, just as he knew that I would always try to evade an indirect question if given half a chance.

Dammit. I'd backed myself into a corner and there wasn't a chance in hell that my father would let it go after that slip.

"At the police station," I finally admitted.

"Nora, are you in some kind of trouble?"

Am I? I wondered idly. My heart seemed more at risk than my physical safety, but I had even less interest in talking to my father about love than I did about a potential threat. The truth would have to do.

Part of the truth, anyway.

"My apartment was broken into when I wasn't home. Nothing was stolen. It might have just been kids screwing around. My neighbor already replaced the door and the locks, and we just set up some security cameras. I'm fine. Everything is fine."

Accurate, if oblique. There would be no mention of the romantic lakeside getaway, no freaking way, and certainly no mention of what the culprit left waiting on my bed.

My father made a sound that indicated he wasn't fully satisfied with that explanation, but for once in his life, he didn't push. "Well, I'm glad it's taken care of. I was thinking I'd come out to visit next weekend, actually. I'm about ready for a change of scenery and I still owe Roberts a beer from the last time I saw him. There's a campground by the lake, so you don't have to worry about entertaining me."

I banged my forehead gently against the new steel door. "It'll be great to see you, Dad. Text me the details."

"I will. You take care of yourself. I love you. See you in a few days."

"Love you, too, Dad. Bye."

I stared down at the phone for a long moment before shaking myself back to reality. It had been too long since I spent any time with my dad, and at least we had a little bit of time to get used to the idea of him showing up in Spruce Hill. I shoved a few more changes of clothes into a bag, secured the locks on my sturdy new door, and went around to Jake's deck to let myself into the house.

Heaving another sigh—was I really so pathetic that my life was boiling down to a series of heartfelt exhalations?—I left my bag on the kitchen table and found Jake positioning furniture around his new area rug.

"I told you it would look great in here," I said.

Jake straightened and surveyed his lair. "You are a goddess among women," he replied, watching my lips twitch. "Everything okay with your dad?"

I plopped down on the couch and threw an arm dramatically across my eyes. "Yes, but he's coming for a visit. I had to tell him about the break-in, though I made it sound like the matter was resolved. It seemed like he was planning to pitch the visit even before I told him."

With a grin, Jake sat beside me and rested his hand on my knee. "So I'll get to meet him?"

"Yes," I muttered. "I conveniently left out the part about being assaulted and then stalked. Oh, and about sleeping here every night. And about banging my insanely hot neighbor. A nd...well, I guess that's the bulk of it."

His laughter earned him a glare, which did nothing to quell that damn dimple. "Well, I didn't exactly plan to inform him that we were 'banging' either, Nora, though I do appreciate that you think I'm hot. But he can't be opposed to you having a boyfriend. You're a grown woman."

"Are you opposed to a background check?" I asked sweetly. "Because that will only be the first step if he knows you're . . ." I waved an airy hand and Jake caught it, kissing my fingertips one at a time.

"Knows I'm what?" he murmured. "Making sweet, sweet love to you at all hours of the night? Exploring every inch of your skin? Giving you countless orgasms until your legs are shaking so hard you can barely stand?"

"I'm glad you find this amusing," I hissed when his teeth nipped at the pulse in my wrist.

Jake's heated gaze settled on my face. "Or did you mean if he knows I'm in love with his daughter?"

My lips parted at the words, but I didn't pull away. His beautiful blue eyes held mine without flinching.

"Are you?" I breathed.

Our earlier comments had been offhand, qualified, lighter somehow. The way Jake looked at me now wasn't any of those things. It was simultaneously intense and scorching but soft and sweet. I could practically feel the emotion flowing from him, twining up my arms and wrapping tightly around my heart.

"Oh, yeah," he replied, brushing his knuckles along my cheekbone.

I knew perfectly well that he would never, not for anything in the world, rush me into saying something I wasn't ready for—but it seemed that the way my expression softened with a breathy little sigh was answer enough for him.

"Well then," I murmured. As I covered his hand with my own, I gave in to a spark of mischief and smirked. "I just dare you to tell him that when he gets here."

The touch of his lips to mine soothed my sudden flare of nerves, but when he deepened the kiss, I nearly forgot all about my father. Eventually, Jake drew back, brushing his nose along mine before flashing a smile.

"Maybe I will. I'd walk through fire for you, Nora—I'm perfectly willing to face your father, no matter how scary he might be."

I thought he might regret that statement by the time he finally met the man, but when he slipped his hands under the hem of my shirt to slide up either side of my ribcage, I decided to put off worrying about it until another day.

Chapter Twenty-Seven

JAKE

To my surprise, Nora resigned herself pretty quickly to her father's impending visit, though she did force me to endure half a dozen one-sided debates about whether she should spend her nights at the apartment while her father was in town instead of snug in my bed. I let her carry out both sides of the argument, choosing instead to bide my time until she was ready for a distraction.

I'd be damned if I would let her scurry away from me just because she didn't want her father to recognize that she was an adult woman with adult needs.

The night before her father's arrival, I caught her chin in my hand and stared deep into those big brown eyes. "Nora, honey, everything is going to be fine. If he hates my guts, I'll let you hold me while I cry my eyes out, but I'll survive, because he's not the one I'm in love with. You are."

Though she hadn't quite come out and said it back, I got a thrill from seeing how she responded to me speaking the words aloud, like she was softening under the warmth of my love for her. Instead of avoiding it for fear of scaring her off, I found that the more I said it, the more she melted.

This time, she slumped against my chest, pressing her lips to my throat as her arms wrapped tightly around my waist. I grinned when she shifted to peek up at me.

"You did that on purpose," she accused, but her eyes were alight with pleasure.

"Did I?" I asked, trailing my lips along her hairline. "I'll say it as many times as you need, as many times as you'll let me. I'm head over heels in love with you, Nora."

With no small effort, I convinced her to stop worrying. Bolstered by a full night's sleep—in my bed, since she'd finally accepted that self-consciousness couldn't lure her away from our current routine—she seemed much more optimistic about introducing me to her father. After a brief phone call the night before, we made plans to meet him for lunch at The Mermaid.

Little by little, most of her small wardrobe had ended up at my house. While she debated what to wear, I tried one final time to imagine how this particular meeting was going to go. Nora told me the last partner she'd introduced to her father had been her date for senior prom, and Captain John Cassidy had scared the poor kid into barely touching her the entire night, even when she'd begged him to dance with her.

Fortunately, I didn't scare quite so easily. In fact, after the hurdles I'd already vaulted over, I was hard-pressed to imagine so much as batting an eye at her father, no matter how imposing he might be. Then again, her father had decades more experience than she did in frightening people away.

I was still mulling that over when I walked into the bedroom, just as Nora pulled on jeans and then a dark blue blouse.

"You, my darling, look beautiful," I said, pausing to kiss the side of her neck.

Nora sighed softly and turned to look at me. I wore my usual bartending attire, hopefully looking clean-cut and respectable. A father's dream for his only child's partner, Nora had joked, but her father clearly wasn't like most others.

She smoothed her hands over my chest in approval and said dryly, "You look wonderful. If I dress up any more than this, he'll be expecting us to announce an engagement."

I smirked but said nothing further, simply took her hand and led her out to the truck. Despite my assurances to the contrary, I *was* nervous about meeting her father. I just didn't want to add to her own anxiety about it.

When I saw her hands clenching and flexing on her lap, I laid my own on the seat between us, palm up.

"Give me your hand."

She blinked at me in surprise, but she placed her hand in mine without a word. Instead of holding it, as I'd done so many times before, I pressed my thumb into the center of her palm and massaged it gently. All of those tiny muscles inside began to loosen, little by little, easing under the warm press of my thumb.

"What are you doing?" she asked finally.

"Whenever you're nervous or stressed, you fist your hands and open them, over and over. I thought this might help you relax a little."

Nora's breath caught on a quick inhale, then left her lungs on a sigh. "It does help."

Though neither of us said it aloud, the misty expression on her face told me that those little acts of thoughtfulness, of kindness and love, also helped. I flashed her a grin and continued rubbing my way across the muscles of her hand until we pulled into the parking lot at The Mermaid.

"It's going to be fine," I said again.

Nora waited while I shifted the truck into park, then she caught my hand and kissed it. "I know it will be," she whispered, "because I'm in love with you, too."

The smile that broke across my face brimmed with such joy that it could have lit the interior of the cab. I lifted my other hand to her cheek and slid over along the bench seat to kiss her, the kind of slow, deep kiss that filled my chest with wave after wave of emotion. When we parted, I closed my eyes and leaned my forehead against hers.

"Then I can handle anything," I murmured.

The bliss was short-lived, however, because Nora suddenly gasped and jerked away, muttering, "Shit, shit, shit."

I turned and saw a tall, broad-shouldered man with the same deep brown eyes as Nora staring at us through the windshield. Captain John Cassidy lifted a single dark brow in our direction as Nora scrambled for her seatbelt. She quickly hopped out of the cab, so I did the same, though I followed more slowly and met the two of them at the front of the truck.

"Hi, Dad!" Nora said brightly, her cheeks beet red.

I'd never seen her blush so deeply, though I was sorely tempted to try to make it happen sometime—in private, of course. She rose on tiptoe to kiss the man's cheek.

"Hi, Bear. Are you going to introduce me?"

"Ah," she stumbled slightly. "Dad, this is Jake Lincoln. My neighbor. Boyfriend. I mean, both, I guess. This is Jake."

Good lord, I'd never seen Nora so tongue-tied—and I was utterly enchanted by it. I forced back the memory of the day she'd accidentally told me I looked hot, smiled politely, and offered my hand to her father.

"Nice to meet you, Mr. Cassidy."

"John will do fine, son," her father said, shaking my hand.

The older man's grip was firm and strong. I caught the barest hint of a smile twinkling in his eyes, so like Nora's, though his expression remained stern. Beside us, Nora still looked completely frazzled, so I took her hand and watched as that simple connection steadied her. When I glanced back at her father, I was dead certain he'd seen it, too.

"This is Jake's restaurant," she told her father as we walked toward the doors.

"It's a family business, technically. My father started it when I was in high school, but my twin sister and I are the current owners," I added with a smile.

Nora's earlier jokes about me being perfect boyfriend material—polite, friendly, charming—would only help if it made up for the fact that her father had caught us making out in the parking lot. Christ, she said she'd never so much as held hands with anyone in her father's presence. I wondered if she felt like she was back in middle school again, floundering under Captain Cassidy's stern gaze, because I sure as hell did. I would help her in whatever way I could, but her fluttering nervousness was throwing off my focus.

"The strawberry shortcake is to die for," Nora added when she realized the conversation had stalled.

I caught sight of her father's amused expression over Nora's head and squeezed her hand reassuringly. Joanna, one of Nora's favorite servers, greeted us with a megawatt smile and led us to a booth on the opposite side of the restaurant from Nora's usual spot.

"This is a very nice place, Jake," John said as we sat. "You must do good business here."

Though it wasn't posed as a question, I understood that I was under review. "Yes, sir, we do. My sister and I took over for my father three years ago when he retired and business has continued to improve steadily. My sister does our marketing, I deal with the finances."

"And tend bar on the side?" John asked. With a small smile, he added, "Word gets around in a small town like this, even to a visitor like myself."

I grinned, though Nora shot her father a quick glare. "Yes, sir. I started bartending after I graduated from college, so it's a good way to keep an eye on things here. Even when my full-time bartender is working, I generally help out a few times a week."

"That seems a bit unusual," he said, looking unimpressed.

"I enjoy it, and it gives me a break from staring at ledgers all day long. I like to be present, stay involved. It helps when we need to make adjustments, see how things are working out, assess business decisions. And it's fun."

John leaned forward and stared straight into my eyes. "Fun," he repeated harshly. "Were you having fun the night my daughter was attacked?"

Every trace of good humor left my expression. "No, sir."

"And instead of reporting the crime, you let him walk out of here?"

"My primary concern was Nora—"

"Well, my concern is this asshole continuing to harass my daughter."

Before I could respond, Nora's palm cracked loudly against the table top. "That is *enough!*" she hissed.

Both of us looked at her in surprise, but her furious gaze was focused on her father, much to my relief.

"I didn't invite you to lunch to bully him about things outside of his control."

"It happened in his own restaurant," her father countered.

"You know why that guy was able to get close enough to touch me? Because I feel *safe* here. Because for once in my life, I'm not itching to leave town. And if you don't think Jake has *everything* to do with that, then your little spy in Spruce Hill neglected to give you the full story. I took care of the situation the way you taught me to, and Jake took care of me in the aftermath."

A stunned silence fell over the table as John's speculative gaze traveled between the two of us. Nora stared him down for a solid minute, but when she glanced at me, I winked at her, impressed.

Nora in a fury was truly a sight to behold, as long as it wasn't directed at me.

"Don't look so smug," she growled, poking me in the ribs as she leveled a glare in my direction.

I smiled over at her even as I rubbed the spot. "Yes, ma'am."

John sat back against the seat, finally relaxing his militant posture as he studied us. "Very well. That tells me everything I needed to know."

Joanna returned with the food, earning herself a wide smile from John Cassidy while Nora and I blinked at his sudden change of mood. We pulled ourselves from our confusion long enough to thank Joanna before she walked away, then we both looked at John again.

"What do you mean, that's all you needed to know?" Nora finally demanded.

"Come on, Bear," her father said gently. "I know perfectly well you don't need a man to protect you. The fact that *he* knows it, that he not only respects it but appreciates that about you, well." He shrugged. "You don't need my blessing or my approval to make your own choices, but I feel a fair sight better knowing you've made a good one."

I waited for Nora's reaction before so much as lifting my fork. Though I might never live it down among the staff if she chose to storm out of there without eating, I'd follow without question if that was her decision. Despite her silence, she was still simmering, so I laid my hand between us on the bench in case she needed it. A bare second later, her hand crept into mine, opening and closing against my fingers as she struggled to control her temper.

"That was low," she told her father with another scowl, but her palm relaxed against mine as I gently squeezed her hand.

Her father raised a brow as he spread the napkin across his lap and cut into his meal. "I was actually hoping Jake here would be the one to rise to the bait, not you, but I suppose it worked out in the end."

I choked on a laugh and Nora turned her glare in my direction. "What's so funny, Lincoln?"

"Bear baiting," I replied with a grin.

"If you know what's good for you, you'll forget you ever heard that stupid nickname," she warned, but she squeezed my hand one last time before releasing it. "So, you get into town and meet up with an old Navy buddy before your own daughter, huh? Was that to thank him for spying on me all this time?"

Her father shrugged, but his lips curved. "Roberts offered to meet for breakfast and I couldn't turn him down. Besides, keeping his ears open for any gossip about my only child is hardly spying." He took a bite and nodded to me. "This is delicious."

"I'll pass your compliments to our chef."

John's smile broadened. "I like a man who doesn't take credit for work someone else has done."

Nora rolled her eyes, so I nudged her knee with mine under the table. She turned her attention back to her father and said, "Jake is also renovating his own house. He's amazingly talented."

"Is he? Is it safe to assume Jake is the neighbor who replaced your door and locks?"

I swallowed another laugh when he put air quotes around the word neighbor. Nora's cheeks burned brighter, which I hadn't thought possible, but she ignored him and took a bite of her own meal.

The rest of our lunch passed peacefully, devoid of any further outbursts or arguments, though I got the impression that Nora's temper still hovered just below its boiling point. I wondered if being around her father always put her in this state—a woman like her surely wouldn't appreciate being treated like she couldn't manage her own life just fine by herself.

Even if John Cassidy seemed to understand his daughter perfectly, the two of them had decades of history that I simply wasn't privy to. I'd just make sure I didn't take any of her glares personally.

The conversation turned away from sensitive subjects, though I couldn't help but feel I was still being thoroughly assessed. Once our meals had been cleared and we were waiting for the strawberry shortcake to arrive, Nora excused herself to use the restroom. I stood to let her out of the booth and then sat, waiting for her father to speak.

He didn't make me wait long.

"Roberts thinks the man from the bar may be the one who broke into her apartment?" John asked quietly.

I nodded. "It seems pretty certain at this point. Nora bumped into him when she was out to lunch with my sister, then we caught him staring at her outside the hardware store the other day. She got a photo of him—it's a little blurry, taken from a fair distance, but it looks like the same guy. I ran after him as soon as I was sure she was okay. He was gone by the time I got over there."

"I'd like to see the photo." John's voice was low and he glanced over to make sure Nora wasn't on her way back. "Am I wrong to assume she's not staying at the apartment alone?"

"No, she's been staying at my house. I'm hoping to keep it that way for as long as she's willing. I have a security system and I feel better with her close by."

Her father nodded. "She'd kill me if she heard me say this, but you take care of her. She's not always as tough as she makes herself out to be."

"No, sir, she's even tougher. But I'll do everything in my power to keep her safe."

Clearly satisfied with my response, John held out his hand across the table. "Welcome to the family, Jake."

Chapter Twenty-Eight

NORA

IN A FREAK TURN of events, my father seemed almost jovial after I returned from the restroom, which made me immediately suspicious. The men were both tight-lipped about whatever had transpired while I was gone, though.

When we walked out into the midday sunshine, I kissed my father's cheek and bid him farewell, then waited until we were safely inside the truck to ask, "What did he say to you?"

"Whatever do you mean?" Jake blinked at my sharp tone in wide-eyed innocence. I merely cocked an eyebrow and waited, so he finally caved and said, "He asked if you were staying at the apartment alone. Or rather, he was already assuming that either you were staying at my place or that I was staying at the apartment with you. I'm still here, so I guess he wasn't too put out by learning the truth. Then he shook my hand and welcomed me to the family."

My jaw dropped at the last part. "He did what?"

"I thought it was a joke, like he just meant it as a token of his approval?" Jake's obvious delight in that assumption wavered when he saw my stunned expression. "Hey," he said gently, touching my cheek, "I'm sorry if that upset you. Maybe I shouldn't have said anything."

I shook my head, though more to clear it than to refute his apology. "No, I'm not upset. That's just...very unlike him."

Jake chewed on that for a minute before a smile tugged at his lips. "So, you think that means he likes me? I thought he was going to straight-up murder me. For making out with you in the truck or for not stopping that asshole from touching you, I wasn't really sure. Fifty-fifty, maybe."

"Let's just put it this way. He made my first girlfriend cry when he asked about her driving record, scared my prom date into not even dancing with me, and threatened a guy I dated in college with a chainsaw, though that one was over the phone. Apparently, you're the first to pass muster. Congratulations."

"Huh," Jake said. For a moment, he paused to consider my words, then he frowned. "Does that mean you haven't really dated anyone past college, or just that you started hiding them from your father for their own protection?"

I tipped my head to one side and replied, "A little of both, I suppose. Nothing like this, that's for sure."

"Well, thanks for not hiding me away. Meeting him was, ah, shall we say, enlightening?" When my eyes narrowed a little, Jake winked and leaned over to press a soft kiss to my lips. "Let's just leave it at the fact that I see now where your badassery comes from."

My laughter filled the cab. "I guess I can appreciate that."

"Good. So what now?"

"I don't know about you, but I need to get some work done," I replied. "For once, I feel like the quiet will actually help. My thoughts are loud enough as it is."

"Your wish is my command," Jake said swiftly, shifting into gear. We drove in comfortable silence, then as we pulled into his driveway, he raised a brow and said, "So, now that I've met your father's approval and you've admitted that you're madly in love with me, will you finally let me fix up Baby?"

"You're a glutton for punishment, Jake Lincoln, but sure, be my guest." Immediately, his blue eyes lit with excitement and I had to laugh. "If I knew you'd be this happy, I would've let you get started days ago."

Jake laced his fingers through mine with a contented sigh. "I feel like I've just cleared the ultimate trust hurdle."

"If that were an Olympic sport, you'd have a dozen gold medals by now."

"Does that mean I deserve a reward?" he asked, smiling hopefully.

I laughed as I hopped out of the truck. "Nice try, Romeo, but not until I get some work done."

He grinned when he caught up with me, then wrapped an arm around my waist and twirled me across the driveway. "Yes, ma'am. I'll get changed and take a look at Baby so I can start planning," he said as he tugged me back against his chest and dipped me low over one arm. "We should go dancing some-time."

"Why was dancing not on Sam's list of your best qualities?" I demanded when Jake swept me upright. "I want to lodge an official complaint. That was a grievous error on her part, almost unforgivable."

Jake caught me in a waltz hold and whisked us up the path-way to the front door. "Indeed. You can lodge your complaint in person if you'd like, because Sam invited us both for dinner tomorrow. I told her I'd let her know, so if you'd rather not, we can stay home and *dance*," he said, bouncing his eyebrows.

"You, sir, are incorrigible," I told him haughtily, but all of my tension over lunch dissipated as he unlocked the door. "But go ahead and tell your sister we'd be delighted to attend. You can show me your moves after I've been a productive adult today, how about that?"

"I'll hold you to it," he murmured, kissing me soundly be-fore he jogged upstairs to change out of his dress clothes.

I couldn't help but smile after him for a long moment, then I grabbed my laptop from the kitchen table and curled up on the leather couch in the Dude Lair. Jake returned in his torn jeans and a blue t-shirt that made his eyes pop vividly against his tan skin, dropped one more lingering kiss on my lips, and disappeared outside to give Baby a more thorough inspection. I shook my head indulgently at his enthusiasm for fixing up my sad little car, but I knew Baby was in good hands.

Unlike any of my work sessions over at the apartment, the words flowed easily here at Jake's house. Even the quiet didn't present its usual—or unusual, rather—level of distraction.

As my fingers flew across the keyboard, I wondered why I was able to focus so intensely here. It occurred to me that I'd never tried to work from Jake's house. Even on days I'd skipped going to The Mermaid, I always retreated to the apartment to work. It was no accident that I'd chosen a solitary career, one that I could do from anywhere in the world, but finding a place where I could be particularly productive was a rarity.

I waved Jake off when he stopped in to tell me he was going out to pick up a few parts for the car, though I vaguely remembered him saying he'd lock the door behind him and asking me to keep my phone nearby in case I needed him.

A text from him came through sometime later, informing me that he was back and working in the driveway. I tore myself from my work to send him a selfie for encouragement, making sure I leaned forward far enough to display a tiny glimpse of cleavage, then laughed to myself when he sent back a row of fire emojis.

It was amazing how light my heart felt just then, how peaceful. Not even my father's involvement in landing me in Spruce Hill could detract from the fact that this place, these people, had changed my life for the better.

Suddenly, my words to my father came back to me and I let my hands hover over the laptop keys as they echoed through the silent room.

Because I feel safe here.

I'd allowed myself to not pay attention to the crowd at The Mermaid that night because I felt safe—safe in Spruce Hill, safe around Jake, safe with my own thoughts. Now, it was like I was finally allowing myself to ignore the silence that had nagged at me for so many years.

By the time Jake came inside, I'd sent off two finished projects to clients and translated more of the novel I was working on than I'd ever finished in a single day. My neck was beginning to ache, so I closed the laptop and set it aside when Jake peeked in at me from the archway into the kitchen.

"How's it going?" he asked.

"Incredibly well, actually. I can't even remember the last time I got this much done. How's Baby?"

Jake smiled. "She's got heart, and soon she'll have enough new parts to have some guts, too." He saw me rubbing the back of my neck and held out a hand. "Come on, that's my job. You've been a productive, responsible adult all afternoon, now it's time to let me take care of you."

Rising, I took his hand and let him lead me straight to the master bathroom. He threaded his fingers through my hair, massaging my neck and scalp as the tub filled with steaming water. I rested my forehead against his chest and hummed with appreciation.

"God, I love your hair," he said softly. "So thick and soft. It always smells like fresh fruit."

"Pears. It's my shampoo and body wash set."

"It's unbearably sexy." While his thumbs dug gently into the muscles of my neck, he pressed his nose to the top of my head.

I scoffed, but didn't move. "And you with the tousled curls and a *dimple* are fighting fair, I'm sure."

He laughed against my hair. "We'll call it a tie then."

After another minute, he reluctantly drew away to turn off the water, then returned to lift my shirt over my head. We finished undressing in easy silence and stepped into the tub. Jake positioned me in front of him this time so he could continue easing the aching muscles in my upper back with his strong fingers.

I melted under his hands, the sensation more intoxicating than any drink he could serve up from behind a bar. Little by little, I relaxed further into him, until it was almost impossible to tell where his body ended and mine began.

With a deep sigh, I shifted, turning sideways so I was curled up against his chest. "Thank you," I murmured.

"For the massage? I consider it my duty and my pleasure, ma'am."

"No," I said, lacing my fingers with his under the water, "for not letting my dad scare you off."

His lips feathered across my forehead. "No one's going to scare me away from you. I'm completely hooked."

"Good, my plan worked."

"Phenomenally. By the way, why does your father call you Bear?"

I groaned against his neck and grumbled, "Not important."

That only piqued his curiosity. "Oh, now you *have* to tell me. Come on. It's cute."

"It is not cute." Jake waited with his usual patience, so I huffed in frustration. "Fine. My dad used to send me little teddy bears from wherever he was stationed. The year I turned ten, he was supposed to be home for my birthday and something happened, I guess he got delayed. Whatever the reason, I was pissed, so I set them all on fire in the backyard."

"You didn't," he breathed, sounding both impressed and appalled.

"My mom didn't even know I'd gone outside. Fire trucks showed up, it became a big huge thing. He shortened it to Bear, but for the first couple years after that, I was known all over base as Bonfire Bear."

Jake's shoulders shook with laughter beneath my head. "Oh my god. You're right, that's not just cute, it's the most freaking adorable thing I've ever heard in my life."

"It's not adorable and definitely *not* funny," I muttered, poking him hard in the ribs.

"Oh, Nora. It is funny, because I can just picture a prickly little version of you in the glow of a burning heap of teddy bears." He laughed even harder as he said it, wrapping his arms tightly around me. "Oh, shit. You have to tell Sam this story."

An annoyed hmph was my reply, but then my head popped up. "Well, now," I drawled, "if dinner tomorrow results in a sufficient number of embarrassing stories about *your* childhood, I might be willing to share it."

"That's a deal I will take." Jake grinned, clearly picturing his sister's reaction. Then, like he simply couldn't resist, he teased his lips across mine. "I am completely crazy about you."

My expression softened at the sweet way he said it. "I'm pretty crazy about you, too," I replied, a little shyly. It still felt foreign to make those admissions.

"Can I ask you something?" He brushed a wet tendril from my cheek, gazing down at me until I nodded. "When's the last time you told someone you loved them?"

My eyes widened as I tried to remember. "Aside from my parents, I assume you mean," I said dryly. "Ah...never, actually."

Jake's lips curved until that dimple twinkled at me like a beacon. It was distracting enough that I spent a solid minute just staring at his mouth before I realized he hadn't responded to my answer.

"What? Why are you smiling like that?"

"No reason. That just makes me extraordinarily happy," he murmured against my lips as he kissed me again.

When the kiss ended, I shifted to face him as I resettled myself on his lap. "Then I'll just have to give you a chance to show me how happy you are."

Jake, as always, was more than willing to rise to the challenge.

Chapter Twenty-Nine

JAKE

MIDWAY THROUGH ANOTHER EQUALLY productive morning for both of us, Sam texted to suggest inviting Nora's dad to dinner that evening. I knew my sister well enough to realize something must be going on, so I called her on speaker while Nora cuddled up against my side on the couch.

"Tell me what you're planning, evil twin," I said without preamble.

Sam heaved a sigh. "Why would you think I'm planning something other than a nice backyard barbecue for my darling brother and his hot new girlfriend?"

A strangled laugh slipped from Nora's lips, but I was undeterred. "Because I've known you my entire life, Samantha. What. Is. Up?"

"Mom and Dad got home this morning and they'll be at dinner tonight," Sam said in a rush, like that would prevent me from understanding the ramifications.

It didn't.

A meeting of the parents, that was what it would be.

On one hand, what better time than when John Cassidy happened to be in town? On the other, I felt like I'd already been run through the wringer, as had Nora. I rubbed my forehead and raised a questioning brow at her.

She only shrugged, so I said, "Fine, we'll invite him. No promises, though. And Sam?"

"Yes, brother dear?"

"John Cassidy is scary as hell, so I hope you're prepared if he accepts the invitation." That prompted laughter from both Nora and Sam, but I was feeling grim as I added, "And you better be ready to clean up a whole lot of blood on the off chance that he changes his mind about murdering me."

When the call ended, Nora texted her father, then tossed her phone aside to drape herself across my lap. "I have to admit, I really like your Dude Lair," she mused. "This couch is super comfortable and perfect for cuddling. And the rug looks fantastic, if I do say so myself."

Wrapping my arms around her, I rolled so I was propped on my elbows, gazing down at her. I lost myself in a vision of the soft shag rug under her back before forcing my mind back to the topic of our parents. "I'm glad you like it. I have plans to get you naked on it while we roll around and appreciate it more fully. Are you okay with meeting my parents?"

The change of subject appeared to give her whiplash. Nora blinked at me for a second before replying, a faint tinge of pink in her cheeks that suggested she was on board with my plan for the rug even if she was considering that last question at the same time.

"Is there any possibility they'll make me cry?"

"Not a chance in hell," I said. "They're going to love you."

"Then it can't be as bad as the risk you ran in meeting my dad, right? Unless they're going to blindside me for putting *you* in danger. I may have to demonstrate my self-defense skills to prove that I can protect you."

I dipped down to kiss her. "My dad looks like a teddy bear compared to yours," I whispered, then gave her a teasing grin. "Just don't set anything on fire, okay?"

Nora burst out laughing while I nuzzled her neck. "I already regret telling you about that."

"What do you say we take the afternoon off from our respective projects?" I asked, gliding my lips along her collarbone.

A sweet, breathy sigh was her only response as she tugged my shirt up over my head and tangled her fingers in my hair.

I THOUGHT I'D MANAGED to take Nora's mind off of our dinner plans until we were getting ready, then she asked, "What should I wear tonight?"

Raising a brow, I pulled on a deep green t-shirt. "I have yet to see you in anything that didn't look absolutely mouthwatering, even when you were actively trying to put me off. Wear whatever you want. This is a backyard barbecue, not a formal interview. You don't have to impress anyone."

Despite my reassurance, she stood there, staring into the tiny sliver of my enormous closet that she had claimed for her things. "I know. Sam always looks so nice, though. Is the blue dress too much?"

"That blue dress is *never* too much. I think it's my favorite thing you own. Every time I see it, all I can think about is the first time I took it off of you." My lips tickled her ear when I came up behind her and wrapped my arms around her middle.

"Am I going to distract you all evening if I wear it?" she asked sweetly, turning her head to bat her dark lashes at me.

"Yes, but then I have all evening to think about what I'm going to do when we get home tonight." I reached around her to pull the dress from its hanger. "Anticipation sharpens the hunger, you know. By the time we get back here, it'll be all I can do not to bend you over the kitchen table and have my wicked way with you."

Both of us needed a minute to regain our equilibrium after that, since we knew I meant every word of it. A little tremor ran through her, a tremor that tempted me to offer a quickie right now instead of waiting until later.

"Is that supposed to be a threat? Because it kind of sounds like a promise," she murmured.

"Oh, it is definitely a promise."

When I reached for her, she dodged away, clutching the dress in front of her body like a shield, but she laughed at the exaggerated leer on my face.

"Right, okay. But my dad might actually pull out a taser if we're late, so you better stop talking like that and let me finish getting ready."

I dropped onto the bed to watch her change and fuss with her hair. "Does he really have a taser?" I asked. The little security store where I picked up the pepper spray hadn't had any on display, but now that she'd mentioned it, maybe I should look into buying one.

Nora grinned over her shoulder. "I don't know, but I wouldn't put it past him. How do I look?" she asked as she turned to me.

With her hair pinned up in a pile of curls, a few dark tendrils floating around her face, I decided this was even better than the last time she'd worn the dress. The slender line of her neck curved gracefully to those shoulders that I knew from experience were both perfectly soft and impossibly strong, able to carry the weight of all her worries without drooping. My heart squeezed tight, as much from her beauty as from her vulnerable expression.

"You are absolutely stunning," I replied, hoping the raw appreciation in my tone served to reassure her. "Ready?"

Nora nodded and slipped her hand into mine. To my surprise, she didn't clench her fingers at all during the drive, though she stayed quieter than usual. Sam lived barely two miles from my house, at the end of a short dead-end street boasting a variety of architectural styles.

"Where did your family live?" she asked just before we pulled up to Sam's pale yellow Cape Cod house.

"Two blocks over. I'll take you past my parents' house on the way home, if you'd like to see it."

"Absolutely. Shit, should we have brought something? I didn't even think about it. I hate walking in empty-handed," Nora whispered when we started up the driveway.

Pausing, I grabbed both her hands and pressed my lips to each palm before waiting for her to meet my eyes. "Sam said absolutely not when I offered. It'd be an insult to ignore her direct orders. In fact, it might even put my life in danger. I'm not sure if you're aware of this, but we own a restaurant. Food is kind of what we do."

Nora gave a strangled laugh, but she relaxed a little and I kept her hand wrapped tightly in mine. The driveway opened to a tidy little yard with a beautiful stone patio—I actually had a bit of patio-envy, though my deck was nice enough after sanding and refinishing it last summer. Casey, dressed in skinny jeans and a gauzy floral button-down, was busy flipping burgers on Sam's impressive chrome grill.

When she let out a wolf whistle at the sight of Nora's dress, I laughed and Nora blushed, then bobbed a cute little curtsy.

"Hey, lovebirds!" Casey called out. "Our illustrious hostess is just freshening up. No parental units have arrived just yet."

Though her cheeks were still aflame, Nora laughed at the phrasing. "There's a throwback," she said. "Nice to see you again, Casey."

The other woman saluted with her spatula. "It's nice to see you too, Nora. You look very fetching this evening." Her hazel eyes twinkled when I wrapped a possessive arm around Nora's waist.

"Get your own woman, this one's taken," I growled.

"What do you think I'm doing here? I've got my own," Casey said, smirking as my jaw dropped.

"That's enough caveman for today," Nora sang as she slipped away. "I'm going to see if Sam needs any help. Casey, maybe you two can arm wrestle or whatever it is Jake needs to work off that extra testosterone."

Our laughter followed Nora as she opened the back door and called Sam's name. When the door closed behind her, I joined Casey at the grill. She arched a brow, grinning at me, and I gave her my darkest scowl.

"What do you mean, you've got your own? Don't tell me you *finally* asked my sister out on an actual date."

Casey smirked. "Look, Lincoln, you know I don't kiss and tell. You want details, ask your twin."

"That is one thing I will absolutely *not* do." My horrified expression melted into a smile. "But I'm happy for you both if there's any kissing to not tell me about. It's about time."

"You know, buddy, not everyone can take one look at their soulmate and fall immediately, ridiculously in love," she teased, but the words were filled with affection—and more truth than she could even know.

As I gazed toward the door where Nora had disappeared into the house, Casey reached over and squeezed my shoulder. I caught her hand and squeezed it in return, then yanked her into a headlock, which lasted all of three seconds before she broke my hold and brandished the spatula like a sword.

Whatever the evening had in store for us, we'd all weather it together. The night would end with Nora in my arms—with the promise of that kind of bliss, I had a feeling we could make it through anything life threw our way.

Chapter Thirty

NORA

"**H**ello?"

"In here," Sam called.

I followed her disembodied voice up a few steps that led into a bright, compact kitchen. Our hostess was fussing with a fruit tray and wearing a red polka dot dress with a frothy petticoat underneath. When I appeared in the doorway, she beamed at me.

"Nora! I'm so glad you're here. You look great," she gushed.

"I love your dress," I said with a smile. "I'm ashamed to admit this is the only one I own. I was hoping you might be up for another shopping expedition sometime soon. This time, I promise I'll keep it together. I think it's time to expand my wardrobe a bit."

Sam popped a chunk of watermelon between her very red lips and blasted me with the full force of her dimple. "Need more clothes to fill a bigger closet over at Jake's?" she asked, lowering her voice dramatically as she fluttered her lashes.

"I didn't move in with him," I protested, then I paused, frowning a little. "Okay, I mean, I sort of did, but not in an official kind of way?"

"Right. You're just staying there indefinitely, sleeping in my brother's bed, and keeping all of your stuff over there," Sam deadpanned.

I choked on a laugh. "Okay, fine. That sounds accurate, yes. Regardless, I'd definitely like to freshen up my wardrobe. While we're on the subject, do you and Casey always hang out this much?"

Sam shrugged, but her eyes twinkled. "We've all been friends a long time."

"And by that you mean you're dodging the question?"

"Absolutely, I am," Sam replied. "Now, if you'll grab that stack of plates, we can bring these out and get this party started."

I grabbed the pile of plates and utensils, then held the door open for Sam. To my amusement, Jake also seemed to be keeping a close eye on the interactions between Casey and his twin as the two of them set the table, trading jokes and glances so hot I felt it even from six feet away.

Jake caught my eye and winked across the table. Apparently the twins were always rooting for each other, no matter what. If

I hadn't already fallen for Jake Lincoln, that would've nudged me right over that particular cliff.

Just as we finished setting out plates and napkins, the sound of laughter came from the direction of the driveway.

All four of us fell immediately silent, looking at each other as though preparing for battle before Sam let out a nervous giggle. Jake took my hand in his warm, firm grip as the full trio of parents rounded the corner of the house.

My father looked like a completely different man today than he had at The Mermaid. He wore a blue Hawaiian print shirt with khaki shorts and—to my absolute astonishment—sandals in place of his usual shining dress shoes. He looked relaxed and happy, with his head tilted toward a woman I would've recognized as Jake and Sam's mother even without an introduction. Their coloring was the exact same as hers, though her caramel hair was accented by strands of shimmering silver among the gold.

Jake's parents were a lovely couple in their sixties, both with laughing blue eyes and ready smiles. The twins' dimples apparently came from their father, whose wife was giggling at something my father had said as they reached the yard, so Jake's dad was the one who called out, "Hey, kids."

"And this must be your beautiful Nora," his mother cried, pulling me into a swift hug. "I'm so happy to meet you. What a wonderful welcome home for us, meeting you and your father."

"I'm happy to meet you, too, Mrs. Lincoln," I replied when she held me at arm's length to look me over.

"Oh, please, call me Cheryl. You are just as gorgeous as Jake's been telling us! And Sam, too," she added, throwing her daughter a smirk.

I cocked a brow in Jake's direction but he only shrugged, grinning, as he shook my father's hand, then embraced his dad in a tight bear hug.

"Dad, this is Nora," Jake said as they turned toward me. "Nora, my dad, Dave Lincoln." I had to tear my gaze away from Jake's sweet smile in order to shake his father's hand.

"Nora, I am absolutely delighted to finally meet you," Dave said.

When he smiled in welcome, that familiar dimple creased his cheek. In another twenty years or so, I imagined that Jake would look just like his father. The man was a silver fox. Later, when we were in private, I fully intended to tease Jake about that fact.

While Dave and Cheryl turned to greet Sam and Casey, I kissed my father's cheek. "Hi, Dad," I said softly.

"Hi, Bear," he said, squeezing my shoulders. As we turned to look at the rest of our little crew, he added quietly, "They seem like a really great family. I'm glad you'll have some support nearby. I hate thinking of you all alone for so long."

In truth, the Lincolns were everything that we were not—boisterous, affectionate, constantly touching one another. Even before my parents' divorce, I couldn't remember a time when my parents had been like that, not with each other and definitely not with me. Somehow, my dad managed to blend right into this crowd anyway, slapping shoulders with Dave in a way I'd never seen him do with anyone.

Jake, bless him, kept his attention focused on me, making sure I was comfortable, pulling me back into the moment when I started to get a little overwhelmed.

"Doing okay?" he asked softly, brushing the pad of his thumb across my cheekbone. I nodded but didn't speak, my eyes caught by his tender expression until Sam announced that dinner was ready.

The meal was accompanied by more lively conversation, though I was interested to note that Sam was not the driving force—she seemed more inclined to tilt her head toward Casey and murmur in an undertone while the parents discussed some of the travel destinations they had in common. My father spoke more during dinner than I could recall him ever doing in the course of an entire day.

Though Jake chimed in readily enough, he seemed content to sit and toy with the little curls at the back of my neck, and I was content to let him. We both enjoyed the simple pleasure of having me tucked against his side as we sat there, surrounded by family and food, love and friendship.

After dinner, the two of us retreated to a corner of the yard that boasted a handmade wooden swing hanging from an enormous oak tree. I sat on it, pushing myself slowly back and forth with one foot while Jake leaned against the trunk of the tree beside me.

"Your family is wonderful," I said.

Jake, unsurprisingly, caught the wistful note in my voice, so he moved to stand behind me and pressed a kiss to the top of my head. Grasping the ropes, he gave the swing a gentle pull and let it go, sending me slowly forward. I laughed a little and tipped back far enough to smile up at him.

"I have no complaints. No real ones, anyway, though sometimes I wished I was an only child when I was growing up," he replied, grinning back down at me. "Even your dad seems to be enjoying himself."

"Yes, he does. I've never seen him like this."

"Like what?" Jake asked as he drew the swing toward him until my back was pressed against his chest. His lips teased my temple as I leaned back into him.

"Happy," I whispered.

A lump caught in my throat at the realization that maybe my parents had never been truly content together, not really. As a child, it was easy to ignore, but now that I felt that joy myself, the memories all felt tinged with the pain of this new knowledge.

"Nora, honey," he said gently, brushing his lips just behind my ear, "the past is the past. And I'm pretty damn happy right now, so it's only fair that everyone else here should be, too."

I turned my head so my lips met his, then Casey called out, "Hey, lovebirds! Ready for a game of horseshoes?"

Jake slowly lowered the swing so I could rise to my feet. All trace of wistfulness evaporated from my expression at the prospect of a competition, and I taunted, "Okay, but I'll probably crush you, so don't say I didn't warn you."

Cheryl and Dave entertained us throughout the game with enough embarrassing and hilarious childhood tales to make up for my father telling them all about my teddy bear pyrotechnics. I couldn't remember the last time I'd laughed so much. By the end of the night, my cheeks were sore from it, but my heart felt full enough to burst.

I watched my father actually kiss Cheryl's cheek as he said goodbye, clasp hands with Sam and Casey, and give both Jake and Dave the one-armed guy embrace that I'd seen other men use, but never John Cassidy. Then he hugged me tight to his chest, an equally rare occurrence.

"I love you, Bear," he whispered against my temple.

I squeezed him back. "I love you, Dad."

When he released me, Sam caught my elbow to discuss plans for another round of shopping. Before my father left, however, I overheard him as he leaned in closer to Jake and murmured, "Walk out to the car with me, would you?"

My heart sank as they walked away. I should have known real life would intrude again the minute I let my guard down.

Chapter Thirty-One

JAKE

THOUGH MY PULSE SPED to a gallop at the quiet words, I stood, leaving Nora nestled between my mother and sister, and walked down the driveway with John. When we reached his gray Honda, he stuck his hands in his pockets and leaned against the passenger side door. I braced myself for bad news.

"Roberts got a name from the host of the bachelor party," John said quietly. "The guy who assaulted Nora is Frank Scarpella. Friends haven't seen much of him after the wedding. They said he told them he was going to visit family."

I blew out a breath. "Let me guess, the family hasn't seen him either?"

John nodded in confirmation. "I extended my stay for another week, at least. I don't expect you to keep any of this from

Nora, Jake, but I wanted to get a word alone with you. Scarpella has no criminal history, no arrests. Maybe he's living out some revenge fantasy based around you two, maybe he's just trying to scare you, prove he's in control. Whatever his game, I don't want the son of a bitch getting anywhere close to Nora."

"He won't," I said grimly.

"Good. Make sure Nora gives you my number. I want you to be able to reach me in an emergency."

I nodded. "Will do, sir."

With a long, searching look, John nodded again. "You love her," he said after a long pause, "and you make her happy. That's all a father can ask for. Thank you for taking care of my girl, Jake."

"I couldn't do anything else," I replied.

It was that simple. I'd go to the ends of the Earth for her.

"She's been running a long time, looking for something, somewhere. I'm not even sure she knew what that was when she started out. Her place, her people. Trust isn't something that comes easy to her, never has been. I knew as soon as I saw you two together that she'd finally found it. And, as her father, I'll only tell you this once—if you break her heart or her spirit, I will absolutely break your knees."

I laughed and shook John's hand one last time. "I'd expect nothing less, sir. I promise you, she's safe with me."

Heart, body, and soul.

The only thing stronger than my newfound dedication to not letting down the man who would hopefully become my father-in-law was my commitment to loving Nora as best I could.

John grinned, his dark eyes glinting in the twilight. "I know. If anything else happens with Scarpella, I'd better hear it from you or Nora instead of from Roberts."

"She won't be leaving my sight for the foreseeable future, though she'll probably kick my ass sooner or later over it."

John gave me a wry smile. "She might, if she weren't head over heels for you, too."

It warmed me to hear her father say it—almost as much as hearing the words directly from Nora's lips, but not quite. If her affection was clear to someone like John Cassidy, then it must be true. I smiled a little and inclined my head in thanks.

"Have a good night, Jake." He winked as he got into the car.

"Have a good night," I murmured belatedly.

For a long moment after the Honda pulled away from the curb, I stared after it, thinking about what he'd said, then I hastened back to Nora's side.

Though I thought she might be eager to head home after the many hours of conversation and chaos that always made up family events for the Lincolns, she surprised me yet again with a tiny shake of her head when I asked if she wanted to go. We all lingered around Sam's little fire pit until well after dark. Eventually, Nora and I were sent off not only with hugs and boisterous farewells, but with huge containers of leftovers, too.

When we finally got into the quiet cab of my truck, Nora laid her head back against the seat and sighed.

"You have an amazing family," she said softly. "Like, fairy tale, picture perfect. Your parents are still so in love even after all this time. I've never experienced anything like it. It makes me feel . . ."

When she trailed off, I waited, watching her with a patient smile on my lips, until she drew a deep breath and continued.

"Hopeful. Like it's possible to find true happiness and seize it, hold onto it with everything you've got."

I took her hand and stroked the back of her knuckles with my thumb. "My parents have had their ups and downs, just like anybody else, but you're right. They're head over heels for each other. Their thirty-fifth anniversary was this past spring, that's why they ended up planning this extended vacation they've been on. You really didn't believe in happily ever after, did you?" I asked, lifting her hand to my lips and studying her expression in the dim interior of the truck.

The existence of true love was not something I'd ever doubted, but it was clear that was hardly the case for Nora. My heart broke for her, the younger version of her who hadn't known what was out there waiting for her, even as it swelled with my love for her and with pride for this remarkable woman who'd made it so far without all the little things that had helped me along the way.

She smiled a little, her expression caught somewhere between sadness and self-deprecation. "No, I definitely didn't.

Haven't. My mom was so unhappy. I don't even know if they were in love to start with, because for as long as I can remember, that's just how it was. He tried to be there for us as much as he could, but I'm not sure it was ever enough for her."

"I can't even begin to imagine what that was like for any of you." I wished I could think of something more to say, but she seemed to understand.

"Sometimes, I wonder if she was happy with Shawn, even for a short while, before it went downhill," she said quietly. "Or if she's happy now. I don't even know what her life is like. Am I a terrible daughter?"

When she buried her face in her hands, I slid across the seat and wrapped my arms around her. "Of course not. Not at all. I hope she found happiness, too, one way or another."

Though she wasn't crying, her shoulders trembled and I kept her tucked tightly against me as we waited for it to pass. In all honesty, I'd expected some kind of aftereffect from the evening. Her simple need to be held was far less dramatic than what I might have imagined. Nora was barely used to sharing her emotions with *me*, nevermind tolerating a prolonged visit with my entire family.

After another long moment, she rubbed her face with her hands and smiled weakly up at me. "Okay. Enough with the maudlin ponderings. Let's go home."

As promised, I took a short detour past my parents' house, a beautiful old Colonial that looked like a dollhouse. It wasn't until she finished exclaiming over it that Nora finally brought up how long I'd been gone while walking her father out.

"What did my dad say to you this time?" she asked. "Let me guess—he threatened to break your knees?"

I laughed. "Well, yes, that was thrown in there, but it seemed like just a token threat, a bit of an afterthought. I don't think his heart was in it." I sobered as I glanced over at her. "The guy from the bar is named Frank Scarpella. His friends said that after the wedding, he told them he was going to visit family. Apparently his family told Chief Roberts they haven't seen him. No priors or history of violence, so all we have is a name to put to the face."

Nora nodded. "I should probably be offended that he gave you the information instead of me, but since he also threatened your kneecaps, I guess I'll let it slide this time."

"You're a hell of a woman, you know that?"

"Yes," she replied simply. "You are truly blessed, Jake Lincoln."

I placed a hand on her knee, my warm, rough palm shifting against bare skin below the hem of her dress. "Oh, believe me, I know," I murmured.

She laughed. "You're a hell of a man, you know that?"

Her echo of my words was equal parts taunting and breathless as my thumb drew heated circles against her bare thigh. "A match made in heaven," I said, my voice low.

"I think you might just be right," she replied. "You know, your parents did a damn good job making you."

I grinned as I pulled into the driveway and shifted into park. "Wanna see just how good?" I asked, waggling my eyebrows at her.

"Yes," Nora said very primly, then hopped out of the truck before I could reply. She danced away when I tried to kiss her, kicked off her sandals while I armed the security system again, and ran upstairs barefoot.

I caught up to her in the bedroom, running my gaze over her flushed cheeks and twinkling eyes.

"Oh, hello," I said casually, but I slowly stalked toward her.

Instead of twirling out of reach again, this time she moved straight into my arms, offering her mouth up to me with a smile. "Hi," she replied, just before my lips covered hers.

There was something different about this kiss, something light and playful, carefree almost, like another one of those fragile glass walls around her heart had crumbled and been swept away like dust in the wind. I was content to follow her lead in this sweet, teasing dance, so I let her propel me toward the bed. When the edge of the mattress hit the back of my knees, I sat, drawing her down onto my lap.

Coherent thought had just about left my mind when Nora drew back and said, "So Sam and Casey are finally dating, it seems."

I blinked at her. "Huh. That's nice."

Then her mouth was on mine and I didn't bother thinking about anything other than how good she felt against me. Any interest in Sam and Casey's relationship, inevitable as it had always seemed to me, flew straight out of my head. All that was left was Nora—the taste of her lush lower lip between my teeth, the soft swell of her breasts against my chest, her heat pressing against the fly of my jeans.

When my palms slid up the outside of her thighs to cup her ass under the cotton skirt of her dress, I froze, my brain short-circuiting until I managed to assemble my thoughts back into some degree of coherence.

"You've been wearing that little black thong all night?" I asked hoarsely.

A mischievous smile lit her face even as she batted her lashes at me. "Of course I have. I did buy it just for special occasions, you know."

"Of course," I repeated, a groan rumbling through my chest. "I didn't realize meeting my parents counted as a special occasion, but I suppose I can see that. And you didn't tell me before because...?"

"Well, I thought you might be too distracted, silly." She trailed her lips along my jaw and I responded by kneading the soft, bare flesh that filled my palms. "Besides," she murmured against my ear, "my parental approval rating might have dropped if they saw the way you're looking at me right now."

"And how am I looking at you?"

Her hands tangled in my hair to tip my head back. "Like you're hungry," she said softly. "Starving, even. And definitely like you have some very explicit thoughts going through your lovely head."

I cupped her more firmly against me and stood just long enough to turn and lay her out on the bed. "I'm absolutely ravenous, and those thoughts are very, very explicit," I replied against her throat. Sitting back on my heels, I threw off my shirt and lifted the skirt of her dress to her hips with tantalizing slowness. When my lips brushed the top of her knee, she wiggled.

"Jake! That tickles," she gasped, then I let my tongue swirl along the inside of her thigh and the gasp turned into a moan.

"You have beautiful kneecaps," I said. I propped myself on my elbows and shot her a quick grin. "Your father did just threaten mine, so I think it's only fair to show yours some heartfelt appreciation. And now look. I discovered they're connected to these truly exquisite thighs, which I've decided deserve equal reverence."

All the air left her lungs in an audible rush as my mouth traveled along her skin. My hands slipped under her ass again, cupping the bare flesh in my palms as my lips grazed her hip bone. When my teeth caught the edge of the sheer black fabric, my name escaped her lips on a strangled, breathless whimper. I slid my hands upward, underneath the waistband, then drew them slowly down her legs, inch by agonizing inch.

"Should I stop?" I murmured, but she only tossed her head restlessly on the mattress.

As I crawled back up, I dropped hot, open-mouthed kisses from ankle to calf, from knee to sweet, softly rounded thigh. When she whimpered and let me spread her legs further, wide enough to fit my shoulders between them, I dipped my head to run my tongue along her center. She arched, her hips lifting of their own volition, and she gasped when I did it a second time.

"What was that?" I asked, drawing back to cock my head at her. "I'm afraid I couldn't hear you."

"Please," she whimpered, then my tongue rolled against her, teasing, circling, lapping at her until she was breathless and writhing beneath me.

I paused again to lift my head, eyebrows raised. "Please stop?" The way she wiggled was answer enough, but I waited for her to say it.

"Please don't ever stop or I might shrivel up and die," she groaned, arching violently against the teasing brush of my lips along her hip bone.

"Can't have that now."

I flashed her a devilish smirk before dropping my head again, then I set about showing her just how much I appreciated her.

Chapter Thirty-Two

NORA

I N THE THREE GLORIOUS days that followed, I learned what it felt like to be welcomed into a loving family. First, Sam, Casey, and Cheryl insisted on taking me shopping while "the boys," as Cheryl lovingly referred to Jake and Dave, worked on my car. Jake had even invited my dad over for the day, but he had a fishing trip planned with Chief Roberts. When Jake told me that, I gave a mock scowl and accused my father of reconnoitering with his Spruce Hill spy.

The next day was family brunch at Jake's childhood home—which, against my better judgment, included a brief but scorching makeout session in his old bedroom—followed by an impromptu trip to a family friend's vacant beach house on the lake.

To my surprise, my dad actually accepted the invitation to join us and enjoyed the day talking about boats and world travel with Jake's parents.

Meanwhile, Jake and Sam spent the afternoon trying to one-up each other with a mix of tragic town lore and ghostly tales about the Spruce Hill Lighthouse that stood proudly in the distance, supposedly home to a lost treasure. Much as I enjoyed the stories, I had to beg them to stop before the competition came to blows.

By the end of those few beautiful days, I was left with a fully stocked wardrobe, a hint of a sunburn, and a heart so overflowing I almost teared up just thinking about it.

That unexpected degree of happiness was why, when Jake walked me out of the house so I could meet Sam for coffee the next morning, finding my closer-to-good-as-new Baby covered in spray painted graffiti almost brought me to my knees.

My blood turned to ice as I stumbled against Jake's side, my fingers tensing into claws around his as he kept me standing. A harsh rasp filled my ears, but I couldn't tear my gaze from the car to see if it was coming from Jake.

The realization that it was my own strangled breathing hit me a second later.

All of the work Jake had put in, all the repairs I'd cooed over the other day, all of my pride and pleasure was obliterated by the tragic sight of almost every inch of my beloved car covered in neon orange and green paint.

"SLUT" was the clearest of the graffiti, written right across the windshield, but I spotted half a dozen more filthy names amidst the chaotic scribbles.

"Oh my god," I whispered, my grip on Jake's arm tightening just to keep myself upright.

When I started to crumble, Jake wrapped his arms around me and swore under his breath, far more creatively than whoever had done this to my car. He tucked my head against his chest to keep me from looking back at the neon mess of words.

"Don't touch anything," Jake warned, already on the phone with the police.

I barely processed his side of the phone call, though I heard the sharp edge of fury in his voice as he spoke. Even with my face hidden in his shirt and my eyes squeezed shut, the nasty words blinked like a fluorescent sign behind my eyelids. When Jake ended the call, he squeezed me tight and started murmuring reassurances that barely registered.

"All your hard work," I whispered into his shoulder. "All that effort."

With his hands on my shoulders, Jake pulled back to look me in the eyes, his expression fierce. "Don't even worry about that. Shh, it's not worth crying over, Nora. I'll fix her back up, good as new. Nothing to worry about, my love, I promise you I will fix everything."

I hadn't even realized I *was* crying, but silent tears streaked down my cheeks and soaked into Jake's shirt when he hugged me close again.

"My dad. He'll want to know, I have to call him."

Jake shook his head. "I'll text him, but Roberts said he'd call him on the way. It's okay. It's okay, Nora. I'm so sorry. I should have parked Baby in the garage."

A strangled laugh broke from my lips. "So he could spray dirty words on your beautiful truck instead? Or on the siding of poor Mr. Jenkin's garage?"

The question made us both look toward the apartment and I lifted my head.

"Is it possible either of the cameras might have caught whoever did this?" I asked, wiping at my wet cheeks.

"Let's check."

Jake pulled up the app on his phone and gave a tense smile when he saw that the camera by the apartment door happened to capture the front half of my car. He scrolled to the second feed, which covered the passenger side. Before he could look too far into the stored video clips, the chief's cruiser and my father's Honda pulled up out front in swift succession.

Roberts gave a low whistle as he took a walk around my little blue car. My dad strode straight to me first, looked me over carefully as though checking that none of my wounds were external, then he gave me a quick squeeze before joining the chief.

"Safe to assume you two didn't hear anything during the night?" Roberts asked.

Jake shook his head. "No, sir, but the cameras we installed at the apartment may have caught something. It looks like one camera angle shows the front of the car and the other one gets the front passenger door, at least. I didn't go through any of the recorded footage yet."

The chief nodded. "We'll take whatever you've got. Give me a timeline here, Jake. John said you were all out at the beach yesterday—what time did you get home?"

"Just after eight, I think," I said.

"What time did you head on to bed?"

Since I was sure my cheeks had gone fiercely pink and avoided looking toward my father, Jake answered for us. "Ah, just after eight, sir."

The chief gave Jake a knowing smile while my dad kept his eyes on the car, his jaw tense. He knew how much Baby meant to me.

Jake added, "We had breakfast and watched some TV this morning. I didn't even look out front. Nora had plans with my sister so I was just walking her out when we saw the damage. I called you first thing."

"Oh, no. Sam," I exclaimed. "I need to call her and cancel. I don't want her to show up and see Baby like this."

Jake kissed my temple. "Go on inside and give her a call, we'll be right here."

The three of them watched me walk back into Jake's house, though when I glanced back through the window next to the door, I saw them all huddled together like they were planning out football plays rather than discussing a stalker who seemed to be getting bolder by the day.

In the end, I sent Sam a text and waited for a reply to be sure she saw it. If I started relaying the detai_s aloud, I had the distinct feeling that I would fall apart again. I gave myself another minute to take a few deep breaths. then slipped back out the door in time to see Jake sigh heavily and rub a hand over his jaw. He must have felt my preser.ce, because he turned and held out one arm to tug me against his side again.

"This has gone far enough," my father mu:tered.

Roberts held up a hand. "Cassidy, let me do my job, would you? I understand everybody is on edge. My team will be out here in a few minutes to take photos, dust for prints. I'm going to set an unmarked car cruising by here around the clock, Jake. I'm sure I don't need to tell you to stick close to Nora and to let us know if you see anything even an inch out of place."

"Of course, Chief," Jake said grimly.

Roberts turned his gaze to the garage apartment with a thoughtful expression on his face. "You know, Cassidy, if Nora's staying with Jake, you could take the apartment, stay close in case of an emergency. Wouldn't hurt to have another set of eyes on things, and I know you can handle whatever comes your way."

"You really think that's necessary?" I asked softly.

My father didn't answer right away, just looked straight at me and Jake before sighing. "Under other circumstances, I wouldn't even consider it. I know neither one of you wants me hovering around while you're finding your feet. If you two would rather I not intrude like that, I'll respect your privacy, but I'm not much help out at the cabin if an emergency arises."

"I think it's a good idea," Jake said, squeezing my hand. "This guy is a coward—a show of force might be enough to scare him off."

I wasn't sure that was true, but it wasn't like Dad would be sleeping in the next room. With my father waiting for my agreement, I finally nodded. "Okay. I'll go get my key for you and give you the grand tour, if the chief doesn't mind?"

Roberts gave us the go ahead as Detective Hanson and her team arrived and got straight to work. We left Jake and the chief conversing in low tones as they reviewed footage from the security cameras. When I led my father up the sturdy stairs to the apartment, he paused to run his hand over the railing.

"Jake did all the work on this?" he asked.

I glanced over my shoulder and saw admiration written across his face. "Yes. Wait until you see inside, he did a beautiful job. His house is even more impressive, but it's not quite finished. He's been doing the renovations in his spare time."

My father seemed suitably impressed, not only with Jake's skill but with the fact that he had clearly poured his time and a great deal of love into something that wasn't his own, in a field that wasn't even his livelihood. Though I knew my father wished he could whisk me away from danger, even after I'd hit thirty, I also knew he was comforted by knowing I had Jake in my corner.

"I have a box at the back of the bedroom closet," I said, "and some clothes left in the drawers, but I can get that stuff out of here."

At that, my father turned and raised an eyebrow. "You sure travel light these days, Bear."

I shrugged, offering a rueful smile as I countered, "I can't really fit too much in Baby, so I've learned to declutter. It's very trendy these days, you know. Capsule wardrobe, minimalism."

"Oh, Nora," he said gently, squeezing my shoulders. He looked like wanted to say more but hadn't the faintest idea where to begin.

"It's just stuff, Dad," I whispered, then my hands covered my face as the tears slipped free again. "It's just stuff," I said again, sniffling. "Even Baby."

He hugged me tight to his chest. "I know how you love that car, Bear. I'll help Jake get her cleaned up. Everything's going to be just fine. I'm sorry I haven't been around for you as much as I should have."

It took another minute or two for me to regain my composure, but I finally scrubbed my hands over my cheeks and stepped back. "I always knew how to reach you, Dad."

He nodded, but he looked utterly unconvinced. "It's not the same. It was easier to just keep reminding myself that you're a grown woman who can handle herself. After your mother left...well. I should have been around more. If I could redo one thing in my life, it would be that. I'm sorry that I didn't make more of an effort."

"You're here now. I appreciate that." I gave him a wobbly smile. After a deep, steadying breath, I added, "I should get back out there."

"Nora," my father said quietly, "I know you've been on your own a long time and gotten used to taking care of everything by yourself, but you and Jake make a good team. Try to let him help you. It's okay to lean sometimes, especially when you're in love with somebody."

His gentle words almost spurred a fresh round of tears. I bit my lip hard until it passed, then nodded. "I really love him, Dad."

My father's smile was sweeter than I'd ever seen. "I know, Bear. I know."

Chapter Thirty-Three

NORA

WHEN DINNER TIME ROLLED around that evening, Baby was safely tucked away next to Jake's truck in the garage and my father had transferred himself and his things over to the apartment. While he nursed a beer alone above the garage, probably contemplating how his adult daughter could have chiseled down her entire life into a single box at the back of a closet, Jake and I were spooned together on the leather sofa, only half paying attention to the movie we'd chosen.

"Holding up okay?" Jake asked, rubbing his cheek against my hair.

Though I would fight anyone who went so far as to call me fragile, at least under almost any other circumstances, I felt a little too rigid after the morning's drama, almost brittle, like it wouldn't take much for me to fall apart.

Again.

As far as Jake was concerned, letting all those pent up emotions out was probably better than burying them inside—he'd told me that half a dozen times, in various ways. Now that we were cuddling, it finally felt like my body was loosening up again, albeit slowly. Those hidden feelings were now creeping back toward the surface, presenting a vulnerability I hated.

"I've been better." I swallowed the lump in my throat. "You really think we can get the paint off of Baby?"

His palm rubbed reassuringly up and down my arm. "I really do. We'll take good care of her."

For a stretch of time, I just burrowed in closer to Jake's body and let him soothe me without so much as a word. If I'd realized people could possess the ability to offer comfort with just their presence, just a warm, reassuring touch, would I have sought that out sooner? Or was it a unique attribute of the man spooned against my back?

Whatever the case might be, I didn't care—all that mattered was that I'd found him, he'd found me, and I wasn't alone anymore.

Once the chaos in my chest finally settled, I rolled slightly to look up at him. "Is it weird that my dad is next door?"

"Weird? Nah. If he could see into the Dude Lair or the bedroom, maybe," he said with a grin. "Fortunately for us, he's on the other side of the house. Besides, he promised me he wouldn't show up over here without texting one of us first."

My eyes widened. "Did he really?"

Jake laughed at my horrified expression. "Look, your dad clearly knows we're sleeping together and I'm assuming he doesn't want to risk seeing anything he'd regret for the rest of his life."

That assurance appeased me somewhat. I rolled over until I was facing him, careful not to knee him in the groin again, nestling in so my nose was barely an inch from his Adam's apple and he had to tug my hips tighter against him to keep me from falling off the couch.

"I love you, Jake Lincoln," I whispered.

"I love you, Nora Cassidy." As his lips brushed my forehead, I sighed, a soft puff of breath against the base of his throat, and he said, "I won't let anything happen to you, you know that, right?"

"I know you won't, and I won't let anything happen to you, either."

"Then we're safe as can be," he murmured into my hair.

"Today threw me for a loop, but you're more important to me than stuff, Jake. I love my car, but in the end, it's still just stuff. You're the only thing I really need. I just...I want you to know that."

I nodded against his chest for emphasis, but I knew he understood what I was saying. Carefully, with one arm already under me, Jake rolled so I was sprawled out on top of him, my mess of curls tumbling around both of our faces like a veil as I looked down at him. He tucked a strand behind my ear and rubbed his nose against mine.

"When they catch this guy—and they will, I have no doubt, because Scarpella is clearly an idiot—we are going to celebrate. And then I'm going to ask you to move in with me, for real this time. You don't have to say yes if you're not ready, but I'll ask you all the same. I thought you might appreciate some warning, so you can get used to the idea."

My lips curved, though I was sure Jake didn't miss the slight hitch of my breath. "I'll try to be ready to answer when you do. It'll take some heavy lifting to retrieve my last box and drawer of clothes, but I also already told my Dad I'd get that stuff out of the apartment."

"One whole box? That's all that's left over there?"

Though I rolled my eyes at the question, echoing my father's incredulity so closely, I countered it by kissing him before I laid my head back down on his chest. "Yes. My dad was similarly shocked, but that's all I've ever really needed. I always rented furnished apartments and grabbed anything else that was missing from thrift stores, then donated it when I moved again."

"Huh," he said, stroking my hair while he considered. "Nora, I think you might be the most low maintenance woman I've ever met. Probably the most low maintenance human being, period. As you can see, we have plenty of room here, so if you decide you want any so-called 'stuff' that I don't have, I wouldn't object. I've spent most of my time thinking about renovating, not decorating, but this awesome rug you picked out spoiled me. Now I find myself lusting after other cool stuff."

I laughed. "I'm sure I could come up with a few things you're missing. And Jake?"

"Yes, my love?"

A flutter rose up in my belly at the endearment. "Thank you."

Gently, Jake tugged a lock of my hair until I propped my chin on his sternum to look at him. "For what?"

Though my eyes were a little misty, I smiled. "For helping me find everything I'd been searching for."

THE NEXT MORNING, SAM and Casey arrived bearing bags and boxes of muffins, donuts, and pastries, along with enough coffee for a small army. My father joined us, at Sam's insistence, and we spent nearly an hour on Jake's deck enjoying a leisurely breakfast. It felt blessedly normal, drinking coffee with friends and family, enjoying the warmth of companion-ship along with that of the morning sun on our faces.

There were a few moments when my heart clenched, when I realized how much these people all meant to me, but Jake steadied me with a squeeze or a chaste brush of lips or even just a glance, showing me how deeply he understood what was going on in my head.

Afterward, Jake, my dad, and Casey, who gleefully in-formed me that she was even better under the hood than

Jake—prompting a burst of laughter from me and a brilliant blush from Sam—set out to clean up my car. The Lincoln twins, damn their dimples, both firmly informed me that it would be better for me to wait to see the finished product instead of bearing witness to the removal process. It was swiftly seconded by my father, so I resigned myself to staying out of their way.

Once the others had disappeared to the garage, Sam and I remained on the deck with our coffee. For the first time since I'd met her, Jake's twin was dressed down, clad in fitted jeans with an old concert tee knotted at one hip. Apparently cleaning up graffiti, even by proxy, called for casual clothes. I didn't feel quite so bad about my denim cut-offs and tank today, since I fit in so well with the rest of them.

"I have a gift for you," she said, passing me a tiny chiffon bag covered in silver stars.

"A gift? For what?" I untied the ribbons and poured the contents into my palm, my breath catching when I saw it was a tiny mermaid tail pendant to match the one around her neck.

She winked at me. "Consider it an official welcome into the family."

It took several seconds for me to get control of the emotions rollicking through my chest, but when I raised teary eyes to meet her gaze, she gave a gentle smile and shook her head to stave off a protest. Then she leaned over and took it from my hands to clasp it around my neck.

"Perfect," she whispered.

I gave a shaky laugh. "Thank you, Sam."

"I always wanted a sister." She grinned. "So now it's mermaid-official."

"Can't get much more official than that. Now, if you're going to hold me hostage, you'll have to fess up. What's the deal with you and Casey? I need juicy details to keep my mind off my lovely stalker," I insisted, in desperate need of distraction.

Sam gave a dramatic sigh, but her expression was serene. "We've been friends for a long time, and I always thought she was more like a sister to me than anything. Or maybe I just picked up on that being the way Jake felt about her and internalized it."

"He said he was relieved to learn she wasn't into guys, so he couldn't ruin their friendship."

"Yeah," she said, laughing. "Once, right after Casey came out in high school, Jake told me he thought she was into me, but I didn't really believe it. Even if it was true, it's so easy to ruin friendships with high school relationships, you know? Then all of a sudden, something changed. I don't know exactly how or when or why. She just makes me ridiculously happy."

"Then I'm happy for you," I said, but I raised a brow. "You were hitting on me at the cafe that day, but it sounded like you were already planning to make a play for Casey even then. What would you have done if I'd taken you up on it?"

"Oh, I was definitely hitting on you," Sam admitted freely. The dimple in her cheek appeared when she laughed and shrugged her shoulders. "Things hadn't changed yet between us, so I was still technically unattached. Jake and I made a twin pact when we were teenagers, vowing never to fight over partners, but he didn't seem to be laying claim too quickly when you first got here."

"I think if he'd done anything remotely like 'laying claim,' I would've punched him in the throat."

"You are pretty fierce. It's hot."

I snorted a laugh. "Thanks."

"But anyway, it was clear you weren't looking for long-term at the time, so believe me, Nora dear, we could have had a beautiful little fling. I guess it all worked out for the best, though, hmm?"

I laughed and raised my coffee cup in toast. "To new beginnings."

Sam touched her cup to mine. "Hell yes. I don't suppose my brother has asked you to marry him yet?"

"Marry him," I repeated, blinking slowly as my smile fell away. "No. I mean, he mentioned officially moving in with him after this mess is over, but marriage is...marriage is a big step."

"One that clearly scares the crap out of you."

Though I didn't respond right away, it wasn't really a question. Sam didn't look at all surprised by my reaction, either. In fact, her patient expression looked a little too much like Jake's at that moment, enough that I had to force my gaze away. I stayed silent for a long moment, staring off toward the fishless koi pond, then nodded.

"Yes, it does. I don't—I didn't grow up with a family like yours, Sam. It wasn't the best example of a loving marriage.

Before meeting your parents, I would have told you happily ever after was nothing but a fairy tale."

Sam laid a hand on my arm. "Hey," she said gently, "I'm not saying he's going to pop the question tomorrow. Jake knows you, Nora, better than anybody, I would guess, and he's the most patient person I've ever met. He'll wait until you're ready to say yes before he ever decides to ask something like that."

With a shuddering breath, I nodded. "I think you're right."

"But the way he looks at you, my god. Hot enough to catch fire!"

With a weak laugh, I scrubbed my hands over my heated cheeks. "Must run in the family. I saw how you and Casey were eyeing each other at the barbecue."

She waved that away, refusing to accept the change of subject. "I swear I didn't mean to scare you, Nora, I was only curious. Things seem to be getting pretty serious between you. I always wished I had a sister instead of that big lout, and I can't think of anyone I'd rather call sister than you. I'm sorry if I upset you."

A tiny smile tugged at my lips, though my eyes glistened with tears at Sam's heartfelt declaration. "It's fine. I just really hadn't thought that far ahead yet. I'm beyond happy and I'm hopelessly in love with him and I like how things are. It's been a long time since I considered anything beyond the next few months."

"You two will find your way. And I will definitely enjoy finding mine with Casey." She bounced her eyebrows at me and grinned.

By silent agreement, we moved onto less fraught topics, including Sam's degree in marketing, her love of real estate, and the history of The Mermaid—all things that required little contribution from me, since my brain was stuck on the terrifying idea of marriage. Still, I loved watching Sam talk, all enthusiastic hand gestures and animated expressions, and I found myself appreciating more and more the way she was able to introduce a topic then dance away before I became uncomfortable.

It had to be a family trait. These twins had stellar genes and a loving upbringing; both of those were abundantly evident in their personalities.

Sometime just after noon, Jake appeared from around the side of the house and insisted that I close my eyes. He led me carefully down the stairs of the deck and along the driveway, gave Sam a sharp warning when she gasped aloud, and dropped a light kiss to the side of my neck before saying, "Okay, you can look now."

Baby shimmered in the sun, completely devoid of spray paint. Even the rust patches marring the original paint job couldn't detract from the car's beauty in my eyes. I moved forward as if in a trance and ran my hands over the shining hood with a sigh that sent Sam and Casey into a fit of laughter.

Maybe it was ridiculous to be so attached to this little car, but I was. She'd seen me through a dozen new places, including bringing me here.

Bringing me home.

Jake never even questioned my love for Baby, though he might tease me occasionally, and now he had washed away all that ugliness with his own hands, leaving behind something that was close enough to beautiful to make my eyes fill with tears.

"You'd think Jake bought her a Porsche," Sam said to Casey in a whisper just loud enough for me to hear.

"A Porsche can't compare to my Baby," I replied, then I threw myself into Jake's arms and covered his face in kisses. "Thank you, thank you, thank you."

He laughed softly against my ear as he lifted me off my feet. "You're welcome. I told you she'd be good as new. Probably better, really, because she wasn't much of a looker before. I guess she's not so bad now that she's shiny and clean."

Over Jake's shoulder, I smiled at Casey and my father. "Thank you both. I didn't think it was possible, but Baby looks wonderful."

Sam snorted in disbelief, but my dad gave me a fond smile. "Yes, she does. And I agree with Jake, she most definitely looks better than when you bought that pile of junk."

"She can hear you, you know." I let go of Jake to scowl at my father while I patted the car affectionately. "But since you did such a good job cleaning her up, I'm sure she'll forgive you."

Sam hooked her arm through Casey's and said, "C'mon, then, our work here is done. Let's get out of their hair so Nora can thank Jake properly."

Though Jake glared at her and my cheeks flushed hot, Sam merely winked, bid goodbye to us all, and strolled down the driveway to her Mustang with Casey.

Even my father couldn't help but smile. "Right, well. I'll be off, too. Enjoy your day, kids, and make sure you keep those cars parked in the garage for the time being."

I gave my father a hug, then Jake clasped his hand. While he headed back toward the apartment, I gave Baby another adoring look.

"I'd be jealous of that expression, if I hadn't been on the receiving end of so many similar ones in the past week," he teased, but he slipped an arm around my waist and pressed a kiss to my temple.

"You guys really did an amazing job," I said, smiling up at him.

"We did, didn't we? Ready to move her back to the garage?"

I wrinkled my nose at him and joked, "Nobody puts Baby in a corner."

Jake laughed, tossing me the keys. I slid behind the wheel and ran my hands lovingly over the dashboard. Baby might not be the picture of vehicular beauty, but the stark contrast between her now-gleaming exterior and the angry insults we'd found the day before made my heart lighter.

However, it was being surrounded and cared for by this little circle I'd begun to think of as family that filled my heart until I thought it might float right out of my chest.

Jake closed the garage door once Baby was safely parked beside his truck. "I could use a nice cold drink," he said after pulling me in for a thorough kiss.

"You might want some lunch, too, or at least one of the leftover muffins."

With a slow, devastating smile, Jake lifted a brow. "Oh? Why would I need such fortification, my darling Nora?"

"Because," I drawled as I handed him a soda bottle, "I think Sam was spot on. I intend to show you just how much I appreciate your hard work this morning."

Jake's blue gaze stayed intently on my face as he set the Coke aside and placed his hands firmly on my hips. "In that case, sustenance can wait."

My laughter swiftly gave way to breathless surrender as we shoved that ugliness even deeper into the recesses of our minds.

Chapter Thirty-Four

NORA

As afternoon bled into evening, I finally told Jake I did actually need to get some work done. He reluctantly agreed, admitting that he needed to update The Mermaid's accounts and prepare some supply orders, no matter what else he'd rather be doing with me, so we ended up sitting at opposite ends of the leather sofa with our laptops perched on our knees.

By now, I knew him—knew us both—well enough to make him stay out of arm's reach. With an amused snort, Jake agreed. Right about now, I was sure he was sorely regretting not being able to reach over and touch me without being obvious about it.

I regretted it, myself.

Though I was usually capable of ignoring him as my fingers moved quickly over the keyboard, Jake spent at least as much of our work time surreptitiously watching me as he spent doing any of his own work. After nearly two hours. I paused long enough to rub the back of my neck and caught him staring at me—again.

I tried to look stern, I couldn't quite hide a smile as I raised a brow in question.

"What kinds of things do you translate?" he asked, lacing his fingers behind his head. We'd spoken a few times about my job previously, but with everything else going on, he hadn't asked for very many details.

I leaned back and tucked my legs underneath me as I flexed my fingers back and forth to loosen them up. "A lot of different stuff, but my favorite thing to translate is probably novels."

His eyes widened. "Like, entire books? That sounds like a hell of a lot of work."

"Yes," I replied, my lips curving at his surprise. "It's a ton of work, but they're definitely the most fun of the projects I take on. With a book, it's not just about converting one language to another, it's about capturing the same feel, the voice and intention of the writer, creating the right atmosphere. It's way more of a challenge, but it's also by far the most satisfying for me."

Jake watched me intently, and I flushed. Even if he was interrupting my actual work by talking about it, I was too caught up in sharing the information to mind.

"Why are you looking at me like that?"

"I like seeing you this way."

I bit my lip. "What way?"

"Excited. Enchanting. Eyes all lit up, like you could talk about this all day. It's beautiful, Nora." He grinned and I had to fight the urge not to shift toward him on the couch. "What kind of books do you translate?"

"A huge mix of things. I intentionally try to keep it varied, just to make sure it doesn't get stale. I've done mysteries, romance, a couple horror, which aren't my favorite thing to read but can be fun to work on. Some children's books. Novels are heavy and time-intensive, so doing smaller projects in between is like a palate cleanser. Picture books are good for that, but I also do articles, documents, sometimes even instruction manuals." Something in Jake's expression made me falter and ask, "Now why are you looking at me like *that*?"

He shook his head, smiling. "You're amazing, that's all."

"Whatever," I mumbled, ducking my head.

He set aside his laptop and held out a hand. "Ready for a break yet?"

I sighed. "I have just a few pages left on this, and knowing how your 'breaks' tend to unfold, I should probably get this done before I let you distract me, tempting as it is."

The smirk on his face told me I'd guessed exactly what kind of break he had in mind. "Okay, you caught me," he drawled, "so how about a compromise? I'll run this stuff over to The Mermaid, place a few quick supply orders, and bring back some dinner for us while you finish up?"

"I would never say no to stuffed mushrooms and strawberry shortcake. Think you can make that happen, hotshot?"

Jake winked and leaned over to kiss me, letting his mouth linger on mine until I finally pushed him firmly away. "I happen to have an in with the owners, so that shouldn't be a problem. I'll lock the door and turn on the alarm. Text if you need me for anything. Or if you get lonely and want some hot selfies to keep you company."

"I will." I laughed, batting away the hand he tried to sneak up my leg. "Go on, Lincoln, get out of here. It's broad daylight, and Dad said he's back at the apartment now. I'll be perfectly fine on my own."

I lifted my face for one last kiss before Jake grabbed his ledgers and laptop and left me alone in the quiet house. For a moment, I simply listened to the sound of silence, then I turned my focus back to the computer screen. If I could finish this project before he got home, we would have the entire evening free.

That prospect would definitely make my current sacrifice worthwhile, though I gave serious consideration to requesting one of Jake's so-called "hot selfies."

The words on the screen swirled around me in a linguistic cloud as I worked. Sometimes the work *was* heavy and time-consuming, but even so, I loved it. And, if I did say so myself, I was good at my job. With the motivation of dinner, dessert, and *dessert* dangling before me, I managed to fly through the remaining pages. Once it was done, I sat back with a satisfied sigh.

"And with time to spare," I said aloud, cracking my aching knuckles.

The project would need another read-through, but the hard part was finished and I was well ahead of my deadline, so I closed the laptop and set it on the coffee table. Briefly, I debated taking a hot shower before Jake returned, but I hadn't paid enough attention to the time when he left and knew that if he got home while I was showering, dinner would end up cold before we got to it.

Texting him to ask was out of the question—if he thought there was a chance of coming home to find me naked and dripping, he would definitely take advantage of it.

The thought made me smile as I stood and stretched out my back. My gaze traveled across the Dude Lair before I wandered aimlessly toward the kitchen, cocking my head from side to side as I considered what decorative touches might be missing. A nice lamp, maybe, to put at the end of the leather sofa. Some artwork for the walls, reminiscent of the kind that hung at the inn.

I'd never put any effort into personal touches, but the thought of adding some to Jake's house filled me with an odd sense of longing.

I'm going to ask you to move in with me, for real.

His words wafted around me while I tried to imagine myself living with him. He'd asked me to help him with finishing the guest bedroom renovations upstairs, but it was still hard for me to picture placing my own stamp on things. It had been a long time since I'd done that even to my own previous homes.

Then I closed my eyes and thought about paint colors, and suddenly it wasn't so difficult to imagine anymore. How did he know just how to reel me in without ever exerting any pressure? The man certainly had a knack for drawing out the dreams I didn't realize I was even harboring somewhere deep in my heart.

I turned, intending to set the table for Jake's return, and caught sight of something on one of the deck chairs.

Probably just a leftover wrapper from this morning's break-fast with the gang, I told myself as I moved to the French doors to squint at it through the glass. Though my pulse kicked into high gear as soon as I laid my hand on the door handle, I forced myself to take deep, calming breaths.

"After all this time, you're still afraid of your own stupid shadow," I muttered, annoyed with my response.

I'd come too far to let myself fall back into those timid habits that made me avoid Jake when I first arrived in Spruce Hill. The afternoon was still bright and I could see the entire yard from where I stood. There was no reason not to go clean up a coffee shop wrapper that had been left behind. The deck was in full view of the windows of the garage apartment, so if I screamed, my father would surely come running.

Jake had shown me how to disarm the security system, so I typed in the code and waited for it to blink green before I went out onto the deck, leaving the door open behind me. The heat of the day felt good after sitting in the air conditioned house for so long. I let my gaze dart once more across the backyard, then bent to pick up the paper and froze before my fingers made contact with it.

It wasn't a wrapper, I realized numbly.

On the deck chair sat the notebook that disappeared from my coffee table after the break-in, with a forget-me-not laid carefully on top. I leaned down to look closer and saw that it had been flipped back to one of the first pages I'd used nearly a year ago, a quick outline listing the salient plot points of the Spanish thriller I'd been translating into English.

Break-in.

Threats.

Vandalism.

Revenge.

The first three were crossed out in heavy black marker, but the last was circled in red.

"Shit!" I whispered, grabbing the notebook even as I reached into my pocket for my phone. The flower fluttered down to land at my feet. Jake answered on the first ring, but I didn't wait for his hello before I said, "He was here, Jake. On the deck."

"I'm leaving right now. Stay on the phone with me. I'll have Bea call 911, tell them to get over to my place right away. Are you still out on the deck? Get inside now!"

"I thought it was just trash," I said as I turned back toward the open door. "It's my notebook, apparently he was using some old translation notes as a freaking guidebook. There was no one out here, I checked before I turned off the alarm, so I—"

The phone clattered to the deck as a hand fisted in my hair, yanking it tight right at the scalp. Tears blurred my vision, but before I could react, the cold edge of a blade pressed against my throat and held me frozen in place. Jake's faint, frantic voice drifted upward from my phone until a low, sinister hiss swept over my skin like ice water.

"Miss me?" he asked, his breath hot against my ear.

With a sharp jerk that sent tears spilling over onto my cheeks, my head was forced far enough back to see a malevolent leer only inches from my face.

Shawn.

"Listen very carefully. You're going to pick it up so I can talk to your boyfriend. Slow and steady. I wouldn't want this knife to slip into your pretty neck, Nora."

At first, my only coherent thought was that he and Frank Scarpella looked like funhouse mirror images. It was no wonder I'd mistaken them for one another, but the twisted light in Shawn's eyes was what really set them apart.

I was right. Frank Scarpella was just a man, but Shawn Milton was a monster.

With the blade at my throat guiding me downward, I crouched, shaking, and picked up the phone. "Jake?" I whimpered.

"Ah, ah, ah. That's not what we're doing. Hit the speaker button. Can you hear me, bartender?" Shawn taunted.

"I hear you," Jake growled in reply. A door slammed in the background like he was leaving his office in a rush. "Let me talk to her."

"I suggest you head home to your woman without contacting the police, or you'll make me very angry. So angry that I'm afraid little Nora won't survive it. If you call the police, she dies. On the other hand, if you arrive alone, I'll give you the chance to say goodbye. Do you understand? Say yes or no, Mr. Lincoln, I'm quite busy at the moment."

"Yes, I understand—"

Shawn dropped the phone and used his booted foot to kick it into the shrubs on the other side of the deck.

I gritted my teeth against a wave of nausea, though I couldn't tell if it was from the pain in my scalp or the feel of his body against my back. My brain scrambled at lightning speed as I tried to decide if it was better to talk or keep quiet, torn between wishing Jake would get here quickly and hoping he'd stay away, because I knew Shawn intended to kill us both.

Between the painful grip on my hair and the knife at my throat, I was at a loss as to how to get out of this on my own without risking serious injury.

Shawn didn't seem to expect a response, since he continued talking as he half dragged, half shoved me toward the house. "You thought you were so smart, didn't you, convincing your loving mommy to block me from her accounts? That was a stupid move, Nora, but now you're going to make it up to me. It's the least you can do."

"Please," I gasped, then clenched my jaw to stop myself from begging.

I stumbled over the lip of the doorframe and felt the tip of the knife prick my skin. A tiny, hot bead of blood welled up before trickling slowly down toward my collarbone.

I'd taken down Scarpella at The Mermaid. Surely I could fight my way free of Shawn.

Words my father had spoken long ago echoed in my head. *Stay calm and wait for the right opportunity, Bear.*

"Oh, you'll say please, all right." Shawn laughed, low and ugly, as he dragged me through the kitchen.

The French doors were still wide open behind us and I nearly screamed, wondering if my father would hear me. Before I could open my mouth, Shawn slammed me against the kitchen island, the edge of the counter striking me solidly in the stomach and forcing the air from my lungs in a painful rush.

Without loosening his grip on my hair or the knife, he pressed in close against my back, close enough that his face brushed my ear. I almost gagged again.

"Do anything stupid and I'll gut you like a fish. Then when your little boyfriend gets home, he won't have you there to defend him, will he?"

For a long moment, he kept me pinned there, the edge of the countertop digging painfully against the bottom of my ribcage. My right arm was trapped against my body by his, but my left was free. I closed my eyes against the sting of fresh tears and tried to calm my frantic heartbeat enough to figure out what the hell to do.

"I was there that night, at your boyfriend's restaurant," he rasped against my ear. "I saw that guy who grabbed you—could've been my twin, huh? The way you flipped out on him, it was because he looked like me, wasn't it?"

"Yes." A shudder wracked my body.

"I couldn't have planned it better myself. He was a perfect scapegoat. Once he was out of the way, I could toy with you to my heart's content and no one would think it wasn't that loser with a grudge against you and your boyfriend."

My body jerked, but there was nowhere to go. "What did you do to him?"

"Let's just say Barney Fife at this hick town's police department won't ever find his body," Shawn replied.

I closed my eyes, wishing I'd done a million things different—that I hadn't brushed off the resemblance between Shawn and Scarpella, that I'd told my father and the police everything from the start, that I'd seen the fucking *truth* right there in front of my eyes.

Maybe if I had, I wouldn't be in this mess.

Then he yanked my head back again, baring my throat to the bite of the blade, and forced me to look at him. I tried to focus on his features, to find some evidence of compassion or kindness I might be able to reach, but there was nothing except cold, hard fury.

"I had to abandon all my plans because of you, did you know that? One more con after your sweet mommy and I would've been set to disappear, but you just had to fuck it up. After you and your boyfriend pay for that, your father is next. He's the one who tracked me down, set investigators after me so I had to go into hiding instead of living the good life. Oh, he's going to pay most of all. I can't wait for him to find his little girl after I finish here."

Though I was sorely tempted to throw out a sarcastic reply about my father kicking his ass, my vocal chords were frozen in fear. I tried to look contrite, but the tears rolling down my cheeks only seemed to excite him. Even though it did nothing to loosen his grip, I managed to grab onto his forearm at my throat without him stabbing me. It was pathetic, but I would take what I could get.

"Now, we're going to go upstairs and wait until your boyfriend shows up. He's going to watch while you make it up to me for your little stunt."

As he wrenched me away from the island and started to shove me down the hall to the stairs, I stumbled again, but my grip on his arm prevented the blade from slicing into my neck. He kept up a steady stream of curses as he forced me to my feet.

I knew, as clearly as I'd known anything in my entire life, that if I let him drag me up the stairs, that was it.

Not only would my life be over—just when it was finally starting—but so would Jake's.

That thought gave me the strength to start struggling. I couldn't do anything about his hold on my hair, but I was confident I might be able to get the knife away from my throat, if I was careful.

Halfway between the kitchen and the front door, I pretended to trip, propelling us into a little side table. Shawn's hold floundered when his foot caught on the table leg, giving me an opening to wedge my hand further between his forearm and my neck.

Just as I was about to yank his arm far enough forward to bite down, the front door burst open and suddenly Jake was there, barely six feet away, looking strong and furious and so beautiful I would've wept at the sight of him if I hadn't already had silent tears running down my cheeks. His chest heaved as though he'd run all the way here.

"Let her go."

Though his jaw was tight, his demeanor was calm until he took in the sight of my tear-stained cheeks, then I felt waves of rage emanating from him. When his gaze hit the drop of blood pooling at my collarbone, his eyes darkened with fury for a split second before he raised his hands to show Shawn he was unarmed.

"Let her go and we can work this out."

"Work it out," Shawn scoffed. "The only thing you'll be working out is whether there's enough left of this bitch for you to identify after I'm done. Close that door and put your hands behind your head, or I'll start slicing into her pretty flesh. We're going to take a little walk upstairs. You'll lead the way, and if you try anything, she'll be the one to pay for it."

Jake lowered his hands and curled them into fists. With the interruption from the side table gone, all I needed was a distraction, just enough for Shawn to either move the knife or let go of my hair, and I could take him down. I wondered if Jake would be able to see the thought, either in my eyes or my expression, but he looked nearly as terrified as I felt.

Before he even moved to close the door, Shawn tipped my head back again with his death grip on my hair. He kept his cold eyes on Jake's face as he ran the flat of the blade down my throat, over the swell of my breast, landing just above the neckline of my tank top. I could have sworn I saw Jake's agonized gaze flicker to the kitchen behind me and wondered what the hell he was looking at, but it was back on me so fast I thought I imagined it.

Then the tip of the knife pressed hard and dragged along my skin, tearing a sharp cry of pain from my throat.

Somewhere between the cold metal of the blade and the warm blood welling up from the shallow cut, I saw Jake nod and threw myself into action. I brought my heel down on the arch of Shawn's foot, drove my free elbow back into his stomach, and then heard Jake's fist slam into Shawn's nose, driving him backward with a sickening crunch.

The knife clattered to the floor as his hands left my body so abruptly that I stumbled forward. Jake swooped in to grab me before I fell, clasping me tight to his chest, but a distinctive buzz and the thud of Shawn hitting the tiles sent my gaze flying back toward the kitchen.

Like a grim avenging angel, my father stared back at us, holding a taser in one hand.

"Get Nora outside," he ordered as he knelt down beside Shawn.

Jake didn't need to be told twice. His arms wrapped tightly around me as we rushed out onto the front porch and down the walk. When we reached the driveway, he turned me to face him, searching my features frantically before his gaze dropped to my wounds.

"You're bleeding," he whispered. Not only that, I was shaking so hard my teeth were chattering, so he pulled me back against his chest, tucking my face into his neck. "Oh, Christ. I'm so sorry, Nora. So, so sorry."

"It wasn't your fault. I thought he was going to kill you." My head moved from side to side against him as a choked sob escaped my throat.

Jake drew back to look at me incredulously, though he didn't let go of me. Even if he'd wanted to, my fingers were clenched in his shirt. I couldn't let go of him, not yet. Not ever.

"Kill *me?* You're the one bleeding, honey. I shouldn't have left. I should never have left you alone, not until that bastard was in police custody." His voice broke when he said, "That wasn't Scarpella."

"It was Shawn," I whispered. "He wanted to kill us all."

The trembling had nearly stopped, but he yanked me back against him, ignoring the blood that smeared across his white shirt. I smoothed my hands across the stained fabric and shook my head again. What felt like a lifetime in there must have been only a few minutes, just enough time for Jake to speed home from The Mermaid.

"It's okay. We're okay. I'm fine, Jake."

The words tumbled out of me like a chant, like a prayer. He looked close to tears himself, so I snaked my arms around his middle.

"We're okay," I whispered again, as though if I said it enough times, it might finally sink in.

"We're okay," he murmured into my hair. Then he gave a hoarse, shaky laugh. "Jesus Christ, Nora, your dad really does have a taser."

Then we were both laughing, crying, kissing, clinging tightly to one another as the riot of emotions paraded through us. Three police cars with flashing lights pulled up out front just as my father marched Milton out of the house, his hands bound behind him with what looked like a dishcloth. Chief Roberts took one look at the three of us, narrowed his eyes at the blood streaking across my skin and Jake's shirt, and passed Milton to Detective Hanson for arrest.

"I've got an ambulance on the way," he said with a nod toward me. "You folks up for giving statements?"

All of us nodded, but I frowned and said, "I don't need an ambulance. It's only a scratch."

Three pairs of eyes stared me down.

Neither my father nor Jake gave an inch no matter how I protested, so I threw up my hands and agreed to let an EMT clean me up while the two of them gave their statements. Reluctantly, Jake handed me off into my father's arms while he went inside with Chief Roberts. When the ambulance pulled up and Casey hopped out of the passenger seat, I narrowed my eyes at her, even though part of me was glad not to have to face another stranger right now.

"Don't shoot the messenger, I'm just doing my job," Casey said with a wink, then her expression sobered as she glanced toward the house. "Everyone okay?"

I nodded. "Jake's inside talking to the police, but they insisted I get checked out first. It's really just a scratch," I said stubbornly, but my dad made a sound of disagreement.

"Let the professional look you over. If she says it's just a scratch, we'll back off." He pressed his lips to the top of my head and gave me one last squeeze. "I'll be inside if you need me."

Though I managed a smile before he headed toward the house, it faded once his back was turned. I cocked my head as Casey threw open the doors at the back of the ambulance and gestured for me to sit. "I didn't know you were an EMT."

"Yes ma'am. Sam dropped me off at home after we left here earlier so I could head in for my shift. I can't say I expected to be back so soon, though."

There was no mistaking the relief in Casey's hazel eyes as she looked me over, even underneath her suddenly professional demeanor. She pulled on a fresh pair of gloves and gently wiped away the blood from my neck before dabbing at it with antiseptic.

"This morning feels like a lifetime ago." I flinched when she moved to the cut across my chest. "Shit, that stings."

Casey gave me an apologetic smile, but there was no mistaking the hard edge that appeared in those hazel eyes. When I raised a brow in question, she shrugged a shoulder and said, "You're one of us now. We take care of our own. And Jake might actually kick my ass for touching your boob, so it's a double whammy of annoyance. None of which is directed at you, of course."

I laughed, though I hadn't felt like there was any humor left inside me even a second ago. "Of course. Don't look now, but he's on his way over here. I'll try to keep him from berating you for groping me," I offered. My gaze locked with Jake's and the smile on my lips widened a little.

"Hey," Jake said softly as he sat beside me. "I see you're in good hands over here." His arm slid around my shoulders and he pressed a kiss to my temple.

"The cut isn't very deep, so you don't need stitches, but that's a sensitive area. Watch for signs of infection, keep it clean, and take it easy for a few days," Casey said, leveling a pointed look at Jake.

He grinned until his gaze dropped to my chest, then his jaw clenched ever so slightly. I caught the flash of lingering fear in his eyes and leaned my head close to his as Casey taped a square of gauze across the wound. Jake's arm, strong and supportive, tightened around me when I winced slightly.

After dabbing once more at the tiny cut on my neck, Casey added, "This one's already scabbing over, so I'll just put a little bandage on it. Make sure you keep it clean, smear a bit of this on it a few times a day." She applied the adhesive bandage and handed us a few tiny sample packs of antibiotic ointment.

Jake clasped her hand in gratitude and Casey pulled him into a swift hug. "Thank you, Casey," he said quietly.

He looked exhausted, as though fear had etched lines of weariness into his skin. With our arms around one another, Jake and I stood to let Casey close the doors of the ambulance. Before leaving, she set a hand on each of our shoulders and squeezed.

"Take care of each other," she told us, "and for god's sake, text your family if you don't want them all rushing over here. Sam's going to want to hear it from you, not me. I'll talk to you tomorrow, but if you need anything, just let me know. We're here for you. For both of you."

My eyes filled with tears of a different kind as I nodded my thanks, then we stood together at the end of the driveway to watch the ambulance pull away from the curb.

You're one of us now. We take care of our own. We're here for you.

It was like a litany of love, tangling around my heart like vines, blooming like the sweetest flower in my chest.

"Are you ready to talk to the chief?" Jake asked.

I could barely stand the thought of letting go of him, but the sooner I gave my statement, the sooner this nightmare would be over. "Yes. Milton is gone?"

"Carted away to be locked up. Good riddance," he muttered.

Before we returned to the house, I buried my face against his neck. "I ruined your shirt," I mumbled.

His soft laughter steadied me enough to draw back, then he cupped my face in his hands and gazed tenderly down at me. "I have others. You're really okay?"

I nuzzled my cheek against his palm. "I'm really okay, Jake. I promise."

"Nora, I'm ready for you," the chief called from the front door.

Jake walked me over to the porch, pressed a warm kiss to my forehead, then sat down on the steps next to my father as I went inside with Chief Roberts.

It was time to lay this nightmare to rest.

Chapter Thirty-Five

JAKE

A FLURRY OF EMOTIONS crackled through my body as John and I stared out toward the quiet street. My gaze landed on the spot where Nora's car stalled the day she arrived in town—it felt like a million years ago, but that memory soothed my jittery nerves, at least a little.

Several long minutes passed before I felt steady enough to say, "I don't even know how to thank you."

John settled his hand on my shoulder. "You don't have to thank me. I should've tracked that bastard down years ago. This is on me."

I didn't agree with that, but I wasn't sure there were any words that could convince him otherwise. John let out a harsh breath and scrubbed a hand over his jaw.

"I should have been there for her after her mother walked away, instead of letting her gallivant all over the country. but I let my own pain get in the way. I buried my head in the sand instead of making sure she was okay."

"Do you really think Nora would let you stop her from gallivanting?" I asked.

A startled laugh burst from his lips. "No, I guess not. I saw your face in there, Jake. If there had been any doubt in my mind that you love her—and believe me, there wasn't—that would've been enough to convince me."

"She's everything to me." The quiet admission hung in the air between us.

"You've done more for her in the short time she's known you than I did in thirty years. You just promise me you'll keep on loving her, and the rest will work itself out."

Though my heart squeezed painfully, I nodded. "Yes, sir, that I can promise."

We fell silent again until Roberts came up behind us and cleared his throat. "We're all finished here. You two car go on back inside."

John stood and shook Roberts' hand. They exchanged a look, then spoke in an undertone so low I couldn't make out any of the conversation before Roberts clapped him on the back and started down the steps.

When Nora appeared in the doorway, John hugged her close and kissed her forehead. "I'm going to head home, let you two settle in. Call me if you need anything, all right?"

Nora tightened her arms around him before she took a step back, her glance flitting over the holstered taser at his hip. "Is that thing even legal?" she asked.

He winked at her but didn't answer, simply nodded to me and strode back toward the apartment. I waited until he was out of view before I slipped my hand into hers, twining our fingers together. She curled into my side, leaning her head against my shoulder.

"If you don't mind, I'd like to hold onto you for the next seventy-two hours or so," I said quietly.

"I don't mind at all. In fact, I can't think of anything I'd like better."

Hand in hand, we entered the house, locking the door securely behind us. Nora paused once we were inside. Slowly, her gaze traveled along the hallway, through the kitchen, out onto the deck.

There was no visible trace of the pain and terror we'd experienced, but the echoes still reverberated around inside my ribcage, making it difficult not to grab her and run away from it all.

For her, I forced myself to keep still, to let her lead the way.

With my hand wrapped securely around hers, she stayed just inside the doorway for a long moment, seeming to draw comfort from my steady presence at her side. She glanced at my face and I lifted a questioning brow, so she tugged me toward the stairs.

Without a word, we went up to the bedroom and pulled off our bloodstained clothing. The impulse to chuck it all into an incinerator struck me hard, but first things first. As my worried gaze lingered on Nora's face, she simply nodded toward the bed and crawled under the covers. I followed, wrapping her in my arms.

It was a long time before either of us spoke. With her head resting on my chest, I let the soft warmth of her fill me with a sense of overwhelming peace. I stroked my fingers lightly over her hair, pausing every so often to press my lips against the top of her head.

"I've never been so scared in my entire life," she whispered eventually, just as twilight began to fall outside the bedroom window. The words trembled from her lips and my heart clenched hard in my chest. "Not even when we thought my mother might be dead."

"I'm right there with you. When he lowered the knife . . ." I broke off, rubbing my other hand over my face. "I thought that was it. I thought I was going to watch you die right in front of me and not be able to do a single goddamn thing about it. I was getting ready to throw myself at the pair of you just to try to deflect it when I saw your dad come in."

She buried her face against my chest, her frame shuddering under my hands as the tears finally came, wetting my skin like a cleansing rainfall. I held her there, stroked her hair, kissed her forehead, wiped her cheeks with my thumbs, until she let out a shaky breath.

"He was there the night Scarpella grabbed me at The Mermaid. He saw it, all of it. He's been watching us."

I tipped her chin up to meet her eyes. "He's gone now. We're safe."

"Yeah." The word was barely more than a breath.

"I love you," I whispered.

Her lips curved just a touch, those dark eyes going warm and soft. "I love you. I know you only wanted to hold me, but do you think...would you mind kissing me instead?"

"I will never, ever turn down the chance to kiss you, Nora."

"I just—I need to feel alive right now."

I rolled to look down at her, studying every inch of her face, committing her features to memory before I lowered my lips to her forehead. With her hands gripping my shoulders tightly, I kissed my way across her cheeks, her eyelids, her chin, the tip of her nose.

"We're both very much alive," I whispered, then at last I captured her mouth.

Though I really hadn't intended anything beyond cuddling her close, Nora urged me to take more—*demanded* that I take more. Her hands tangled in my hair even as her legs wrapped around my waist. Without shifting my lips from hers, I rolled again so that she was straddling me.

"Take what you need, my love," I murmured. "Anything you need. Everything you need."

With wild, intense abandon, Nora took and took and took, but she gave freely, too, offering everything she had to give into my keeping.

Together we rode through the hurricane, shedding our terror along the way until we both felt fully alive with the forces rising between us and with each other. When at last she collapsed, quivering, against my chest, I could only laugh breathlessly and tighten my arms around her.

"I think you should ask me now," she whispered. She lifted her head to peek up at me, saw my confusion, and smiled a little as she snuggled closer. "To move in with you. For real, this time."

My deep inhalation lifted her as air filled my lungs and love swelled in my chest. "Nora Cassidy, will you move in with me? For real?"

Her lips dropped to my chest, just over my heart. "Hell yes, I will."

"Here?" I asked. At her puzzled look, I gave a little shrug. "I wondered if it might feel, I don't know, tainted? We could find another house, or build one, or—"

Nora stopped me with a finger over my lips. "No. No way. You've poured so much love into this house. I feel it every time I come through that door. This is home, Jake. *Our* home," she added simply.

I kissed her fingers. "God, I love you."

"Good, because I love you, too."

We fell silent for a long moment, waiting for our pulses to slow. I breathed deeply to draw in the sweet scent of her, like golden pears and sunshine. Everything I needed was right here, in my arms and in my heart. The wonder of it welled inside me until I was practically floating away.

When Nora finally lifted her head again, I saw a flash of familiar mischief in those pretty brown eyes.

"Besides, Sam and I picked out the most perfect bubblegum pink for the third bedroom. I'm going to get started on it next week," she informed me, managing to keep a straight face even when my expression turned to horror.

All of my worry evaporated as I rolled us back over so I was looking down at her. "Like hell you will," I growled.

I lowered my head gently, though, to kiss her lips, her jaw, the graceful line of her throat, then I paused to look at the tiny bandage and the white square of gauze adorning her fair skin. A shudder went through me.

"Nevermind. You can paint it any color you want, as long as you'll stay."

Her smile was sweet and radiant and filled with everything I loved about her. "I'm staying," she said softly, and sealed it with a kiss.

Epilogue

Nora

MY DAD STAYED IN town for two weeks after the incident. Though he was subtle about it, it was obvious he wanted to be absolutely sure I wasn't going to have a post-traumatic breakdown before he left. I accepted it good-naturedly, even if I occasionally rolled my eyes at Jake over my father's gentle fussing.

I wasn't about to stand in his way, not this time.

After Jake told me about his pained confession on the porch step, I understood his need to rectify the course that had been set so many years ago.

Together, we stood on the front porch and waved as Dad drove away. When his car was gone from view, I leaned my head against Jake's shoulder. At my soft sigh, he wrapped his arm around my waist.

"He'll be back to visit," he reassured me, but I shook my head a little.

"I never meant to stay here for more than a few months, you know," I told him. "I thought I might even leave before Mr. Jenkins got back from Florida."

"And now?"

"Now I can't imagine wanting to be anywhere else."

His arm tightened ever so slightly around me. "Good, because I don't know what I'd do without you. I'm hooked."

"I'm still not entirely sure how you weaseled your way in, but I'm glad you did, Jake." I turned my head to kiss the edge of his jaw.

"Me too," he said softly, nuzzling the top of my head in return.

It felt almost strange to be alone again after the barrage of attention we'd had since Shawn's arrest. Jake's family had been a near-constant feature in our lives, not that I could complain. From meals to distractions, they'd been the best possible support system I could imagine. Still, my introvert self had been longing for more than a few scattered moments of peace and quiet.

I'd also gotten to see Spruce Hill's gossip mill in action, though Jake stood guard to keep any nosy townsfolk from confronting me directly.

And if nightmares plagued my sleep now and again, at least I had Jake there to hold me.

"I think we should get a dog. There's an adoption event at the park next weekend, a few local rescues will be there."

My body jerked at Jake's pronouncement, but everything inside me softened at the expression on his face—like love and contentment were shining out of every pore. Any anxiety I might have expected at the thought of settling into a life together had simply vanished beneath the force of that glow.

"Okay," I said simply.

"Excellent. I was thinking we could name it Taser." His grin shone bright as the summer sun overhead.

I burst out laughing, dropping my head to his shoulder. "You're a goof."

"But I'm your goof, so you're stuck with me."

"Believe me, Jake, there's no one on this planet I'd rather be stuck with. And Taser's actually not a bad name for a dog."

"So, next up, adopt a dog. Then what? Painting that bedroom bubblegum pink? Filling the koi pond with fish? Learning a few new languages? I don't speak French, but I do know all about French kissing."

I laughed. "That all sounds lovely, but I'm starting translation work on a romance novel this week. I decided I need a break from violent content, so for now, I'm only going to work on happily ever afters."

His lips curved slowly upward into the kind of dimpled smile that always made me go soft and dreamy.

"Well, that sounds just perfect," he drawled, dropping his mouth to mine, "because happily ever after is exactly what I had in mind."

Also by

RACHEL FITZJAMES

Keep in touch! Sign up for Rachel's newsletter at https://rac helfitzjames.com/ for FREE bonus content, sneak peeks, sales, and news about upcoming releases!

SPRUCE HILL SERIES

Unpacking Secrets

A Lonely Road

Canvas of Lies

Crumbling Truth

Playing for Paradise

Sinister Returns

Treasured Legacy

Lucky Save

Wrenching Hearts

Flash of Danger

Acknowledgements

While this book has undergone more sweeping revisions than most, one thing remained the same throughout every iteration of it: Nora is unabashedly herself. I worried this book was too quiet, that Nora was too prickly among my usual feisty heroines, but to my surprise—and delight—Nora is probably the character I've received the most comments about readers relating to. And since Nora is probably the most like me among my main characters, that was a heartwarming discovery. So to everyone who loves a black cat character with a wall of thorns around her heart, thank you. I hope you enjoyed her story, because even the most prickly among us deserves a happy ending.

As usual, thank you to my family for listening to my endless ponderings, for encouraging me to make this dream come true, and for helping every time I'm in need of a name, outfit, or pet.

For every random lighthouse road trip, every set of nice pens and piece of artwork, every Pinterest board—you guys are the best.

Melissa Rotert, always and forever, thank you for tolerating all the kissy bits in order to make sure my characters are using contractions instead of speaking like Regency aristocrats. Above all, thanks for adopting this black cat introvert into your life. Love you everything.

To my CPs, Christie Curry, Christina Brennan, and Briana Newstead, I can never thank you enough for convincing me this book shouldn't be scrapped as "too quiet." Your love for Nora and Jake kept me plugging along when I might have given up, and I adore this pair so much, it would've been a shame to abandon them!

Heather Frances, huuuuuge thanks to you for solving my "this needs something but I don't know what" problem and making this book a hundred times stronger with your insights! Tobie Carter, Lindsay Barrett, and Charisma Williams, thank you all for being my cheerleaders and sounding boards, I am so lucky to have met you all. And to the romance writing community at large—I so appreciate every one of you for being so generous with your wisdom and enthusiasm.

About the author

Rachel Fitzjames is the author of a contemporary romantic suspense series set in the fictional town of Spruce Hill, NY. She started writing on her brother's ancient computer back in the early 90s and never looked back, though her first short story about an underground cat thievery ring was sadly lost. With a degree in geography inspired by wanderlust, Rachel has a keen appreciation for the escape that the romance genre allows. She is a lifelong resident of Western NY and created Spruce Hill in order to give a little bit of home to all of her characters.

Connect with Rachel at her website, https://rachelfitzjames.com/, or on Instagram and Threads at @rachelfitzjames.